The Dalkey Persuaders

Niall & Pauline
BRACKEN

BLACKWATER PRESS

Editor
Aidan Culhane

Design & Layout
Paula Byrne

Cover Illustration
John Short

ISBN
0 86121 983 X

© 1998 Niall & Pauline Bracken

Produced in Ireland by
Blackwater Press
c/o Folens Publishers
8 Broomhill Business Park,
Tallaght, Dublin 24.

DALKEY

Self-contained journey's-end Dalkey.
Coarse-cut stone castles and harbour walls,
Head-swivelling views of coast and countryside,
Grey and permanently green hills,
Fickle ocean.
Serpentine streets with other-era shop-fronts,
Churches, pubs, clackety-clack of trains trundling through.
Grand houses, sweet summer smell of night-scented stock,
Mellow odour of earth and rotting leaves in autumn,
Old money.

CONTENTS

PROLOGUE

The 'johnny-come-latelys' of Dalkey confronted the day in their own way.

Cas Maitland stuck out his tongue at himself in the bathroom mirror, and then peered through the window and decided it was a peach of a day, but he wouldn't be free to enjoy it. Fifteen minutes later, with one or two early bathers arriving at the sandy harbour near where he lived, he reluctantly drove away from the sparkling sea views and into the city. Tiny tension lines were already beginning to form on his face.

Pam O'Regan sat back in the carriage of the train and flicked through a magazine. Her old car was out of commission again. She could have waited and taken a lift from Cas, but she preferred to be on her own in the mornings. She liked an early start to her day and enjoyed the brisk walk from the railway station on Westland Row to the agency. Sunny Dalkey gave up its sunniest resident for the day.

At Bulloch Harbour, Paul Bennett positively skipped out the front door of his new quay-side home and, with his briefcase tucked up under his arm, stopped to stare down at a gleaming, white, red and navy blue liveried six-berth cabin cruiser moored in the water below. What a little beauty! He must find a way of acquiring it.

In no humour to admire the scenery, Martin O'Neill crouched over the wheel of his car and fairly raced into the city, disregarding the hangover gathering above his brow. On mornings such as this he regretted his decision to come and live in a terraced house in picturesque Dalkey, and vowed once again to move nearer the agency. He threw the stub of a cigarette out the window and lit another.

Liz and Des Downey left their Victorian-style lodge on Sorrento Road, and Des nosed their car down into Dalkey village, chauffeuring Liz to her job as usual. The morning light hit the crenellated castle in the main street, and several people dodged out from early morning Mass to catch the train, giving the place a parochial air. Liz was already preoccupied with the moves she would make that day.

Ted Flynn stood looking out to sea in the bright pillared porch of his house, and breathed deeply, as the sun burnt off the early morning mist and coloured in the day. If bougainvillaea bloomed on the old stone walls around here, with this view you could feel you were living on the Riviera, he thought. He got into his Mercedes, drove down the gravelled driveway and out onto the Vico Road, and headed into Dublin for another exciting day. Ted was in a position to make excitement the norm rather than the exception.

At the other end of the social scale, Bruce Bellingham enjoyed being an old Dalkeyite. He was unshakeable in his belief that the Bellinghams of Dalkey were descended from Sir Edward Bellingham, the Viceroy who landed there in 1548 when Bulloch Harbour was the premier port of Dublin. As chairman of the huge Arkwright & Dobson conglomerate, he had the money, position and power to enjoy the deferential nods and 'good mornings' which greeted him as he sauntered to the railway station.

His home was a large grey rambling pile set high above Dalkey in one acre of neatly tended gardens. Bruce Bellingham loved Dalkey in the proprietorial way that dukes and earls love their estates, and while he kept his distance from the hoi polloi, he knew every inch of the village and surrounding areas thoroughly and he felt a sense of personal betrayal every time one of the big houses went up for sale and some johnny-come-lately moved in. Of late he was given to musing how life in Dublin was changing. Where once established Protestant families had upheld the social values, the burst of progress in the sixties, and now here in the seventies, seemed to have sidelined them in some respects: the young men no longer came for references for pensionable jobs in old firms like Guinness's, Jacobs, Dockrells and Findlaters.

CHAPTER 1

Cas was furious. Marco Caspar Maitland was 28 years old. He was tall with broad shoulders and dark wavy hair, and eyelashes that women would kill for. Cas Maitland wasn't fully aware how heart-flutteringly attractive to women he was.

At the long Georgian boardroom window he looked down at someone in a car inching along Merrion Square in Dublin, fruitlessly looking for a parking space.

Yet again Ted had lied to him. My God, but he would tackle Ted straight away before the board meeting, and sort things out once and for all! This couldn't go on. After all, he was now Managing Director of the damn place.

The door connecting Ted Flynn's office and the boardroom opened and Liz Downey, Ted's executive assistant, came in with an armful of note pads, and a handful of ball-point pens. She began to lay them out neatly on the long boardroom table, positioning a pad and pen exactly in front of each chair.

'The board meeting will be delayed,' she said, giving Cas a sympathetic grimace. 'Ted is on the phone to a client – Tim Cranby. Tim has another complaint about the TV schedule. I've told Martin and Jim I'd let them know when Ted was ready for the meeting. And Birdie phoned to say she can't make it, for some convoluted reason I couldn't understand.'

Cas brooded. A few minutes later Ted Flynn, Chairman of the advertising agency, Flynn & Malby, stepped into the boardroom. 'Sorry, Cas, sorry, Liz. We'll have to defer the board meeting indefinitely. I have to go and see Tim Cranby. He wants to see me immediately. He's apoplectic about the Baby Faire TV schedule. The Media Department, curse them, have bought some time slots around the "Week by Week" current affairs programme. Tim says that nobody who watches current affairs is interested in baby products, and I agree with him.'

Ted Flynn had light, sandy hair and good regular features. They said he looked a bit like the Duke of Edinburgh as a young man. He had an animated and charismatic manner, but when cornered, his character changed; his eyes became hooded and his tongue played with a loose tooth – and he lied freely. When crossed he was ruthless. He was taller than most. His nickname throughout the advertising industry was 'The Giraffe' – and when people were talking to him, he inclined his head towards them, giving the impression that they were receiving his full and undivided attention, thus gaining for himself the reputation of being a good listener. It also allowed him to put a concerned and controlling arm around their shoulder. When he shook hands, he placed his left hand over the clasped ones, or under the person's elbow, to convey the full strength of his commitment. Normally to the forefront of fashion and trends, Ted always wore bow-ties which, unintentionally, gave him a dated and conservative look for the 1970s.

As a child Ted had lived in extreme poverty with his parents in Black's Lane in Dalkey. His father had gathered swill from house to house for a piggery outside the village, and Ted had helped him. At 19 he had set out for London from Dun Laoghaire on the Mail Boat with one cardboard suitcase held together with the belt of a gabardine raincoat. From there he had gone to Australia, where he spent many fruitful years, ending up in Hong Kong, and then Bangkok, before returning to Ireland, an acknowledged expert in advertising and marketing, with several prestigious awards under his belt confirming his natural talents in these fields.

Although Ted Flynn was Chairman and majority shareholder of Flynn & Malby Advertising Limited, he always insisted on a consensus from the other directors on every decision made by the Board. He would keep a meeting going all night until the others were exhausted, and eventually agreed with his point of view just so that they could go home. He claimed he valued other people's opinion, but actually he was a bully, with a bully's lack of confidence. Occasionally Ted would show great concern for someone and go to extremes to help them. He was highly creative and involved himself in the minutiae of agency business, and most of the agency's clients were impressed by him and thought that, as an advertising man, he was the best thing since packaged milk.

On her husband's death, Birdie Malby had inherited 25 per cent of the company, but she did not participate in the day-to-day running, although Ted had given her a small and insignificant job in it.

The other four directors, Martin O'Neill, Art Director; Jim Reilly, Financial Director; Marco Caspar Maitland, Managing Director and Liz Downey, executive assistant, each owned five per cent of the shares as a result of a bonus scheme implemented a few years previously, when money had been tight. Ted had an agreement with these four that if any of them left the agency, he had first refusal on their shares.

'You'll have to get rid of that one Celine in Media,' said Ted. 'She doesn't know a bee from a bull's foot.'

'It was Celine's assistant who made out the schedule,' said Cas.

'Who?'

'You know the young one who wears the skimpy hot pants.'

'Her? Good God, imagine going through life knowing your arse was your best feature!'

'You approved the schedule, Ted,' said Cas. 'You initialled it.'

'Dammit, am I expected to be responsible for everything in this agency?' said Ted. 'What are we paying all these people for?' He waved his arms in a circle.

'Actually, I wanted to talk to you about Celine,' said Cas. 'She came to me for a salary increase and I turned her down. Then I understand she went to you, and you agreed to an increase. This sort of thing can't go on, Ted.'

'I didn't.' Ted's voice was raised. 'She's telling you a downright lie. She came to me and I said she must see you.' Cas didn't know whether to accuse Celine Dunphy or defend her.

'Go and see her and talk to her,' said Ted. 'Look,' he changed tack. 'I've got to go. I'll see you when I get back and we'll talk to Celine together.' He disappeared into his office.

Liz looked at Cas and wrinkled her nose.

'You know he's not telling the truth,' said Cas. 'Celine swears he promised to bump up her salary.'

'I know he's not,' said Liz. 'I'll talk to him when he comes back but he's gone for the day now.'

'Blast it,' said Cas. 'By the time I see him again, this whole episode will be history.'

'Anyway it's not his fault about the TV schedule,' Liz said, changing sides neatly, as she frequently did. 'He didn't have time to look at it closely when he initialled it. It's not fair. He has too much to do.'

'He wouldn't have so damn much to do if he stopped interfering in other people's jobs and stuck to his own. He just can't seem to delegate even though he says he wants to,' said Cas.

Liz Downey had been Ted's highly efficient secretary in his previous job, and he had brought her with him when he left to start up his own agency. She had lived, with eight brothers and sisters, in a small Corporation house in Oliver Plunkett Villas in Monkstown Farm, and it had been her searing ambition, from 13, to climb the social ladder as far and as quickly as possible. Her first, and only miscalculation had been marrying handsome Des Downey. However, she soon realised that while Des was averse to exertion generally, and his philosophy of life was firmly based on the laissez-faire principle, he was at least malleable and compliant. Whatever Liz wanted to do was alright with Des. She planned to hitch herself to an ascendant star.

Liz managed to wheedle a number of loans from the agency, and together with several substantial bonuses and reimbursements of mythical expenses sanctioned by Ted, she and Des were able to move from a minuscule apartment in Monkstown to a compact, elegant up-market Victorian lodge on Sorrento Road in Dalkey, which was, much to Des's joy, within a short walking distance of Dan Finnegan's pub. Liz was a good-looking woman in a sharp-featured way, fastidious in her appearance. Her eyebrows were groomed to near-extinction and her finger-nails were flawless. Her strict dietary regimen kept her a permanent size ten, and she had a ready smile which rarely developed further than her lips. She walked with a quick up-and-down movement, her naturally curly brown hair bouncing like a TV shampoo advertisement.

As Ted's executive assistant/girl Friday/shareholder/director/surrogate mistress, Liz was a powerful figure in the agency, but surprisingly, she was without an official title. This was unusual in advertising circles, where labels and appellations were as plentiful as pints at a Rugby club get-together.

* * *

Cas stretched out his hand and squashed the alarm clock into silence. It was half past six in the morning. It was also Saturday. Throwing back the bed-clothes he jumped out of bed and was half-way across the bedroom when the hangover struck. Bang! The little man at the back of his head began working his pick-axe ferociously, while his mate used a pneumatic drill with savage effect on his forehead. He groped his way to the kitchen where there was a glass of water, two Alka-Seltzers, and aspirins already lined up on the counter waiting to be consumed. God, he thought, he must have been very drunk the previous night. He couldn't remember making these elaborate preparations. What was he doing up this early on a Saturday morning? Then his mind cleared briefly. Going painting. Bloody hell! Pam had persuaded him to go down to the harbour, crowded with summer craft, to catch the early morning light in water-colours. He had painted the little boat-filled harbour in oils several times before, and he knew that if he worked quickly he could achieve a pretty good dawn effect.

Cas was a talented weekend painter, and as such had received recognition. To be a full-time artist was what he had wanted ever since he could remember, but it was not to be. He had attended the National College of Art, but had been persuaded by his father to take the course in commercial art and graphic design. From this he got a job in a small advertising agency, and after studying advertising at the College of Commerce in Rathmines, progressed to a top creative job in a larger agency. He later joined Flynn & Malby, one of the up-and-coming advertising agencies in Dublin. Then, on Ted's insistence, he had become a collar-and-tie executive, thus cancelling his artistic ambitions.

He was born in Ireland, of an Italian mother and an English father who was a surgeon. When his parents met and decided to get married, his father hadn't wanted to live in Italy, and his mother hadn't wanted to live in England, so they chose neutral ground. Cas's mother was a beautiful woman and was said to be descended from one of Florence's important, but less famous, painters. She herself was an able sculptor and Cas had inherited her talent, with an added touch of lazy genius. His mother had wanted Cas to become a full-time painter, but his father's pragmatism had prevailed.

The telephone rang. Cas unhooked the hand-set from the kitchen wall. He knew who it was.

'Hello,' said Pam. 'You're up.'

'And regretting every minute of it,' said Cas.

'Come on, you were all for it last night.'

'Hmmm.' Cas took the coffee saucepan from the cooker.

'We're not going on a cross-country trek, we're just going painting. You got a head?'

'Yes'.

'Serves you right. I'll be down immediately.' She hung up.

Pam lived in the apartment above Cas's garden flat, in a big house near Sandycove harbour. The telephone in the hall outside her door could be switched to act as a internal line with Cas. She used it infrequently to call him, preferring to barge in unannounced using the hall-door key which he had imprudently given her six months ago. The entrance to Cas's apartment was by way of a wrought-iron gate which led to a rose-festooned courtyard. The frosted glass front door opened into a small, bright hallway, and a large lounge cum dining-room was the main feature. A well appointed kitchen with a bar counter was illuminated by diffused lighting, and through an archway were two bedrooms. Cas used the larger one to sleep in, and turned the other into a studio, because the light there was good. On an easel, a portrait of Pam, started some months previously, stood unfinished. Tubes of oil-paint and clusters of brushes in jars abounded. Suits in dry cleaners' bags and shirts fresh from the laundry lay on the spare bed.

Pamela Dorothy O'Regan, known as Pam D'Or to her friends, was an attractive, big-hearted, big-bosomed, blonde, bubbly young woman with an appetite for life – and Cas. She was in love with Cas, although he was not in love with her. She knew this and she didn't care. Although they were seen by many as a suitable duo for the long haul, she exerted no pressure on him for an engagement ring. Some people thought she was wasting her time on Cas. Pam thought otherwise. She had long term plans for the man in her life, whatever others thought. She didn't discuss their relationship with anyone, but kept herself busy between playing badminton and going out with her girlfriends for laughs and drinks. Her system for getting her man had worked for others, so why not for her? For a man it was easier to fall into marriage with a girl he had been seen around with for years, she believed, than to lose friendships in both their immediate circles. This seemed to Pam to be the way to land Cas as her mate for life. She loved him dearly and believed that he would one day realise that he loved her too. Meanwhile she was having great fun all round. Pam worked as secretary to Martin O'Neill, the Art Director in Flynn & Malby, and she had moved into the flat above Cas from her family home in Rathgar, the better to be near him at all times. How she found the flat, or even knew it was vacant was a total mystery to Cas.

Although he liked women and sex, Cas had never been fully in love. He was fond of Pam and happy to bask in the attention he received from her, but privacy and freedom were the things he prized. Very occasionally she spent the night with him if they had been out somewhere together and had returned late. He discouraged Pam from staying overnight too often.

Once down at the harbour, they set up their easels. They worked in companionable silence, Cas swiftly and deftly painting with total concentration, gradually over-riding his hangover, and Pam picking away in amateurish fashion, just happy to be near him.

CHAPTER 2

Martin O'Neill was examining some baby photos for possible use in a press and magazine campaign for Baby Faire with one of the studio artists, when Cas burst into his office.

'Martin, I have to talk to you.' Martin dismissed the artist and turned to face Cas. He lit a fresh cigarette from the one he was finishing, and crushed the stub in an overflowing ash-tray.

'It's Ted,' said Cas.

'Again? What's it this time?' Martin sucked smoke through his teeth.

'I'm off the Allied Oils account,' said Cas.

'Which you brought into the agency.'

'That cuts no ice with Ted. He's been to see the chairman of AO but he brought Paul Bennett with him and indicated to AO that Paul is now handling the damn account, and not me. Ted boosted him to the skies. So much for my being the new Managing Director of this kip. Why does he do it?'

'We've all been asking that for years. Why does he do anything? The man's a schizophrenic. In this case he's probably working on "The Lord giveth, the Lord taketh away" principle. If you brought the account to the agency, you can bring it with you if you ever leave. Handling the account gives you too much power. So, the sooner he stops you having direct contact with the client, the better. Allied Oils is a valuable account.'

'Too much power? Then why make me Managing Director? Remember the board meeting. He insisted I take up the post and then demanded it be ratified by unanimous decision of the directors.'

Martin shrugged. 'You're a valuable asset, Cas. And you're a hard worker, and dedicated to Flynn & Malby. Anyway, Ted needn't worry. You'll never leave here. Once an F&M man, always an F&M man. Go and talk to him Cas. He put his arm around Cas's shoulders. 'Give him hell, old mate. Don't let the bastard off the hook.' Martin enjoyed making snowballs for others to throw, particularly Cas.

'Liz says he's gone to a meeting. I'll see him when he gets back.'

Martin couldn't resist a quiet smirk as Cas left the room.

Flynn & Malby was a substantial advertising agency by mid-1970s standards. For its size, the shares in the company were spread quite widely, but of course Ted Flynn retained full control with a majority shareholding. He even had it written into the articles of the company that legally he could override or revoke any decisions of the Board, so great was his terror of losing control of the company he had founded. His insecurity stemmed from the fact that in an agency in which he had worked previously, there had been a junior management heave which succeeded in leaving the top brass more or less on the side of the street. Ted had further complicated matters for himself when he resigned flamboyantly to start his own advertising agency with Frank Malby as junior partner.

Frank was a talented commercial artist. He remained in awe of Ted's creative energy until he died of cancer caused by stress, only four years after the foundation of the company. When Ted resigned from his former employers, some of the companies which had placed their business there left also, and later appeared as Ted's new start-up clients. Ted was accused of stealing the clients of his erstwhile colleagues, and of a lack of ethical standards – all of which he hotly denied. 'I have lured away no accounts whatsoever. If clients come to me, there's no way I'm going to turn them away', was his counter-reaction. This was untrue, and he lived in the shadow of the day some executive of Flynn & Malby would leave and take accounts with him. This insecurity produced in him an ambivalence, so that while he wanted the best people around him, he was always afraid that they would be persuaded to go elsewhere and, with an insider's knowledge, poach his business.

Shortly after Flynn & Malby got on its feet, Ted became an ardent supporter of the political party in government, and donated large sums to its fundraising committee, which operated in secret from a room in a Dublin hotel. His spectacular success in securing government advertising contracts was noted with suspicion by rival agencies, but any special treatment was vehemently denied by Ted and the government departments claimed that they always chose the 'lowest tender'.

Ted was a consummate salesman and was much envied in the advertising industry in Ireland. Highly creative and plausible, his failing was that he always promised more than he could deliver. When confronted with this, he lied to get himself off the hook. Many of his sophisticated clients knew this and dismissed 50 per cent of his claims, continuing to work with him, and preferring to take advantage of the undoubted high quality of the agency's work. The others, on the other hand, just took their business away. Consequently, while he was always talking new business into the agency, he was also losing established clients, almost at the same rate. This 'revolving door' situation was in danger of causing growth stagnation, and the other directors were concerned.

'The thing is, he knows it, but he won't admit it,' Liz said to Cas.

'We have to use his strengths, and cover for his weaknesses,' said Martin O'Neill. 'He'll never change.' Martin was not above being devious, himself. While he despised Ted's mercurial character, he admired the fact that he had got on so well in the world. Martin had lived in Dublin's inner city and had come from a background of poverty and educational disadvantage, but with a doggedly earned scholarship had got himself into a middle-grade job in CIE, the national transport company. While there, he discovered that he had a creative talent. Over a period of time he had written and lavishly illustrated a number of magazine articles and co-written a series of documentaries for Radio Eireann, as well as drawing cartoons for one of the evening papers. It was the budding of a remarkable creative talent, and when Ted met Martin at a party, he was impressed by him. He also enjoyed Martin's sense of humour. He had already heard from someone in Radio Eireann about Martin's writing talent and, with great acuity, he offered him a job in Flynn & Malby as a visualiser. Martin smelt big money and took the plunge and the job. Within half a year he had taken Frank Malby's place as the senior creative person in the agency, and after two years, Ted appointed him Creative Director.

Martin liked women, but what was more important to him, they liked him. They liked the way he stood, feet apart, rough-hewn, with his grey-green eyes and red hair, now grown long as befitted his image, the inevitable cigarette in his hand, daring them not to like him. They soon succumbed to his rapid-fire, wry remarks. Martin was fun to be with. He had married at an early age, choosing a pretty but uneducated girl. Now that he had come up in the world, he was shedding everything and anything which impeded his progress. This included Imelda, his wife.

For no reason that the doctors could advance, Imelda had gone deaf after the birth of their first child. Unable to keep up with the pressure of a top advertising executive's social life, she became increasingly estranged from Martin, and eventually she turned to drink for comfort, with disastrous results. Ted had great sympathy with Martin in what he perceived as Martin's predicament rather than Imelda's. Celine from the Media Department was Martin's current conquest.

* * *

On most evenings, two or three members of the staff of Flynn & Malby were to be found lowering a few drinks in O'Dwyers in Mount Street but it usually wasn't until Friday that serious sessions got going. From five o'clock onwards – frequently from even earlier in the afternoon – sometimes from lunchtime, they filtered in, one by one, until a large knot of them occupied a corner in the back lounge bar, where they got steadily and noisily drunk. All except the Accounts Department, who, as if it had been written into their job descriptions, were declared teetotallers. The odd one from Accounts who did break ranks and consume an alcoholic drink, did so in his or her local, or as far away as possible from the contaminating camaraderie of the 'creative' side of the agency.

It was Celine Dunphy who started the ball rolling one Wednesday. Martin O'Neill had gone to London to iron out some problems with the film laboratories regarding a double-head of a Bartons Flour television commercial, and Celine was feeling bored and neglected. She demanded that Jack Bacon take her for 'a drink' to O'Dwyers.

With Martin on the trip to London were Will Rooney, a copywriter and Len Fenton, the assistant advertising manager of Bartons, although it was absolutely unnecessary for either of them to accompany him. The making of the commercial was at an advanced stage. Len Fenton had said that he wasn't happy with the film and would withhold his approval until he saw the final result, and much to Martin's irritation he demanded that a three-man delegation go to London to 'sort things out'. Len knew a good 'freebie' when he saw one and deliberately ignored the fact that in the end his own company would be paying the bill.

At Heathrow airport Len left them, pleading 'other business.' When Martin and Will were finished their meeting, Will went on his own to visit a striptease club in Soho. There in the front row was Len. Embarrassed, he left hurriedly. Later Will went to another strip joint and there again was Len. The scene was repeated in a third location. Eventually Len begged Will and Martin not to mention anything back in Dublin, and Martin reckoned they wouldn't have any trouble getting the commercial approved after all.

Jack, or 'Hairy' Bacon, as he was known, because of his long hair and beard, was an exceptionally talented commercial artist from the North of England. The hair was thick and luxuriant, but the beard was a failure and always looked like wisps of theatrical hair spirit-gummed to his chin. Much of Hairy Bacon's spare time was spent double-jobbing as a clarinetist under the name of Lenny Goodman, playing with a small band at tennis club dances, and as such he was much in demand.

He was married to a solid, bundle of a woman, also from the North of England. He loved her and his only son dearly, and he was a dogged provider. The trouble was that with drink taken, he stole things. At lunchtime this particular Wednesday, Hairy met an artist friend from one of the other agencies. They started with a glass of lager each, and without realising it, quite a substantial number of pints were consumed. Hairy was slightly unsteady on his feet when he arrived back at the agency in a taxi, and his art department colleagues spotted that he was under the weather when they found him watering his plants for third time. Hairy Bacon's desk was surrounded by a *cordon sanitaire* of potted plants in all varieties and sizes, including several species of ivy which trailed and curled determinedly over shelves, around his free-standing room-dividers and up his angle-poise lamp. According to fellow artist, Eric Timmerman, some of the plants looked suspiciously like cannabis. It was Hairy's routine to water all his vegetation first thing every morning before starting work, and when he went away on holidays intricate instructions were left with a bribed member of the staff for their care and maintenance.

Hairy sat at his desk throwing balls of Cow gum into a jam jar. He divided his time between watching a juddering air-brush compressor advancing across the wooden floor to bang repeatedly against the Grant copier, and studying a junior repairing a piece of carpet around the absent studio manager's desk, which he had cut deeply with a Stanley knife when he was trimming a mounting board on the floor.

Eric Timmerman was doing his best to isolate Hairy from the prying eyes of the management when Celine came into the department and joshed a malleable Hairy into taking her to O'Dwyers, while the others covered for him. They drove to the pub. A nucleus formed, to which other members of the agency attached themselves as the afternoon and the evening wore on, until around nine in the evening a rip-roaring session was in full swing. Cas joined them. He had been to lunch in the Stephen's Green Club with Terry Brady, an executive from RTE and a brand manager from Arkwright & Dobson – son of one their directors. Their afternoon had been spent unprofitably, drinking and playing snooker in the club.

The group now began to break up into smaller knots of people as rounds of drinks went down at different speeds. A well-oiled Eric Timmerman stood at the counter, addressing Celine with a stream of supposedly humorous, suggestive remarks, as was his wont when he had a few. Eric was dressed in a blue, floral, torso-hugging open-necked shirt, with a gold pendant nestling in what looked like a chest wig, and red trousers so tight that people wondered how he managed to walk without doing himself an injury. Celine was trying hard to keep in eye contact with Eric and pretend that she too was enjoying the slagging, but many brandies and ginger ales had impaired her concentration and her eyes kept slipping down his chest and stomach to the front of his trousers. After one of Eric's best attempts at a saucy remark, and unable to contain herself any longer, she lunged forward, glassy-eyed, and grabbed the bulge tightly like a hawk closing its talons on its prey. Then she passed out, still clutching Eric. Consternation ensued, and as if some type of alcoholic rigor mortis had set in, her fingers had to be prised off Eric, one by one. By the time Celine was revived, helped by another large brandy and ginger ale, Eric, who had been slumped against the bar gurgling something in Dutch, was nowhere to be seen.

Closing time arrived and they all assembled on the pavement, deciding where to go. Some favoured the Oul' Cod restaurant, some Zhivago Niteclub or Maxims, and others made conflicting plans for alleged parties in different locations. A few made for the dubious ATS nite-spot in Nassau Street. Hairy, who had not been around for Celine's act of revenge, appeared clutching a huge metal ashtray, which he had stolen from the hallway of the Majestic Hotel.

Suddenly they realised Celine was missing, and Hairy began to worry. Nobody knew where she was, and someone vaguely remembered seeing her phone a taxi in the pub. Now Hairy, who had originally brought her to O'Dwyers, became frantic with drink-induced concern, and insisted that they all get into Eric's car and drive to her house in Morehampton Road, where she lived with her mother, to see if she had arrived home. He had been there once before to deliver a file, and insisted he knew where the house was. He was firmly convinced that the taxi man could well have had his way with her, in her brandy and ginger-aled condition.

A rowdy group piled into Eric's station wagon, disturbing his dog in the process. They set off slowly, eight in the car, not counting the dog. Eric closed one eye, the better to focus on the road, and found that by concentrating on the kerb he could keep the vehicle moving in approximately a straight line. Hairy still had the remainder of his pint with him, which he held against the roof of the car in order to avoid spilling any when they went over bumps. The ashtray bounced ominously on the roof rack.

They called to five houses on Morehampton Road before they found the right one, and an ashen-faced Mrs Dunphy opened the hall-door in a hastily pulled-on dressing gown to eight boisterous men and a barking dog. Hairy explained the reason for their concern three times in a drink-thickened North of England accent, but Mrs Dunphy, by now rigid with fright, was unable to understand a word. Eventually, Hairy, losing patience with her dimness, and conscious of this waste of good drinking time, pushed past her and ran upstairs to check every room until he found Celine. There she was, fast asleep across the coverlet of her bed, wearing a vast, pink diaphanous nightie and snoring loudly.

Much relieved, Hairy quickly closed the door and came down the stairs. He wrapped his arms around Celine's mother and gave her a big kiss, before departing with the others into the night, taking with him a silver candlestick from the hall table.

Cas and Terry Brady had gone to Zhivago Niteclub in the meantime, where they were barred from entry. They spent a fruitless half hour trying to gain admittance, during which Brady knelt on the pavement to reach the low-placed letter box opening and shouted up through it, 'I'm a very important person. Let me in, or I'll have you on the nine o'clock news, and you won't like it, you bastards!'

* * *

The door of one of the houses built into the rocks at Bulloch Harbour in Dalkey opened softly and a woman slipped out, carefully carrying a china mug of tea. The sun had just risen and was shooting streams of gold across the surface of Dublin Bay, and this was what Tessa Bennett had come out to see. Early morning was her own special time, and although she often slipped back into bed for a doze to reward herself for being clever enough to see the day come up, she loved this early, private communing with her beloved Bulloch Harbour and the views from it. Now that they had moved here, and she didn't have to go to work, she could relax and bring her children to school later.

It was glorious living out here in Bulloch. Of course the mortgage was heavy, as the house, originally a fisherman's cottage, had been completely renovated and extended to the rear, but her husband, Paul Bennett, was making his way upwards in Flynn & Malby, and the future seemed agreeably bright, financially and every other way. Paul's enormous coolness about life seemed to impress everyone, and he had no bother in talking the building society and bank managers into giving him a large mortgage to buy this house and a loan to furnish it fully. The house was built with six others against a great sheltering rock and the harbour in front of it was full of bobbing boats. In addition there was a small attractive front garden. Sometimes she sat on one of the seats along the short pier with the children, watching a rising tide lift all the boats together.

There also seemed to be a rising tide for Paul in Flynn & Malby, as the agency's turnover had increased dramatically, and Cas Maitland, a young man about his own age, had recently been appointed Managing Director.

Bulloch in Dalkey was their favourite place along the coast, the spot to which they had driven in the long summer evenings, to park the car and watch the sun drop slowly behind the spires of Dun Laoghaire's churches along the bay. They often watched it from 'their' seat at the end of the pier and wished they could live there. Then one evening, when they had left the children, Jake and Stephanie, aged six and eight, with Paul's parents, they drove down as usual to Bulloch. Something was different – there was a 'For Sale' notice on one of the quay-side houses. For sale? At Bulloch Harbour? Houses in such a choice spot never had a 'For Sale' notice on them, but went on the books of estate agents to meet the waiting list of prospective clients with ready money.

Tessa reacted first. 'For goodness' sake, what are we doing just sitting here looking at it? Let's knock on the door and try and find out what they're asking for that darling house. It will sell in a day or two, if they leave that sign up.' They got out of the car and called at the house, where an anxious-looking woman brought them into her cleverly furnished and spacious front room. Tessa remembered every detail of that first visit.

'I shouldn't really be showing the house this late in the evening,' the owner said, a worried look crossing her lined face and spoiling the effect of her impeccable grooming. 'My co-owner and I were not quite in agreement as how we should dispose of the house, now that we have to go back unexpectedly to Britain for business reasons.'

'You are selling, aren't you?' Tessa asked carefully in response to this surprise opening announcement.

'Well, I decided this afternoon to put up a "For Sale" notice, to see what it would attract in the way of interest and you are the first to react. It hasn't been put on any auctioneer's books as yet, but I have to get this sale going, and quickly. You must think it all rather odd,' she added, embarrassed.

'Not at all, not at all,' Paul murmured pleasantly, taking over the exchange from Tessa, as he usually did. His excitement was mounting as he looked out through the filmy white curtains of the beautifully furnished livingroom on to the harbour front. What a backdrop for the Bennetts! Tessa and he could entertain here and advance his position significantly in the advertising world. They could eventually have a boat and take business contacts out cruising. He jerked back to reality and decided to play this strange opportunity carefully. The woman seemed to be stealing a march on someone by rushing a sale, and as they passed from room to room, his resolution grew. Eyeing Tessa behind her back, he picked up her excitement and, conspiratorially, they drew the owner out on the possible price.

The house was surprisingly roomy inside, with every square inch cleverly adapted for family living. It even had two bathrooms, though admittedly one was small, but it would do fine for the children. A long room converted from the attic was a real bonus, as it was already furnished as a superb master bedroom with a view over the harbour. A good architect had left his mark here. Before they left, Paul made her an offer for the fully furnished house, which would swallow up quite a lot of his monthly salary. They left their telephone number with the owner and strolled, mesmerised, back to their seat on the pier, eyeing one another like two children who have discovered a bag of sweets behind the couch in a relation's house, and don't quite know what to do about it.

Some days later, they received a call from the lady at Bulloch. Were they seriously interested, and if so, could they come out and clinch a deal without delay? Paul went to his building society and played the performance of his life to obtain the necessary rejigging of mortgage facilities. His recent salary increase, with the promise of more to come, won the day in the end, and he phoned an auctioneer to put his own house on the market, to complete his decision. They went out that afternoon to Bulloch, and clinched the deal. Then, within six weeks they bid a cheerful goodbye to the semi-detached house in the estate, and although Tessa would miss some of the other mothers living around, she could see the dramatic increase in Paul's already steady confidence in himself, and thrilled to it. She could depend on him to do whatever was best. Equally delighted with the move, she had formed the habit of pulling on a track suit in the early morning, if it were nice enough outside, and bringing out her first mug of tea to watch the day come up over Dublin Bay.

Paul absolutely loved it. He loved swishing in to town before the early morning traffic in his new Ford Capri 2000 GL, leaving this gorgeous backdrop knowing that it was all waiting for him on his return. The children were ecstatic at the idea of living beside a harbour and Tessa had backed him all the way. He already had his eye on a smart six-berth cabin cruiser, and one evening, as he stood admiring it, the owner had come along and mentioned that it would be coming up for sale at the end of the season. He was really on his way now.

Paul Bennett was a useful member of the agency team. He had been brought in by Ted as a Senior Account Executive essentially because of his political connections, and, to a lesser extent, because he was a respected member of Fitzwilliam Lawn Tennis Club – although he hadn't played a game in years, and the select Milltown Golf Club – although he only played occasionally. In the agency he was regarded as an asset by some, and as a lazy floater by others, but he was highly successful at handling clients. Before he joined Flynn & Malby he worked as Brand Manager for Roylon Fabrics, and at his interview Paul had insisted that the agency pay his yearly club subscriptions. This airy demand, along with others in a similar vein, had impressed Ted.

Paul Bennett liked money and all that it brought with it. He never spent where others could be induced to do so, and indulged in small meannesses, such as arriving a few minutes late for any daytime appointment in a hotel, so that the pot of coffee would already have been ordered, and all he needed to do was ask for another cup. Although he could well have afforded to buy those modern cassettes of his favourite music, he preferred to borrow them from the local library, and the small sums he saved in such ways totted up to extra money to be used when cutting a dash on family holidays at good hotels. He was often heard to say that there were no real holidays in the life of an advertising man, since excellent contacts could often be made while on vacation at home or abroad.

Paul's wife, Tessa, was a sweet, very pretty but generally unassertive young woman, who came from a Waterford business family, and who had received a good portion on her wedding day. Paul had liked the assumption that some money would come to Tessa on their marriage and he wouldn't have settled for less when choosing a wife, but they were well suited as a pair. Paul liked to refer to her in company by playful names, thus keeping himself in the commanding position in their relationship. He felt well pleased with his domestic life, having a wife who loved him, and whom he felt he loved too, two healthy children, and now the kind of home to which he had only aspired, and a nice financial cushion between himself and the world in his rising position in Flynn & Malby.

It was his ambition to become one of those authoritative, floating figures which grace exclusive sports clubs and company boards, and who patronise expensive holiday resorts in Ireland such as Kinsale or Baltimore in West Cork. He knew it never occurred to anyone to question the ability, intelligence or credentials of such men, once they are seen to be rich, and he intended to take his place among their number in due course. He had seen them at race meetings and other social venues, and read about them being at the best parties, unassailable, sometimes irresponsible people. He wanted to be the kind of person who is approached for references by young men who are a lot more intelligent than they, but who need a seal of approval for whatever it is they are about to embark on. Paul Bennett reckoned that if he were ensconced in a prosperous advertising agency, he would join the 'Heavies', and no one would ever quite be able to work him out. That was the way he liked things, and that was the way he intended things to be. But one small rumour clung to him like stick-weed. There were whispers around town that Charles Bennett was not his father. His mother, it was said, had had a brief fling with a well-known Dublin accountant and Paul was their love-child. His distinctive looks gave him away, the gossips said.

Paul was proud of his little son and daughter, although he didn't see all that much of them. Left alone with them on a Saturday morning when Tessa sometimes needed to go out alone, he would stay in bed as long as he could before getting up to look after them, and would be chafing at the bit by noon to slip into more sociable company, regarding himself as having been with the children 'all morning.' If Tessa arrived back earlier than arranged, or if anyone suitable called, who could be prevailed to stay until she returned, the Capri would be seen sliding up Harbour Road and into town, where he could catch up on the Saturday morning gossip in the Horseshoe Bar of the Shelbourne Hotel. He was conscious that he was setting up a system of slithering through life comfortably, and he secretly congratulated himself on his style, not stressing himself unduly, but having a good time with the aim of making other people pick up the tab.

He was liked by some in the agency, who sought to imitate him, and he carefully cultivated a hail-fellow-well-met personality, genial to all, never causing dissent, and cloaking his speech in a jargon designed to keep others at bay and to prevent any conversation from becoming too serious, in case commitment could be sought from him. Owing money to the bank was termed being 'in for a grand or two', and anything unpleasant or calling for responsibility on his part was evaded by means of light airy phrases and easy quips. He never used bad language, except as the punch line of a joke, and, quite happy with Tessa, he never flirted with other men's wives, felt really fond of them, or sought to be specially friendly with them. Fondness for people, especially for women, who could be astute and call for straightforwardness, was avoided by Paul. Straightforwardness would mean honesty, and honesty in relationships invariably brought commitment, and this was not at all Paul Bennett's bag, to use one of his own words. It was true that he brought in accounts to the agency, albeit small ones, but he constantly had the air of being four phone calls off a million, and this caused a reaction of optimism in Ted, and generally made him pleasant company. He was singularly devoid of creativity and was careful to conceal the fact by cleverly picking the brains of others, without their quite knowing it, flattering them into impressing him with their ideas. A think-tank was his idea of acquiring creativity, and he regularly organised such sessions to his own benefit.

A redeeming feature in Paul's character was that he was behind most of the jokes and mischief in the agency and he was always prepared to lighten the day with a few belly laughs. Cas was not usually involved, as he sought to maintain a certain distance in his role of Managing Director, but, nonetheless, he immensely enjoyed such carry-on.

When Ted asked Junior Account Executive, Karl Cunningham to come up with an inexpensive but effective local promotion for Wilton Peas, Karl jumped at the chance. Fired with enthusiasm, he decided not to discuss the assignment with the creative people in the agency as was routine, but instead to come up with his own, original idea, and take total credit for it in due course. Confusion over credit due for creativity was a recurring feature of agency life.

Having heard about a clown who rented himself and his wife out for promotions, children's parties and appropriate events, Karl Cunningham went single-mindedly after him. Blobby Nose and his wife – a contortionist called the India Rubber Woman – were an elderly Cockney couple who, seeing an imaginary gap in the children's entertainment market in Ireland, had moved to Dublin to improve their standard of living. Blobby Nose jumped at the engagement when Karl offered it to him. A binding agreement was reached.

The plan was that Blobby Nose and the India Rubber Woman would set themselves up on an open-sided trailer in the car park of one of the major supermarkets, flanked by pyramids of tinned Wilton Peas, posters, flags and bunting. They would move from one supermarket to another every week for six weeks, and would entertain the children and in this way draw mums and dads to the large display, dispensing leaflets offering money off the next purchase of Wilton Peas in the process. Blobby Nose would ask the children riddles and give small prizes for correct answers.

The first step was to present the promotion as a fait accompli to the client, and Karl duly invited the marketing manager and his team to the agency for a presentation of Blobby Nose's attributes and the promotion generally. He requested that Ted and Martin sit in, and as it was only expected that a brief meeting would be required, discussion would then pass to other products under the same brand name. Karl had bigger plans: when everyone was comfortably seated in the boardroom, the door of the adjoining office was thrown open and Blobby Nose raced in wearing full make-up, spotted costume and shoes with extended toes, blowing a bugle. He was followed by a scantily clad India Rubber Woman.

Round and round the table he ran, yelling his set piece in an unmistakable Cockney accent, waving his arms and stopping here and there to pose chuckling questions to the mystified, mohair-suited marketing men. The India Rubber Woman stood in the corner and turned herself into unspeakable shapes. Thrilled with the effect, an excited Karl could not be persuaded to call off Blobby Nose and his mate, in spite of horrified glances from Ted and Martin.

Cas, Liz and Paul were in the adjoining office and heard the whoops coming from the boardroom. Paul, who knew a comic situation when he heard one, was for going in to see what was happening, and each of them in turn slipped quietly into the room, with thought-up excuses, Liz with extra coffee, Paul with pencils and pads and Cas with an imaginary telephone message. They tried to keep straight faces, but hurried from the room, exploding uncontrollably, unnoticed by the hypnotised audience. Blobby Nose was blowing up balloons by this time, and twisting them into unrecognisable shapes, reminiscent of his wife, who by now had adopted a decidedly dubious posture in the corner, which had the undivided attention of the marketing manager, who stared agape.

Eventually Ted's fingernails digging into Karl's arm made him realise that perhaps the performance had gone on long enough. Blobby Nose and the IRW were extracted from the room, leaving consternation behind. Now that Blobby Nose had been contracted ('You get two for the price of one') and would have to be paid, it was eventually decided to let Karl go ahead with the deal.

Then came the actual promotion, when Blobby Nose took up his position on the trailer, surrounded by countless cans of Wilton Peas. He proceeded to ask the children riddles, and although it was not part of the plan, to give away tins of peas as prizes. Meanwhile the India

Rubber Woman was winding herself into intricate and obscene configurations. A crowd gathered, and more and more people milled around, adults now as well as children, shouting answers at Blobby Nose and demanding tins of peas as prizes. Children tried to clamber up on to the trailer. Blobby Nose turned nasty and trod on their fingers. Admonished by a frightened Karl that he should only have handed out leaflets, Blobby Nose said he didn't care one way or the other, but with the supply of free peas suddenly cut off by Karl, the crowd turned ugly and a fracas broke out. Blobby Nose was pushed aside by youths who leapt on the trailer, scattering the display in all directions and knocking over the India Rubber Woman who bumped through the crowd in a ball. Opportunists gathered up the peas and disappeared. The Gardaí were called.

Back at the office once more, Karl was summoned to Ted's office to give some explanation, which might be used to mollify the client, but as none was forthcoming, apart from the ghastly error of judgment in hiring Blobby Nose in the first place, Karl was banned from any further contact with the Wilton account.

Among the abandoned merchandising materials were large quantities of stickers with Blobby Nose's head on them, originally intended for handing out to children as badges. Paul commandeered the stickers and set about decorating the agency with them. Everywhere Karl went there were reminders of the ill-fated promotion and for weeks stickers appeared on towels, on cups and saucers, all over his desk, in drawers when he opened them, in his brief case and on his overcoat, stuck to the soles of his shoes, and even in toilet bowls, until Karl piteously begged for the torture to stop and Cas gave an order that all this had to end before Karl was carted away with a nervous breakdown.

'Make sure that Wilton gets kid glove treatment in future,' Ted said grumpily. 'That account is worth a lot of money to us.'

Nobody could call Ted parsimonious – no steadier hand when it came to loosening the purse-strings. But his innate sense of what was right and proper in terms of cost-effective advertising came into play when Western Distillers informed him that they had commissioned a top British firm of marketing consultants to devise a brand name for a 'new' 14-year old special Irish Whiskey which they intended to launch on the British and Irish markets. They had also retained the consultants' associated design company to produce a Western Distillers corporate logo. The cost would be astronomical, but well worth it, the Managing Director said. That kind of work was always expensive, but the consultants had a reputation for being one of the best in Britain.

Ted objected passionately on three counts. One: the cost proposed was outrageous; Two: he had always had a bee in his bonnet that there was a lot of mumbo jumbo talked about devising logos and brand names by people with vested interests, who deliberately made it more complicated than it really was; Three: it was totally unnecessary to go to England for such a service anyway – as was the norm.

He decided to invite the top executives of Western Distillers to a meeting in the boardroom of Flynn & Malby and to make a presentation to them as to why Flynn & Malby should be given the task of creating the new brand name and logo, and not the UK company.

The resultant submission showed Ted at his intuitive and creative best, and gave a glimpse of why he was so well thought of by so many tough, discriminating businessmen, and why, despite his shortcomings, he had built an advertising agency to which many companies were happy to entrust their substantial advertising budgets.

'Good advertising and marketing money, as well as time are wasted when virtually any mark could be a logo, providing it isn't obscene, insulting or being used elsewhere,' Ted claimed. 'A logo only becomes effective when it is recognised as being associated with a company or institution through advertising, promotion and publicity, and has little or nothing to do with the intrinsic design.

'As for brand names, similar thinking applies. Usually a massive amount of research is carried out to ascertain which word or group of words best suits and describes the product. People are asked penetrating questions. Questionnaires are filled in. Information is collated. Meanings and shades of meanings are investigated. Names are selected. These are scrutinised from every angle and for every nuance. And a brand name is finally chosen. But is all this really necessary?

'Take "Guinness", for example. How did that brand name come about? Not through research. It was simply the name of the man who invented it! And when he put his name on the bottle, it ceased to be his surname and became the name of a bottle of stout. Then through promotion of all kinds, it became one of the most famous and successful brand names in the world.'

He went on: 'Just think, if his name had been O'Reilly, you could just as easily be asking for a "Pint of O'Reilly, please!" whenever you went into a pub.'

He gave a two-hour performance, covering every angle and doggedly pressing his theories. For a man often given to waffle, as Cas and Martin saw it, he was reassuringly incisive when he wanted to be.

Ted won the day. Flynn & Malby were given the assignment, and Western Distillers saved themselves a considerable amount of money.

CHAPTER 3

'Rita Flynn on the line,' said Cas's secretary. 'You want to talk to her?'

'Put her through'. Cas liked Ted's wife, Rita; she was good fun and she lacked Ted's deviousness.

'Hello, Rita?'

'Cas?'

'Yes. What can I do for my favourite person called Rita?'

'It's what I can do for you, my love. Boy, have I got a job for you!'

'I have a job, Rita – or didn't Ted tell you?' Cas doodled elaborately on his blotter.

'Ah, but this is after hours, my love,'

'Double jobbing?'

'Sort of. Two young friends of an American cousin of mine are coming to Ireland. I don't suppose Ted mentioned it?'

'No.'

'Well, they are. Don't be difficult, Cas. These are two lovely, single girls from California, flying into Dublin this weekend. What are the chances of you and one of your bachelor friends taking them out on the town some night?'

'No chance.'

'Come on Cas.'

'What age are they and what do they look like?'

'About your age and beautiful. I talked to one of them on the phone and they sound gorgeous.'

'Beautiful – on the phone! Anyway, do I have a choice?'

'No.'

'Okay. When?' Cas sighed.

'Friday,' was Rita's whiplash reply.

'Right, I'll talk to Barry Rogan and see if he is as big a sucker as I am.'

'It's about time you met a nice girl and settled down,' said Rita.

'I've met lots of nice girls.'

'One is all that's required. Monogamy is back in fashion – or haven't they told you? Anyway, the girls will be staying in the Shelbourne Hotel. Call for them at eight o'clock sharp next Friday. They're college pals and know one another well. One is Laura Burbridge-Otis and the other is Chloe O'Leary.'

'She's the one with the Irish connections.'

'Clever boy. In the dim and distant past, maybe.'

'Okay, okay. Will do.'

'Thanks, love. Be in touch,' Rita laughed and hung up.

Ted Flynn's wife Rita puzzled a lot of people. Since Ted rarely appeared in public with her, they felt he shouldn't appear in public with her at all. It spoilt their conjectures that just maybe Ted was having a long-standing affair with his colleague and board member, Liz Downey. Even when groups in the social magazines showed Ted in a semi-circle of business associates with Liz among them wearing her supercilious look and a crazily expensive sheath dress, the long expected split between Ted and Rita never materialised. How could Rita go on taking it – people asked themselves, annoyed at being kept waiting so long for some scandalous developments. And how was Liz's husband, Des, so accommodating that he allowed his wife be photographed widely with Ted at parties and on formal occasions. Did he not feel aggrieved?

The solution to the last question could be found in the fact that Ted was paying Liz handsomely for her company, and it was well worth it to Des to play along. Not an energetic type, his modest salary in Dockrells hardware company could never have paid for the breaks he took with Liz to very expensive resorts, when she was able to ease herself out of Ted's grasp. Of late it had not been unusual for Ted to accompany the two of them and to make up a nice little threesome for Cap d'Antibes, Cannes for the Film Festival, or Venice for the Biennale art festival. They had even made it to Glyndebourne for the opera season one summer, although not one of them had the slightest notion of enjoying opera. What they did enjoy was the strolling by the river in evening dress, the hamper meals on the lawn and the rubbing of shoulders with world opera figures, whose names made music lovers' mouths water. And photographs of these sorties somehow always seemed to make their way into the papers and the good magazines. Where was Rita in all of this? Was she not furious, her own set asked themselves, as they leafed through *Creation, Social and Personal,* and the *Irish Tatler and Sketch,* studying the hand-picked glamorous events and participants. Rita refused to be drawn.

As it happened, Rita had stopped minding that kind of thing. She had cared in the beginning, but Rita Flynn *née* Doyle knew she had exactly what she wanted from life – more in fact. Yes, of course it was annoying to see Ted go off on these jaunts, but she knew in her heart of hearts that three children, plenty of money and an amazing amount of personal freedom was what she had married Ted for, and they remained the reasons why she intended to stay married to him. She had come to the stage where she treated Ted more like a difficult eldest son than a husband, someone who had to be humoured and occasionally hauled over the coals. Here they were, excellently housed in a handsome home on Dalkey's Vico Road overlooking Killiney Bay, admittedly not yet paid for, as the mortgage was huge and would take a lifetime to pay off. Flynn & Malby was making more money each year and Ted appeared to have the Midas touch, and she knew that she would never be able to keep up with the amount of social life he seemed to have to handle to keep things rolling, the social life which was his life's blood. He'd been like that when she had married him.

Rita Doyle met Ted when she was having a brief bloom of youth. Not a particularly good-looking girl, she was nonetheless full of life, and she had realised that maybe money and a large family was more in her line than marriage with the rather earnest young man she had been dating for several months, who had just asked her to marry him. The young man had interviewed her for the job of wife rather than courted her, and presented her with an engagement ring, which she had taken for the glamour of it. Then his suggestion of a pre-marriage course to 'get budgeting straight for once and for all' had put her off the idea of marrying him so soon, and she had handed back the ring with a view to looking for a man with a bit of money.

She had spotted Ted a few months afterwards at a race meeting in the Phoenix Park, for Rita dearly loved to place a bet and frequently went to race meetings with her girlfriends. When the crowd drinking in the bar had arranged to go on somewhere for dinner, Rita had met

Ted in the group, and had been surprised when he decided to pay her attention, and eventually asked her out. Something in her direct attitude had interested Ted.

What they had in common was a liking for money, and to the amazement of their respective groups of friends, they had embarked upon a quick romance. Rita's rather large child-bearing hips had appealed to Ted, as he felt he was ready to settle down and start a family, and he didn't fancy any of the super slim young women who pursued him. He had the idea that someone like Rita could be the right person to form the backdrop against which he could lead a colourful life, and being a slick salesman, Ted had sold her on the idea of a short engagement and marriage.

Rita was the daughter of a north Dublin motor mechanic who owned a small garage. Her father had come into some money through an accident claim and he had invested it wisely for his only daughter, hoping she would bring home a young man who was going places, and who would lift her up a peg or two above him and his retiring wife. Although he hadn't immediately taken to Ted as a person, he had not stood in the way of Rita's marrying, but had given her a considerable sum of money on marriage. She had intimated to Ted that this was forthcoming, which had added to her allure for him while they were still dating. They had married quietly and honeymooned in London for a week.

With the rising fortunes of the agency, their suburban house had been exchanged for a larger one, and then a larger one again, until eventually they had gone full out and bought a villa high up over the Vico Road with breathtaking views on three sides. The house had been built by people who had retired from active service in India, and it had colonial features which had made their acquaintances and their separate friends squirm with envy.

* * *

'Bit of a laugh,' said Cas, when he met his friend Barry Rogan that evening for pints in the Queens pub in Dalkey, and told him about Rita's American girls.

'Could be, but we're taking a big risk. At least, I am, you've signed on the dotted line. They could be awful looking. The Misses Lumpy.'

'Fifty per cent odds,' said Cas. 'That's not bad. I've risked more at the bookies.'

'I don't fancy your one,' said Barry Rogan.

'Which one is mine?'

'Sweet Chloe O'Leary. Mine's Laura Burbridge-Otis. Oh God, what a name to conjure with.'

Cas took a deep drink of his pint and wiped the froth from his mouth.

'Burbridge-Otis. She could be black.'

'Jesus, I've never been out with a black woman before,' said Barry.

'Do you know that your eyes have glazed over? said Cas.

'Thinking of the strange, dark and mysterious does that to me,' laughed Barry. 'And what about darlin' Chloe O'Leary?'

'Red hair. Drinks cranberry juice. Is deeply into physical education. Daddy's a cop.'

'She might let you educate her physically, then. With a bit of luck.' Their predictions about the girls grew wilder and wilder, and their hopes of a fun night out increased under the influence of Guinness.

* * *

Pam O'Regan threw herself into a chair. She was tired after a strenuous day in Flynn & Malby. She liked her job, but her boss, Martin O'Neill could be very demanding, and he was taking her willing personality a bit too much for granted. She looked at her watch. Quarter to seven. I'll go down to Cas and persuade him to take me out for a meal, or at least a drink, she thought. His car was parked outside the flat, so she knew he was home. She hadn't seen him all day. The poor lad was working too hard – and she had a fragment of information which would interest him. She went to the mirror and repaired the gaps in her make-up, and then brushed her straight, blonde hair into shape. A modicum of Ma Griffe perfume restored her faith in herself and she decided to go down without phoning.

Pam turned the key in Cas's door and went straight in.

'Anyone at home?' She heard a grunt. 'Where are you?'

'In the bath.'

'Oh good!' She turned left, opened the bathroom door and went in. Cas was lying full length, relaxing in a Radox bath. Pam stood on tip-toe, tilted her chin and peered into the bath. Cas grabbed a face-cloth and placed it strategically.

'Pam, must you come barging in?'

'No. It just happens that I like doing it. I see I'm welcome anyway.' She giggled and Cas threw a loofah at her.

'Go into the lounge and pour yourself a drink. I'll be out in a few minutes.'

'Okay. I heard something today which should interest you.' Pam went out and poured two gin and tonics. She took a few sips of hers and then slipped into Cas's bedroom. Pulling back the bed-clothes, she jumped in and pulled the duvet up to her neck.

'Pam?' came from the lounge.

'I'm in here.'

'What are you up to?' He came into the bedroom. Pam's face peered over the bedclothes at him.

'Come to me, you beautiful boy,' she said in a mock sexy voice.

'Pam, stop it. I have to go out. I'm late as it is.'

'Are you not going to make love to me, then? Did you hear what the construction worker said to his girl-friend after he made love to her in the cabin of his JCB? Did the earth move for you?'

'Sorry, Pam D'Or. I have to be in the Shelbourne in three quarters of an hour for an appointment. Now get up out of that.'

'Oh well,' said Pam resignedly. 'A girl can but try. Anyway, Celine and Co. wanted me to meet them in Fitzgeralds for a drink and go on to a Chineser, so ...' She sat up in the bed. 'Listen, do you know what I heard today?'

'No. What?'

Pam watched him appreciatively as he got dressed. 'You know the Giraffe is going to Leitrim for two weeks' fishing.'

'Yes, of course. He goes fishing this time every year.'

'Well, this time Martin's going with him.'

'What?'

'Yeah. I wondered if you knew.'

'No, I didn't.' Cas was annoyed.

'And they've been having whispered discussions in Martin's office recently. They're cooking up something, Cas. But maybe you know what it is?'

'Christ, no. Going away on holidays together? That's a new one. Martin and Ted are like chalk and cheese and Martin has no interest in fishing.' Pam suddenly felt sorry for Cas. He didn't realise how two-faced Martin could be. As Martin's secretary she certainly did. She knew he was deeply jealous of Cas.

'Look, what about a meal out tomorrow night?' asked Cas.

Pam laughed and climbed out of the bed. 'Sorry old chum, booked solid tomorrow.'

It was exactly eight o'clock as Cas Maitland and Barry Rogan stood in the lobby of the Shelbourne Hotel, positioned to see their dates come down the stairs or out of the lift. They had asked Reception to phone Miss Burbridge-Otis and Miss O'Leary in their rooms and had been told that the ladies would be down immediately. Cas wore a red sweater and black trousers, and Barry a mauve casual jacket and grey trousers. They had decided on the Brazen Head as the place to bring the girls for a few drinks. Some place really Irish, Barry had said. Then, maybe, on to the singing pubs and a late night snack somewhere. First, if they liked the idea, a sight-seeing tour of the city by car, to fill up the evening.

As various women came out of the lift or down the stairs, Barry poked Cas in the side and said nervously, 'I don't fancy yours.'

'What you lose on the swings you gain in the tunnel of love,' said Cas. Inevitably the women they were looking at went straight out the front door, or turned left into the Horseshoe bar.

'I bet you a fiver these two are ours,' Barry said.

'Done,' said Cas. Two extremely attractive and elegantly dressed young women were stepping out of the lift. Barry elbowed Cas and chuckled.

'There, you owe me a fiver.'

'Not bloody likely,' said Cas, peering into the tea lounge.

'Caspar Maitland?' said a husky American female voice. Cas spun round. Jesus, it was them!

'Yes,' said Cas. Barry was struggling to regain his advantage.

'I'm Laura, and this is Chloe,' the husky voice said. 'Sorry for being a little late. Chloe had a slight difference of opinion with the zip on her dress.'

'Hi, I'm Chloe.' Chloe stretched out her hand. Her voice had only a trace of an American accent.

Cas beamed, smitten. 'This is Barry Rogan, a friend of mine.' God, he thought, these are two of the most beautiful women I have ever seen. He checked them over. Laura was petite with carefully styled blonde hair and stunning blue eyes. She was dressed in a beige low-cut, short evening dress, which showed off her lightly tanned skin perfectly. Chloe was red haired, but it was dark red, like the colour of a squirrel's coat. We were right – she has red hair, Cas thought. Her eyes were nut brown and amused and her skin was creamy, her lips full. She wore a green and black patterned dress, which flowed over her.

'You ladies come from Hollywood, by any chance?' asked Barry with obvious admiration.

'Bullseye,' said Chloe. 'Why do you ask?' She laughed.

'It's just that you're not quite what we were expecting,' said Cas.

'And what were you expecting?' Laura asked. 'We were expecting a Mr Jass'

'Mr Jass?' said Barry, puzzled.

'Yes,' added Chloe, 'Hugh.'

'But who's Hugh Jass?' asked Barry. There were a few seconds of complete silence, then they all burst out laughing. The tension was broken, and they were set for a good night.

'What we really meant,' said Cas, 'was that you're in evening dress and we're just casual. We were going to bring you to the Brazen Head, the oldest pub in Dublin.'

'We like pubs,' said Chloe firmly.

'Still, you must have been expecting more. You're dressed correctly for an evening date and ....'

'So what', said Laura. 'Our fault. We weren't sure where we were going, but who cares? Come on. Let's go to this pub. It's got to be great fun. It sounds real neat.' She slipped her arms around the waists of the two lads and steered them towards the door.

'I'm looking forward to this,' said Chloe.

They ended up in the Gresham Hotel, still enjoying themselves hugely, and all four wanted to meet as often as possible while the girls were in town. They would be in Ireland for two weeks and planned to spend a week in Dublin and another in the west of Ireland.

Each night Cas and Barry took them out for a meal, or as Cas was a theatre fanatic, to a play, or just to a pub, and on some of the days, one or other of them brought the girls sight-seeing. They were on a roll, all four of them.

They even went to Glendalough, the sixth century monastic settlement in County Wicklow and for a joke Barry invented an 'old Irish custom', making a group of visitors hold hands around the famous hundred foot high round tower. He said that it was a tradition to make a wish, which was sure to come true, and later, when they were leaving, they saw groups of Germans queuing to hold hands around the tower, firmly establishing his newly-minted legend.

Barry cooked a meal for the four of them in Cas's apartment the evening before the girls set off for Connemara, and afterwards Cas showed them his paintings. Chloe thought they were superb and Cas promised that one day he would paint her portrait.

While Laura and Chloe were away, Barry phoned Cas at the office and asked him to meet for a drink, as he had a big favour to ask of him.

'Okay, what's the favour?'

'You know my Aunt Vi.'

'Sort of,' said Cas.

'She's very old now and she lives alone in the Moira Hotel in St Andrew's Street.'

'Well, what about her?'

'She wants to see me because she thinks she's dying. Would you come with me? I don't want to go on my own. She's a bit of a tartar, but she sort of likes me. I haven't seen her for ages but I can't turn down the message I got that she wants me to come. I'm afraid she'll savage me for not coming regularly, but I know she'll tone down if someone else is there.'

'I'll go along with you,' said Cas.

That evening, after a few drinks in the Old Stand, Barry and Cas went visiting.

'Number 42, through that door and down the corridor. Last door on the right,' said the receptionist.

Vi Moran, now 84 and alone in the world wasn't actually Barry's aunt. She was his late mother's sister-in-law, and reputedly wealthy, with no one to whom she could leave her worldly goods. Barry was not disinterested. He knocked.

'Come in you fool, it's open.' A good start. Barry grinned at Cas and shrugged. They went in carefully.

'Hello, Aunt Vi.'

'And about time too,' she snapped. Vi was sitting up in bed, wearing a fur cape as a bed jacket. The room was quite small and the rumpled bed was spread with a confused array of objects, mostly of silver and gold, ranging from candle-sticks to perfume spray bottles. The air was a sickening mixture of heavy perfume and cigarette smoke.

'About time,' she repeated. Barry kissed her lightly on the cheek.

'Sorry I haven't been in more often, Aunt Vi,' he mumbled.

'This is a friend of mine, Caspar Maitland.'

'He needn't think he's going to get anything from me,' said Vi.

'I don't think he's looking for anything, Aunt Vi.' Barry was embarrassed. Vi waved a long cigarette holder with a lit cigarette in it.

'All this will be yours. All this and more. You'd visit me more often if I told you more on that score.' She indicated the items on the bed. 'Look, take this, for example.' She fondled a figurine of a shepherdess and sheep-dog. 'This is worth a fortune.' Cigarette ash fell down on the counterpane. 'What's this other young man doing here?' It was hard to understand what she was saying, as her voice was slurred.

'He's a friend, Vi, I told you already.' Her hand shook as she stubbed out her cigarette and replaced it with another.

'When I die, you will inherit everything I have, Barry. You know that? I feel it is only a matter of time. The hotel is making arrangements to transfer me to a nursing home. I hate nursing homes, but there you are.'

'Don't talk nonsense about dying, Aunt Vi,' said Barry. Cas suddenly realised that Vi's old age and infirmity was compounded by the fact that she was drunk out of her mind.

'Aunt Vi. You're not going to die for quite a long time, believe me,' said Barry, trying to keep control of the discussion.

'See if I don't,' was Vi's intoxicated reply. They stayed some time, while Vi arranged and rearranged her valuables on the bed, like a child setting out its toys. When at last they were able to leave, Cas gulped for air outside the door.

'The words "money isn't everything" spring to mind,' he said.

'She's been giving me that line about leaving me all her wealth for years,' said Barry. 'I wouldn't mind it if she did, but anyway she's not going to die for a while yet'

They went back to the Old Stand for a night-cap pint.

* * *

While Ted Flynn's wife Rita had more or less what she wanted in life, apart from Ted's company, on which she had given up, there was still one side of her as yet unexplored – Rita, the businesswoman. For a long time she had an ambition that she would like to open a teashop and make her own money and lifestyle. She had been too busy for anything of the sort while she had been bringing up her family, more or less single-handedly, but now that the last one was leaving school and would choose a career, underpinned by Ted's income, Rita was busy laying her plans. Ted might be gracing the pages of the social magazines in the company of Liz Downey and colleagues, but she, Rita, had him when she needed him: Christmas week for family shopping in Grafton Street, family functions, bank holidays and some Sundays.

Ted had taken to being away more and more from early summer onwards, either up at the fishing lodge in Leitrim entertaining clients, or buzzing around the continent attending advertising award events, and so he would be out of the way. Rita set about investigating her idea of a smart teashop where she would meet new people, day for day, and where she would have the achievement of stacking up a nice little pile of money for herself.

She was a naturally good and competent cook, and as the daughter of a businessman, albeit on a small scale, she understood how to handle money and stay in credit. She would present Ted with a fait accompli. She would use her investment of her father's gift, which had grown nicely over the years. Ted had never asked her for any of it, preferring to feel that she had some security of her own.

Rita fancied Sandycove seafront as a location, with its established year-round circulation route and scenic views. It was near Dalkey and easily accessible from home, and accordingly she notified an auctioneer in nearby Glasthule, and sat back prepared to wait until the right thing turned up. Ted might well object that he wasn't consulted and fly into a temper, but she knew that if it came to a slanging match, she had enough to make him back down. Rita wasn't stupid, and if half of Dublin thought that he and Liz Downey were having a long-running affair, she had plenty of ammunition. She felt sure that they didn't really have such an alliance, but if others thought they did, she would serve him this – and he wouldn't like it at all.

A call came from the auctioneer more quickly than she expected. He thought he might have found just the right premises for her, and would she like to view it? Rita dressed casually, not to give the idea that she was made of money because she lived on the Vico Road. She drove down to Glasthule in the Mini Ted had got for the children. The hall-door level of a tall house on the seafront, close to Glasthule, was the place he had in mind, and Rita liked it right away. Since there were several small hotels and restaurants in the area, there would be no problem about conversion for commercial purposes. The large front window was semi-circular and commanded an excellent view of the bay, with Howth across the water looking like a large-snouted porpoise snoozing in the sun. The area at the back of the main room was suitable for conversion to a kitchen, and toilet facilities were already installed from the time it had been converted to an apartment. It was really a question of making up her mind either to go for it, or to drop the whole idea.

She went ahead with it. Her savings would cover the rental of the premises, and the necessary new catering equipment, as well as a smartening up of the exterior. It would also stretch to her new décor. She had thought it out well in advance and she had fallen for a scheme when she first consulted a designer. The colours would be simple, red, white and black, with white predominating. A black polished soft-tiled floor would make for quietness, and white walls with suitable paintings and framed photographs would give an effect of coming to rest. Furniture would be modern 1970s, well designed and easy to clean, and table cloths would be checked, red and white, and black and white. Table flower arrangements would soften the effect and make the place welcoming. She would call it simply, 'The Teashop'. Since it would be some time before the work was completed, there was no hurry about deciding on the bill of fare. The next item on the menu was to tell Ted.

'Ted, I've something important to tell you,' Rita said suddenly, sitting back in her outsize chintz-covered chair after dinner. The standard lamp behind her shadowed her face theatrically in the fading evening light.

'Mmmmm?' Ted was sprawled on the settee with one foot on a foot-stool, and *Campaign* magazine opened and unread across his chest. His eyelids were heavy and his reading glasses had slipped down his nose.

'Are you listening to me?'

'Yes.' A pause. 'What is it?'

'I'm going into business on my own shortly,' Rita said pleasantly, as if she were saying that she intended to buy new curtains for one of the rooms.

'Good. That's nice.'

'I am ... going ... into ... business ... on my own ... shortly,' Rita repeated, in a louder voice.

Ted sat up and took off his glasses.

'Going into business on your own?'

'Oh stop repeating what I say, and listen to me,' Rita said, snapping in spite of her resolution to play this calmly. 'I intend to own and run a teashop, on a good circulation route, in an attractive location.' It sounded like a rehearsed speech. 'I've done my research and the one thing missing along the Sandycove seafront is somewhere interesting to sit down and have a proper morning or afternoon tea.'

'Good God, Rita, you can't be serious.' He was sitting up alert.

'Of course I'm serious.'

'When did you come up with this dazzling idea?'

'Recently.'

'But you've no business experience. You don't know about catering, or running an enterprise of this kind, or anything like that. You've no idea what it takes to run a business. For God's sake, woman, you haven't got yourself too deeply into this, have you?'

'If you consider signing a lease, arranging to have the place done up, ordering fittings and furniture going in too deeply, well, yes, I have.'

Ted was fuming.

'Why the hell didn't you tell me about this before now, Rita? What are you up to? What were you thinking about? You've no right to get into this mess without consulting me.'

'It's not a mess. And why should I consult you?'

'Why? Why? Because I do know something about business.' His voice was a mixture of anger and sarcasm.

'And I am your husband. Remember? You should rely on my judgement.'

'Look Ted. I knew exactly what your reaction would be. Completely negative. So, I went ahead. Anyway, I didn't see you as the person to consult. You're never here.'

'That's absolute nonsense. Of course I'm here.'

Caught off guard and embarrassed, Ted went over to the drinks cabinet and poured out two whiskeys and sodas. He handed one to Rita and sat down.

'Look Rita. I'm bloody angry about this. Not only should you have checked out your scheme with me first, but you've gone into something financial without consultation. Where did you get the money for this hare-brained idea anyway?'

Rita got up and turned on several lamps dotted around the room from a central switch beside one of the large mahogany bookcases flanking the marble fireplace. Then she stood by the window, staring out at the lights which glowed in clusters around distant Bray Head. She sipped her drink.

'Don't worry, I'm not asking you for any cash. I've used my own, the money that Dad gave me.'

'That was a mistake.'

'Why? It's my money to do with as I wish. It's got nothing to do with you.'

'I was hoping you wouldn't touch that money, Rita ....'

'Why not?'

'So that it would always be there – in an emergency.'

'What emergency?'

'Well if ever – oh, never mind. This whole thing is bloody ridiculous.'

Rita swung around. 'Ted! First of all it's my money. Secondly you've got your agency and your own lifestyle, and you do as you damn well please. Thirdly, my time is my own to use as I wish. Now that the kids don't need constant care, I'm off to do something with my life. I have one, you know, strange as it may seem. And anyway, you're not the oracle when it comes to business. Okay?'

Ted was dumbfounded. Seldom at a loss for words, he was stymied now. And with that Rita downed her drink and left the room rather grandly. He was too offended to ask her to stay, and soon she was lolling in a perfumed bath, pleased about the way she had handled him. She went to bed after her bath, and heard him going up to his room. Knowing that Ted had an early departure for the airport for London the following morning, Rita was quite happy that there would be no immediate opportunity of resuming the topic which had proved so disagreeable to him. Ted only spoke in monosyllables over breakfast the next morning, and left in a huff. The way was clear for The Teashop.

CHAPTER 4

Tessa Bennett was generally content with her lifestyle, and she rarely missed her job as a physical education teacher which she had before the children were born. She felt she had everything in control. Jake and Stephanie constituted the perfect small family, and Paul was doing really well in Flynn & Malby, with Ted giving him more and more responsibility. As a couple, this meant that they were not worrying about financial matters. Just one small cloud appeared now and then on her personal horizon, and that was that Paul seemed to expect her to spend a great deal of time without him.

She didn't exactly resent it, as she had freedom while the children were at school, and there were sufficient social occasions attached to agency life for her to get out and around and occasionally put on the style. It was just that it didn't occur to Paul that they should spend time together in an unstructured way. He always liked to know where he stood about spending time at home, and was inclined to budget his company, unlike when they had been courting, when he had all the time in the world to spend with her outside working hours.

Tessa presumed that most married couples had as satisfactory a life as she and Paul had, in that they had a partnership, a family and a future. She hadn't looked for more at first, and was reasonably content. Still there was the niggling feeling that it would be nice to enjoy Bulloch Harbour and the surrounding area together. On a sunny evening, the mood would be just right for doing something with the children, or together if she had a sitter, but as the hands stole up to nine o'clock on his watch, Paul would want to slip off for a pint locally. Sometimes he brought Tessa with him, but he went anyway.

This morning she dressed in a track suit and new runners, and tied her thick, fair hair back in a sporty scarf. She planned to jog through Dalkey and up the Vico Road, and then back as far as Dun Laoghaire via Sandycove seafront. It was a particularly scenic route as it followed the variations of the coast, and she would run or walk until she was thoroughly exercised, and had her mind filled with pleasant thoughts.

As Tessa came along by Scotsman's Bay, she was impelled to slow down and rejoice in the view, and she walked the remainder of the seafront enjoying it. Half way down she spotted a place simply called The Teashop, with red and white striped blinds. It was open for business and she wondered how she hadn't noticed it before. Feeling like a break after her jog, she turned in the short path and went through its open and welcoming door.

'Tessa! It is you, isn't it?'

'Rita. It's you, isn't it?' They both laughed.

'My goodness, Tessa, it's so long since we've met that I hardly recognised you, particularly in that casual outfit. Were you doing something athletic?' Tessa's face was pink from the exertion.

'Yes, running, walking and jogging. I've been bitten by the new keep-fit bug.'

'Come and sit down and make yourself comfortable. I can offer you a good pot of tea and something nice to go with it.'

Tessa sat down and surveyed the room.

'This is fantastic. Are you working here? I didn't hear about this place opening.'

'I'm the proud owner and this is my first day. In fact, you are my very first customer – my handsel, to bring me luck. I only opened an hour ago, would you believe, and my heart is in my mouth in case I don't make a go of it. I've had this in mind for some time, and now I am finally, Rita Flynn, Prop. I'm still at sixes and sevens.'

'Oh, but the place is lovely, Rita. Of course you'll make a success of it. Mind you, Paul never mentioned that you were going into business. But then, you can't depend on men for news, now can you?'

Rita looked a trifle sheepish. 'Well, I was a bit bold about it, I suppose. I was so keen to get it going that I – well – neglected to mention my plans to Ted until the last minute. When I did tell him, he wasn't all that pleased, so maybe he hasn't been broadcasting it around the agency. Never mind. He'll come round in time.'

Tessa was amused, but admired Rita's strength of purpose and cleverness in implementing her ambitions.

'I only hope I have as much go in me when my family no longer needs me, Rita,' she said. 'Oh God, that sounded terribly bitchy, but you know what I mean.'

Rita laughed and patted Tessa's hand. 'Now, what about that pot of tea? I have six blends. And a homemade scone or two with special raspberry jam, or maybe a cream cake? It's on the house. Next time, you'll be a paying customer, I hope.'

Tessa sat down at a table by the window and as Rita went off to prepare her snack, she noticed the rack of newspapers and magazines for customers and the general effect of the décor, and was filled with admiration for the older woman. This would make a splendid half-way house for her runs or jogs, she decided.

Rita returned with the tea and scones and left Tessa to enjoy them along with the view, busying herself behind a screen where there was a small office section. So far Tessa was the only customer, but surely a clientele would spring up in a short while.

Rita was pleased with her client. She had liked Tessa when she met her at the occasional reception. She hoped now that Tessa would find The Teashop a relaxing place, and bring along her friends in due course, or at least spread the word. When Tessa left half an hour later, Rita had seven customers and she felt her teashop had been launched on the right track.

* * *

In Dalkey village, a newly arrived restaurateur surveyed the premises he had been engaged to make over and convert into an up-market venue. Included in his brief was winning new patrons for this restaurant, and he intended to be ruthless about it.

Roddy Ogilvie had come from Scotland, where he had managed restaurants at various times in Glasgow, Edinburgh, Stirling and Aberdeen, and it was very important for him that this Dalkey assignment would go well. Tall and good-looking, with fair hair that could have come from Scandinavia, his clear eyes had a compelling look and he had a perfectly shaped nose that gave him a somewhat haughty air. As a divorced man, with a string of affairs on his CV, he had decided to make a break from his home country and look around Ireland for opportunities of every kind. He had approached the owners of a restaurant in Scotland and put it to them that he would be very interested in opening a restaurant for them in Ireland, with a view to setting up a similar series of venues if the first one prospered. On the basis of their agreement he had taken over The Twig, a medium-sized premises in Dalkey main street, with a dwindling trade.

Roddy Ogilvie had focus and ambition, and was not overburdened with principles. As a boy, he had worked in restaurant kitchens to get the money together to train in catering and restaurant management, and he had seen wealthy clients waste food without a worry in the world, and how canny restaurateurs often made a good living out of this. As a student in catering college he had displayed a ruthless streak and had used every trick in the bag, feeding himself on his days off by bringing out food that would not be missed.

One thing he had learned from watching rich people relaxing – they liked to be made feel rich, and he had studied them. People with new money wanted to be seen to be wealthy, and unpriced menus was one way of pandering to this. Roddy knew how to make people feel rich – and noticed. Now Dalkey would add another exclusive restaurant to the few already there, and hopefully a local clientele would spring up, joined by the carriage trade.

He decided that he would get fresh air and exercise every day, now that he was working in a scenic area, and adopted an early jogging routine every morning. He took to rising early and moving quickly and silently along the Vico Road, one of the loveliest in Ireland. Normally Roddy was back in his apartment after his run by nine o'clock, but one morning he was delayed by business telephone calls and took to the road nearer to ten o'clock. Just heading out of Dalkey he caught up on a pretty young woman moving along smoothly in a relaxed rhythm, and obviously enjoying her morning run. He set himself a challenge. He'd get to know her, and he bet himself he'd ask her to lunch in the newly renamed restaurant, The Aristocrat, and impress her in more ways than one. If he won his own challenge, he would have made a nice new contact, and possibly a new conquest. A polished operator, Roddy Ogilvie jogged quietly past Tessa Bennett, not even giving a companionable nod, but intending to turn around at the top of the road and come back a short time later, and meet her head-on. From the merest sidelong glance he thought her remarkably pretty.

Arriving at the top of the road, he turned back and ran down the slope, rejoicing in the beautiful morning and the prospect of meeting this lovely young woman. Before they drew level he stepped off the path. 'I hate to stop you, even for a moment,' Roddy said. He was grinning, but breathing heavily as he continued to run on the spot. 'I've come out without my watch. Could you tell me the time, please? I had to turn back rather than risk missing an appointment.'

Tessa stopped and nodded. She bent down and put her hands on her knees until she had recovered her breath. 'Coming up to twenty past ten,' she gasped, looking at her watch.

'Thanks. Sorry for disturbing you. Big sin among joggers.'

Tessa smiled and renewed her run. She noted the charming way he had rolled the 'r' in joggers, and pronounced it 'jawgerrs'. Roddy Ogilvie ran on, well pleased with himself. This would do for a first encounter.

* * *

Cas replaced the flipcharts. The presentation had gone exceedingly well. He could hear Ted chatting animatedly with the directors of Western Distillers as they went down the stairs from the boardroom to the hall-door. He heard guffaws as they shared a joke.

Flynn & Malby already did some work for Western Distillers, but the task of launching the new brand of whiskey on the market would be an enormously exciting one, and it would be a valuable contribution to the agency's coffers.

He fingered the boards which displayed the design for the new label, and the artist's impressions of the several possible bottle shapes. There was no doubt that Ted and he had made a very good presentation team, when it came to pitching for new business. During the presentation, Ted had reached over and put his arm around Cas's shoulder, and begged the Western Distillers executives to listen carefully to Cas Maitland because he was one of the best creative thinkers in the business – if not the best. And a great client contact-man to boot. Damn Ted for being so two-faced.

Ted, Martin and the Western Distillers team went together to dine in Snaffles basement restaurant, Cas having asked to be excused, pleading he had urgent work to attend to. It was always at this point that he felt he had enough of Ted, and to dine with him and the client was just too much for him today. Watching Ted go through his various routines could sometimes be beyond endurance – sincerity, deep sensitivity, light-heartedness – all the tools of a through-and-through salesman. When they left, he went down to the small room which acted as a kitchen for agency staff, and one of the secretaries who fancied him made him a sandwich and coffee to take back to his office. He put his feet on the desk and relaxed. God, but he was tired.

He closed his eyes and thought about Chloe. He was madly in love with Chloe O'Leary. But what was he going to do about Pam? Poor old Pam, he hadn't been out on a date with her for over three weeks now. He'd have to tell her he was in love with Chloe – madly in love. She'd understand. Hopefully. Christ, but Chloe was a beautiful woman. Witty too, and full of fun. Sharp as a razor, though. She had mentioned that she wanted to set up a business in Ireland. She said she could use an Irish partner. What did she mean by that? What sort of a business, and what sort of a partner? Something to do with her work in Hollywood, he suspected. Did Barry know about it? Was Barry in love with Laura Burbridge-Otis? He thought not. But then he didn't know. Men didn't know these things by instinct like women do. Did Barry know that he, Cas, was in love with Chloe? He'd have to get her on her own. He'd love to do a painting of her. Full length. Nude. What a subject.

The telephone rang.

'Cas?' It was Pam.

'Hi.'

'You still working?

'Yes.'

'Will you be long?'

'Not really. I've two letters to answer and then I've finished. Where are you phoning from?'

'I'm upstairs in my office. I was working late. Will you take me for a drink in O'Dwyers? Or dinner?'

'Pam, I ...'

'Go on. I haven't seen you in yonks.'

'I've been tied up,' said Cas.

'I know. What about a drink?'

'Well ... okay. See you in the hall in ten minutes.'

'Done,' said Pam.

'Okay?' Cas opened the car door for Pam.

'Yep.' Pam sat into Cas's car. He could hear her tights rub together as she settled her legs, and could smell her recently applied Ma Griffe perfume. It always meant Pam to him.

'I'm dying for a drink,' said Pam. 'I'm exhausted.'

'Me too,' said Cas. They drove the short distance to O'Dwyers as if there were no Chloe O'Leary in the picture.

* * *

Roddy Ogilvie set about the assignment of sorting out and relaunching the newly-named restaurant, The Aristocrat. He ate there each day for two weeks, as well as having the odd walk through the kitchens to unnerve the chef and his assistants. He secretly formed the opinion that while the foot soldiers were excellent, the officers would have to go. The chef and assistant chefs were in for a nasty surprise, while the front of house staff were quite safe. He had found the chefs wasteful and poor on detail, while he considered the reception and table service competent and friendly. The much vaunted friendliness of the Irish was useless if it was not based firmly on competence, and the balance of the two was what he sought to maintain at The Aristocrat. He privately interviewed a chef and assistant chef who had been sent over to him from Scotland, and decided to take them on. He would have to call a staff meeting first.

'I'm glad to have this opportunity of speaking to you all together,' he began, 'and I look forward to making The Aristocrat the most talked-about restaurant in Dublin. Unfortunately, there will be a 50 per cent cut in staff, which won't please some of you, but perhaps it is best to let you have the bad news right away.' He explained his decision and there were gasps of horror from some, and sighs of relief from others. 'These changes will take effect from the first of next month, and in the meantime the restaurant will close from tomorrow for redecoration and refurbishing. That's all I want to say at this point. Thank you all for the work you have done since I took over. Kitchen staff please arrange to come to me in the back office between three and five o'clock, where I will give you any money due to you, and all relevant cards and papers. Thank you everybody, thank you.'

The staff dispersed in shock, and a few hours later, feeling well pleased with himself, Roddy went off to his apartment to change and go jogging. He did it as briskly as he had dismantled the restaurant staff, as this was his way of tackling tasks, pleasant and unpleasant, and he looked forward to climbing Killiney Hill so that he could feel monarch of all he surveyed.

On the same afternoon, Tessa Bennett realised that she didn't have to collect the children until an hour later than usual, as they had a music class, and so she set off running lightly from Bulloch Harbour. She found herself thinking that running is a solitary business, and wishing for a little company. It was difficult to find a jogging pal, and better to set out whenever the weather was good and take advantage of it. The afternoon picked up and as she reached the Vico, she decided that she should stretch herself a little more and climb up to the obelisk on the hill. It only took her a few minutes and when she reached the top, she found she wasn't alone there. A man stood looking down at the bay, apparently lost to everything except the contemplation of its beauty. Behind the crescent beach, the Wicklow hills stretched to the horizon, with the large and small Sugar Loaf mountains clearly outlined against a pale blue sky, looking like cardboard cut-outs. The man turned around abruptly.

'Oh hello, there,' he said, 'I didn't hear you come up.' Tessa hadn't intended to disturb him in his reverie.

'Hello,' she said politely. He came over and stood near her, smiling.

'And hello again, we've met before.'

'Oh ... on the Vico Road, when you stopped to ask me the time.' She turned her face into the light breeze.

'That's right. Now, there's a coincidence. The gods must have sent you here to give me a lovely surprise.' Tessa regathered her hair and replaced the band on her head.

'I don't know about that,' she said tartly, 'I just came up here to get a bit more exercise and take in the view.' She inhaled deeply, then relenting in her tone, she said, 'It's so clear today, you feel you could reach out and touch it.'

'I'm from Scotland,' he said suddenly, striking a more formal note, seeing that his flirtatious opening hadn't been taken up. 'We have splendid scenery there, but this is certainly out on its own. I'm a city boy, you see. If this weather holds, I might be tempted to short-change my working hours.'

'I know what you mean,' murmured Tessa, liking the taste of companionship, but not wishing to push the acquaintance further. The man was very attractive, but she rarely took the lead in social encounters, even in the safety of Paul's gatherings and receptions.

'Roddy Ogilvie,' he said, stretching out a hand to shake hers, and when Tessa involuntarily reciprocated, she liked the feel of his firm, friendly, short-held grip.

'Tessa Bennett,' she said. 'I don't live far away, and so I feel obliged to make use of the amenities. I have children to pick up from school every day, but I really enjoy getting a bit of exercise before I do. It makes it less of a chore and more of a pleasure. I'm afraid I'm a bit of a jogging nut and I spend more time at it than I should.' She bent down and touched her toes several times.

'I run a restaurant in Dalkey', said Roddy. 'Do you know The Twig in the main street? Well, I've taken it over and I'm in the process of transforming it into The Aristocrat. It'll be a more up-market job.'

'The Aristocrat? A memorable name,' said Tessa.

'In Victorian times Dalkey was called "The Aristocrat of seaside resorts".' He turned and faced her and she could see the laughter lines forming around his eyes. 'Maybe you know some ladies – including yourself – who would like to be invited to the opening?' he said. He was standing closer to her than she was to him, or so it felt.

'Well ... that's kind of you ....' Tessa made a face.

'Where shall I send your invitation?' He pressed his advantage. Tessa hesitated, but it was too late to back out. Anyway it would be churlish to do so.

'Coonawling Cottage, Bulloch Harbour, Dalkey.'

'What a charming address. I'll be delighted to do that.'

Having obtained what he wanted, Roddy Ogilvie was too experienced to delay and he moved to resume his run.

'I've enjoyed meeting you – again,' he said. 'Until then.' And with a disturbing smile he turned and ran off leaving Tessa alone on the summit. Tessa stood there, pleased with the encounter in one way, but taken aback at the same time. She had just accepted an invitation to lunch from a total stranger. Why? – she asked herself. Maybe she was feeling a little lonely with Paul so tied up with work. Life was becoming a bit of a dreary-go-round. The previous weekend had been hopeless from a family point of view, with Paul sleeping late on Saturday and then going off to watch a tennis match in Fitzwilliam in the early afternoon. Although Tessa hadn't wanted to go to the actual match, she felt Paul could have made an effort to have her join him with the crowd in the clubhouse afterwards. It would have meant bringing the children, or getting a sitter for them, but it hadn't come up at all. She knew that if there was a meal arranged for that evening, he would let her know in time to get someone to come in, but as it turned out, he had arrived home at six, expecting the usual fare, and it was too late for them to arrange to do anything. Paul had slipped down to the pub later. Sunday hadn't been much better, as it had rained and he had watched a match on television while she brought the children out for a walk in wellingtons and rainwear. Paul had done some agency work at home that evening, and suddenly it was Monday again.

She ran back down to Bulloch with a light step, suddenly relieved of all her negative feelings. It was a big wide world, after all, and maybe she wasn't getting out enough herself.

The invitation went out to as many clients of the former Twig as there were names and phone numbers in the reservation book. With his new Scottish chefs taking over the kitchen and his front of house staff in attractive uniform, Roddy felt he was on to a winner. For his décor, he chose country mansion dining-room style, with good antique furniture, circular mahogany tables and an interesting sideboard. The plates were imitation ironstone, all in keeping with a gentle well-bred atmosphere designed to bring in an 'arrived' clientele. And busy though he was, he did not neglect to send an invitation to Mrs Tessa Bennett, 'Coonawling Cottage', Bulloch Harbour, Dalkey, Co. Dublin.

Tessa's invitation arrived the morning she was rehanging some curtains which had been dry-cleaned. She had earlier made some calls to contacts with a view to finding some PE work at one of the schools, and she was feeling brisk and energetic. She was secretly pleased that the stranger hadn't forgotten their brief encounter, as it must mean that she hadn't lost her touch after all. She greatly missed having a close girlfriend or sister nearby with whom she could have laughed over it, but she hadn't yet found the luxury of a confidante in her neighbourhood. Coming from Waterford she had no immediate family in Dublin and the estate from which they had moved hadn't yielded a friend close enough to whom she could show the invitation. Maybe she was better off not showing it to anyone, and not to Paul, certainly, as he wouldn't have understood how she came to accept it in the first place. She left things as they were.

A week later Tessa drove the children to school and returned to get ready for lunch at The Aristocrat. She had a relaxing bath and put work into her hair, making it shine and back-combing it into a slightly bouffant style. It felt good to be dressing up for lunch and she chose a new navy cotton suit which laced at the sides to a perfect fit, and showed off her hard work in achieving her figure by taking regular exercise. Lots of silver jewellery completed a chic, daytime look, and when she slipped into a pair of expensive navy court shoes, and looked at the total effect, she was charmed with her own reflection. Now to observe Dalkey society.

Roddy came over as soon as Tessa entered the restaurant.

'It's good to see you. Is a friend coming?' he asked.

He's looking really handsome, Tessa thought.

'No. I'm on my own. Is that alright?'

'Perfect,' he said. 'Would you like to lunch alone, or would you prefer if I put others at your table?'

'Thanks, but no. I'd like to lunch alone, if I may, to enjoy the food and observe the scene. Anyway I'm feeling a little anti-social and nervous.' She giggled and was immediately annoyed at herself for doing so.

Roddy grinned and said in a mock hoarse whisper: 'You're among friends. May I call you Tessa?' He put his hand on her arm and held it in a firm grip, and steered her to a small table at a window corner, from which she had an excellent view of everything and everybody. This was promising, and she anticipated a pleasant lunch, in its own way. When the place filled up with fashionable people, and a really good meal was served, she began to loosen up, and enjoy herself immensely. It was nice that Roddy had sensed that she wanted to progress at her own pace, and at the close of the meal when he had had a liqueur served, and said a few words, he slipped over to her table and asked her how she had liked it all.

'It was superb,' she said. 'I've really enjoyed myself.'

'Tessa, you will come again, won't you? Will you come back next week? I'd love you to try out some of our specialities, new items I plan to offer, and you could let me know what would hit the jackpot with the customers. Will you come this day week? Say yes.'

Taken by surprise, and delighting in the feeling of being a person in her own right, and not Paul's wife or the children's mother, and helped by the two glasses of good wine and a liqueur, she found herself saying, 'What a lovely invitation, Roddy' She was conscious of using his name for the first time. 'I'll come,' she said. Then she added carelessly, 'It'll be fun.'

Delighted with her reaction, Roddy escorted her to the door, and looking straight into her eyes said formally for the benefit of bystanders: 'Goodbye so, and thank you. So kind of you to have come.'

Tessa walked back through Dalkey, thinking of the lunch and how she seemed to have siphoned off Roddy Ogilvie's attention, even though he had so much else on his mind. Why did she feel so taken over by him? Should she tell Paul about the lunch and make light of it? A little voice inside her firmly told her to enjoy this on her own and leave Paul out of it. After all, it was just an invitation to lunch, and not a personal one. No harm in that. And then she remembered the old maxim learnt many years before – 'if it's no harm, don't do it'. Why not, she questioned herself, why not indeed?

Tessa was suddenly feeling on top of the world. Her lunch at The Aristocrat had brought a new dimension to her life in Dalkey, and while she was attracted to this stranger from Glasgow who had brightened up her image of herself, she didn't regard herself as being under a compliment to him. It felt good to be an attractive woman, and to be married and getting on with her family life, but still retaining her individuality.

This was exactly what Roddy Ogilvie wanted her to feel.

Now she thought it was time to show the children more of Dalkey and the surrounding areas, so that they would grow up appreciating their environment. She would start with a family picnic on Dalkey Island, with plenty of stories about pirates to please Jake, and so she made a booking to be rowed across the sound by a family from Coliemore Harbour, who had been carrying on that business for generations.

The Saturday she chose dawned bright and sunny and Paul said he would join them. Tessa packed the lunch basket with care, and the children ran around in circles excited about the boat ride and the day on the island.

'Will the wild goats want to eat us?' Stephanie wanted to know.

'Oh no. Those goats always have plenty to live on. They eat everything on the island and they even go into the water and catch fish,' Tessa answered. 'I once saw a goat swimming along with a fish in its mouth on the far side of it.' She had been there with a group from the school where she worked as a PE instructor when she first came to Dublin. Now she was catching some of the excitement of the children, and was looking forward to the trip. She also wanted to photograph the coast from a new vantage point with the idiot-proof camera Paul had given her for her birthday.

'I'll be on the look out for pirates,' Jake said. 'I'll push them all back into the sea.' As Jake spoke, the phone rang and it was someone for Paul to ask him to meet them urgently in the Gresham Hotel on business. When Paul told her he wouldn't be able to come on the picnic after all, Tessa felt sad, thinking what a lovely family day they could have had, if Paul didn't always have last-minute changes of plan.

The boat was waiting for them at Coliemore Harbour and they crossed Dalkey Sound with its swirling currents and were deposited safely at the rocky landing place on the west side of the island. From the mainland it looked smaller than it was, and soon they were going up through the rough scutchy grass and fern to the area around the small ruined church. Tessa had a real moment of conscious peace as she gazed at the coast line stretching all the way to Wicklow Head, with the Sugar Loaf mountain doing a good imitation of Mount Vesuvius in the background, its cone reaching into the sky.

The children loved it. Tessa produced each person's favourite food for the picnic, photographed the children playing around the Martello Tower at the other end of the island and even brought them up its dark, musty old staircase to see the panorama from the top. She felt it was a foresight of their life in Dalkey and rejoiced in it. They'd have to come back with Paul. Wasn't he already talking about buying a boat at the end of the season? She couldn't blame him wanting one, living by the sea with the children always begging to be brought out in boats.

'Look Mummy,' said Stephanie. 'There's a goat over there eating thorns. He'll choke.'

'He's not actually eating the thorns,' said Tessa, 'he's eating around them.'

'I hate thorns,' said Stephanie. 'They hurt you. Jesus had a crown of thorns and they hurt him. Thorns are sad.'

'Dalkey used to be called 'Deilg Ei' in the olden days. Deilg Ei means Island of Thorns and that's how Dalkey got its name.'

'Is Dalkey a sad place?'

'No, not really.'

'Is it still full of thorns?'

'No. Well, maybe for some ...'

The only other people who came to the island that afternoon were two fishermen who set up their rods and lines near the landing place, and Tessa left them to their own company and their quest for fish. The goats also kept to themselves, and Stephanie eventually asked to go up and meet them where they were solemnly assembled on the highest rock, the wind ruffling their ragged coats.

A week later Tessa dressed in casual clothes, a light all-round pleated skirt, a short jacket and silk turquoise shirt. Smart brown leather knee boots and a good matching shoulder bag completed the look, and pleased with life she strolled down Dalkey main street shortly before lunchtime. There was no denying it, she felt excited and the shine in her eyes and glow in her cheeks owed more to anticipation of her lunch date than to regular exercise. She went into The Aristocrat.

Roddy came forward to welcome her and she immediately knew they were on a new footing. Two people, mutually attracted, were meeting to further that attraction, whether or not they would admit it. She shivered slightly as he took her hand in his and led her to the same corner table as before, pulling out her chair for her. She had a sudden yearning to go on with this surprising friendship.

Roddy well knew how to court a woman and to make her feel alive and special, and he knew, with the experience of a clever seducer, that Tessa Bennett was caught in his net. She would try to get away but he would hold on to her fast. A little thrill of expectation ran through him as Tessa sat down and he pulled up a chair opposite her to chat for a few minutes.

'If you don't mind, Tessa, I won't eat with you as I'm on duty. I'd like to bring you small portions of what I think you might enjoy from the menu. This is an important sampling exercise, as far as I'm concerned,' he added, laughing. The double meaning did not escape Tessa, but somehow it was too late to pull back out of this growing relationship even if she wanted to, and she too laughed, but nervously. This man attracted her greatly.

She hadn't ever felt like this before, and the alternative was to grab her bag and slip out of the restaurant and out of this man's orbit once and for all. There were other places where a person could go running and jogging. She did have her Morris Minor, after all. But she did none of these things and instead she stayed and enjoyed it all, as Roddy discreetly plied her with delicious items from the kitchen. A few parties came in to lunch and he and his staff gave them first class attention, with Roddy slipping back now and then to see how she was getting on. And when she stood up to leave, his hand tightened on her arm.

'Next week, this day next week. Meet me at three o'clock when I come off duty. Please.'

'Roddy, I can't. I've enjoyed my lunch, but you know I can't go on meeting you.'

'You can. In jogging gear. At the obelisk. Please say you will. I'll be there, waiting for you.' And before she could disagree, he moved back inside the door of The Aristocrat. The feeling of his hand on her arm remained as a pledge as she walked away.

When Tessa picked up the children from school that afternoon, she was preoccupied.

'Are you day-dreaming, Mummy? You're all dreamy. Can I go to town with the others on the class outing on Monday? Can I?' She hadn't heard the question the first time the child asked it. She had more on her mind.

Paul came in that evening and was unexpectedly chatty while she was busying herself around the kitchen. Things were hotting up at Flynn & Malby, he said, and he wanted to tell her all about it. Something about a big new account. Western Distillers had been in recently and there would shortly be news about the agency getting a new product to launch. Typical of Ted not to give full details, and to leave him panting, but he could read Ted's body language and he seemed to want to put Paul right in there in the action instead of Cas. Tessa felt she must be giving off rays, as Paul even put his arms around her while she was at the cooker, and said they should go out at the weekend and have a bit of fun to celebrate.

CHAPTER 5

The presentation was going well. Five people sat around the board-room table, three from Flynn & Malby and two from the client-company. Ted stood at the top with a flip-chart and easel, and he ringed salient points on the chart with a felt-tipped pen as he spoke. Most of the information was a regurgitation of researched facts, given to the agency at a previous briefing by the client, Dilmans of London, who were trading in Ireland as the Booth Chocolate Company, an old-established firm which held seven per cent of the Irish sugar confectionery market. The early part of the presentation dealt with the marketing of Booth's 'Goal' chocolate bar, and the advertising campaign which the agency had devised for it. The latter, and lengthier part of the meeting was devoted to Booth's new chocolate bar, 'Pickolo', which had already had a massive success in Britain, and had been launched on the Irish market only two years previously where sales, as yet, had been unspectacular. There were plans for a large advertising budget increase for both products.

The English Marketing Manager of Dilmans and his assistant had just expressed approval of Flynn & Malby's proposals for 'Goal', and there was a noticeable relaxing of tension in the boardroom. Cas twiddled the spoon on his coffee cup, Martin sat back smoking, with his arm over the back of his chair, and Paul, the Account Executive on the account, doodled pound-signs on his note pad.

With a magician's flourish, Ted unveiled the boards on which the new colour advertisements for the Pickolo campaign were mounted. Posters and other items would be derivatives of these designs, he said. He then went through the layouts one by one, explaining in a confident and persuasive tone the creative thinking behind the design of each advertisement. The Dilman executives were suitably impressed. Ted pointed out that, as the research demanded, the full colour photographs depicted people in 'reward' situations. This meant that the advertisements were devised to appeal to mainly middle-class women – their target market – who, having completed a task, were now rewarding themselves with a well-earned bar of chocolate.

The Marketing Manager of Dilmans beamed, and silently tapped the fingers of one hand against the palm of the other, applauding the presentation, and indicating his pleasure. His assistant immediately nodded his head vigorously in agreement. The agency had won the day, hands down.

Then, to the horror of Cas, Martin and Paul, Ted produced another advertisement layout, unscheduled, which featured a young woman shopping. When Ted was on a roll, he was unstoppable.

'This,' said Ted, 'is the clincher.' Cas, who detected flecks of spittle at the corners of Ted's mouth and knew the signs, closed his eyes and pinched the bridge of his nose, as a wave of panic swept over him. Paul dabbed away the beads of perspiration forming on his upper lip, and Martin crushed an empty cigarette packet until it was a solid lump of cardboard, and patted his pockets repeatedly in the vain hope that a fresh pack would materialise.

What in the name of God was Ted up to? He must have gone directly to the art department and had this extra advertisement made up, without telling anyone.

'We carried out an extra piece of research ourselves last week,' said Ted buoyantly, 'which proved conclusively – without a shadow of doubt – that twenty per cent of middle-class women who buy Pickolo, purchase a bar before going shopping. They slip it into their handbag in case they haven't time to stop for coffee. All the women interviewed said that they could get through their tasks without stopping, if they had a secret bar of Pickolo. This advertisement is based on that premise.'

A shadow passed over the marketing manager's face.

'This is new territory, Ted,' he ventured.

Cas fancied he felt his legs go numb from the knees down. Ted was lying! He was making up imaginary bits of research, which he claimed the agency had undertaken, just to impress the clients. Why, oh why was he doing this now, when the client had already approved the campaign?

'It's an extraordinary claim,' pressed the marketing manager.

'Paul will back me up on this one,' Ted said, waving an arm in Paul's direction. 'His wife was directly involved in the research.'

Cas and Martin looked at Paul, whose face was bleak. Paul was remembering that Tessa had told him that she had been in town a couple of Saturdays previously, and had just bought herself a bar of chocolate and bitten a piece off it, when she met Ted making his way to the Shelbourne Bar. She had been slightly embarrassed, and in a throw-away comment she had said that she hadn't time for coffee, and was getting up a bit of blood sugar before tackling all she had to do. They had laughed and chatted briefly before making off in different directions.

So that was Ted's bloody survey – one person! A vague chat with Tessa was the sum total of it.

'Doesn't match up to any experience I've had on the English market,' said the marketing manager doubtfully. Cas could see the whole presentation slipping away. There was a short silence and Paul said faintly: 'This is a survey of Irish women.'

The marketing manager brightened. 'Of course, of course'. The meeting was wrapped up and drinks were handed around. Ted excused himself and slipped back to his office. Shortly afterwards the Dilman duo departed, well satisfied. Minutes later, Cas, Martin and Paul, all three furious, went to Ted's office in a posse to demand an explanation as to why he had lied as he did. Ted wasn't there. He had left the premises to go to another meeting, and, as was typical, the whole episode was never fully sorted out.

Several months later, an extract from an ongoing piece of research showed that 20 per cent of all women who had bought a Pickolo bar, or a directly competing product within the last few days, had bought it prior to going shopping. Blast Ted!

The entire advertising community enjoyed telling yarns about Ted. Some were true, some were not, most were loosely based on fact.

* * *

Barry ordered a pint and took it to a corner table in the pub, where it was quiet. He needed some time alone to take stock and pull together the fragments of thoughts jumbling in his head.

An only child, Cas's friend Barry Rogan lived with his father over a small newsagents near the library in Dun Laoghaire. Although his father worked hard and stayed open late and at weekends, the shop only produced a modest income. After Barry's mother died, one thing kept his father going, and that was the goal that one day Barry would become a doctor. He worked every hour that God sent him to achieve his ambition for his son, but after his first year as a medical student, Barry knew that medicine was not for him. He stretched his studies to two agonising years, rather than offend his father, and he never forgot the day he told him that he couldn't go on. His father was behind the counter, polishing under-ripe bananas with brown shoe polish to give them better eye-appeal, and he slumped down on a stool and stared into space without saying anything for a full ten minutes. The sight of the anguish in his eyes brought a lump to Barry's throat, and Barry served the customers who came into the shop, and tried to persuade his father that it was all for the best. His father didn't speak to him for three days.

Eventually, Barry got a job as a representative for a pharmaceutical company, calling on doctors. Salary and commission were reasonable. Shattered dreams can never be put back together again, but Barry told himself that one day he would make his father proud of him.

He thought about his Aunt Vi, having received a message that she had been transferred to Jervis Street hospital, following a fall. She had lain on the bedroom floor for several hours before she was able to attract one of the hotel staff by tapping on the skirting board with her ring. Now she had just suffered a severe stroke and it was reckoned that if she had another, which was likely, she would die within the week.

Poor Vi. He didn't want to think about the money she had promised him, but he still couldn't put it out of his mind. If it was as much as she had boasted, he would be set up for life. Anyway, a lump sum of money would be a great help if he were to go into business with Chloe.

Chloe had been reticent about her business plans, but he knew they had something to do with films, and that she wanted Irish partners. She had been evasive about her work in Hollywood, but he imagined that a woman as beautiful as Chloe must be an actress whose name was still unknown, or even a studio starlet. Anyway, she seemed to have plenty of money. He'd ask no questions for the moment, he'd just wait and see. She said she would come back to Ireland in a few weeks – without Laura – as she was in the way of getting airline tickets at a considerably reduced rate. But Barry was convinced Chloe was on the lookout for a husband in Ireland, and that was why she intended to return so soon – and hang the expense! That was why she wanted to set up a business in Ireland – she hoped to live here.

* * *

Ted stood in the doorway of Ballyowney Lodge, smiling from ear to ear.

'That's what I call a good day's fishing. The fish were queueing up like buses.' He dropped his fishing accoutrements on the flagged hall and sat down on a settle to pull off his waders. 'Give me a hand with these boots, will you Liz?'

'Where's Martin? Did he catch anything?' asked Liz.

'I don't think so. He's on his way. He stopped to do a sketch of the little bridge. He's more interested in drawing than fishing.'

Liz helped Ted out of his waders. 'Gin and tonic?'

'I'd love one.'

'Celine, will you pour out three gin and tonics?' asked Liz in her best boardroom voice.

'Certainly.' Celine jumped to her feet eagerly. Ted took his drink and went into the little parlour in his socks, and sat down by the fire, spreading his hands to it.

Ballyowney Lodge was a fishing lodge, purpose-built in the Georgian style and beautifully furnished. Situated outside Ballinamore in County Leitrim, it was a hundred yards from the picturesque Woodford river which, with the defunct Ballinamore and Ballyconnell canals, joined the river Erne and the river Shannon together. With 28 lakes within a five-mile radius, it was a fisherman's paradise. The lodge was owned by Colonel Wentworth, who lived part-time nearby, although many people thought Ted owned it – and he never bothered to correct them.

To be accepted by the local people, Ted had managed to worm his way on to a County Committee which planned to restore the old canals disused since 1869, and reopen them for pleasure cruising. His standing with the local inhabitants was important as on one occasion, at four in the morning when sleep had deserted him, Ted had seen from his bedroom window a group of men with guns, drilling by the light of a full moon in the lower field attached to the lodge. When he mentioned this to a customer in the bar of the Sliabh an Iarann Hotel in Ballinamore, he was told it was 'just the IRA lads'.

He had an arrangement to rent the lodge every year for the summer months, and he always brought Liz and Des with him as the core party, inviting several others to join them, usually clients. Sometimes Ted invited business people he had met in passing. He would arrange to let them use the lodge on their own, and always picked up the tab for them, as he found this an excellent way of putting them under a compliment to him.

This year he had something very important to discuss with Martin, and he had invited him as his guest for the first time.

'Bring someone with you – you know ...!' He had laughed and slapped him on the back, but Martin had brought Celine from the agency and Ted had been annoyed about it, because she was on the staff and he couldn't talk freely about the agency when she was around. Martin never got things like that quite right, thought Ted but Martin would be a good ally if events turned as he thought they would.

'All that fresh air nearly killed me,' said Martin when he came in, pulling on a cigarette.

'Did you catch anything?' asked Celine softly.

'Yes, one,' said Martin.

'Only one?' laughed Liz. 'After all that time!'

'I consider catching one a major triumph.'

'How many did you get, Ted?' Celine ventured.

'I lost count.'

'Three,' said Martin with a grin. 'I checked your basket in the hall.' He poured himself a large brandy and ginger ale from an array of bottles set up on a side table.

'I threw them all back,' Ted lied automatically. 'Listen Liz, are you and Celine thinking of going for a walk? I want to talk to Martin privately.'

'We've been,' said Liz, 'but come on Celine. Where's Des, by the way?'

'He's still hard at it,' said Martin. 'And will be for some time. He's after a particular fish, and he said he wouldn't leave until he had him onto the bank.' They got up and went off to the kitchen to help the housekeeper with dinner, leaving the men to talk.

'That poor fish is doomed,' said Ted. 'Des will pursue it until he drops, so he can regale the Dalkey lads in Dan Finnegan's with stories of his fishing prowess. You know Des, his stories are always well past their amuse-by date.'

Martin laughed. 'Cas was telling me that everywhere Des goes he sends cards back to his friends in Finnegan's, and that they refer to them as Des Downey's "boast-cards".'

'Des is to bragging what Peter O'Sullivan is to horse-racing commentaries. He keeps going with mounting excitement, his voice rising and rising until he reaches a mouth-frothing climax.' Ted drained his glass. 'Look ...' His mood changed abruptly. 'To more serious matters.'

'Yeah, what's it all about, Ted, you're being very bloody mysterious,' said Martin, frowning.

'Another brandy and ginger?' said Ted, motioning with the bottle.

'No, I'm fine for the moment.'

Ted poured himself another drink.

'It's Arkwright & Dobson,' he said slowly. 'We may be losing the account.'

'Christ! Why? When did you hear?'

'About three weeks ago. I had a sixth sense something was about to happen, but it was only confirmed to me two nights before we came up here.'

Martin was mindful of the fact that Arkwright & Dobson was the biggest account at Flynn & Malby. Bruce Bellingham was the majority shareholder in the company, although it had long since ceased to be a strictly family business, and when he had taken over the chair Bruce's natural flair for commerce had allowed him to expand its activities considerably. Reflecting his autocratic personality, his art deco office, which was wood-panelled and had stained glass windows and an open coal fire, hadn't been changed one iota since the 1920s. Bruce liked it that way. In most other respects he was forward-looking, Martin knew. Apart from Old George, who had been his father's general factotum and whose sole job now was to tend the fire in the chairman's office, Bruce insisted on surrounding himself with personable young men, well-trained executives with modern 1970s business ideas. Arkwright & Dobson was a huge conglomerate, manufacturing products under licence as well as a marketing company acting as an Irish agency for a spread of foreign manufactured products – mostly British. Its core business was a range of food products manufactured by Tilley UK Ltd, whose Advertising Manager was a man called Keith Oldham.

'I was out for a stroll a couple of Sundays ago,' said Ted. 'I walked down to Dalkey village and dropped into the Queens for a nightcap. Keith Oldham was there with Cas and Paul. I thought, what the hell was Keith doing in Ireland without my knowing it – and in Dalkey with Cas and Paul. Then, two nights ago I went into the Horseshoe Bar in the Shelbourne with Liz, and there was Oldham again, drinking his skull off as English people do when they come to Ireland. We had a drink with him and he sort of implied that some disaster was about to befall Flynn & Malby. I sent Liz home in a taxi and took Keith down to the United Services Club – and fed him more drink. When he was really in his cups, he let it all out. He had heard – and he was absolutely positive it was true – that Arkwright & Dobson are planning to take all their business – not just Tilley products – away from Flynn & Malby. He heard it "in confidence" during a night of high passion with Bruce Bellingham's secretary.'

'Sweet God. This is terrible!' said Martin. 'Our biggest account.'

'There's worse,' said Ted. 'Listen to this. Bruce Bellingham plans to set Cas Maitland up in an advertising agency of his own, and to give him the total A&D business, plus the advertising accounts of several other companies which Bruce is director of. Like Henry Noblett, the wine and spirit merchants.'

If what Ted said was true, and it appeared to be, there was trouble ahead. Martin was aware that Bruce Bellingham had thought Cas was going places when he met him several times in the Stephen's Green Club, and had chatted to him to show he was in the mainstream and not just an old codger. Bruce thought that Cas was a clever young fellow and was sorry he hadn't someone like him in the family to carry the Arkwright & Dobson standard. When Cas was handling the account, Bruce had been very impressed with his efficiency and creativity. Then Paul had been put on the account by Ted, and Bruce thought he seemed pleasant enough, very extrovert and determined to succeed. Then, to complicate matters, Ted started to contact Bruce, going over Paul's head. Martin knew that Bruce felt it was important to have this side of the business well looked after these days, with so much competition about.

'I don't believe it,' said Martin, drawing heavily on his forty-somethingth cigarette of the day. 'What the hell are we doing here? We should be back in Dublin sorting this mess out. I've always thought that Cas was a bit of a sneaky bastard, and by Christ that silver spoon he was born with will choke him one day.'

'The problem is – wait for it – Cas doesn't know anything about Bruce's plans for him as yet.'

'Are you sure?' Martin was incredulous.

'Almost certain. Keith said so. I know Cas better than any of you. It would have come out by now. He's not devious. And I know that Bruce thinks the sun shines out of Cas.'

'Is that why you took Cas off the account?' said Martin, as though he had made a brilliant deduction.

Ted looked startled. 'Nonsense. He's better off running the day-to-day affairs of the agency than handling clients.' He sipped his drink. 'I can't go to Bruce Bellingham directly about this, of course. He would be furious at the leak of information, and if things went wrong, the repercussions would be terrible. And there's worse.' Ted was getting agitated, as the drink was beginning to affect him. Martin lit another cigarette.

'You know the trouble we're having with Baby Faire?' said Ted. 'Well, if the way the meeting with Tim Cranby went the other day is anything to go by, we could lose that entire account also.'

'Yeah,' said Martin. 'I've had a rough time recently with them myself.'

'That's why I had to get away and think this whole problem through,' said Ted, 'and that's why I need you here to talk it all out privately. Obviously a board-meeting couldn't be held, because Cas couldn't be left out of it.'

'It might be worth talking to Jim Reilly, though. After all, he is the company accountant.'

'I did, and that's where the real problem lies.'

'Shit! This gets worse, Ted. What's Jim up to?'

'No, no. Not Jim himself, he's alright. He doesn't know the full story, of course, but he did say in passing that if we were ever to lose the Arkwright & Dobson and Baby Faire accounts, the whole agency would be in danger. We're very overstretched financially at the moment, apparently. Those bonuses we paid ourselves two months ago are contributory, and the extra premises we acquired next door haven't helped. Plus other bits and pieces. I know, I know, Jim warned us against the new premises at the time, but that's history. We can't go back on things now.'

Ted took another drink and said, guiltily, 'As you know, my director's loan from the company is substantial. Well, that's not helping any.' This was a rare omission indeed by Ted, and Martin noted it immediately – Ted saying that he was taking too much money out of the company to finance his lavish lifestyle!

'If we don't get that extra business from Western Distillers, then we're in Queer Street,' said Martin.

'Precisely.'

'We'll have to watch Cas closely.'

'I'm not sure that Cas is the problem,' said Ted. 'I can't quite put my finger on it yet, but give me time. The person to watch may well be Paul Bennett.'

* * *

Ted Flynn had extraordinary talent and a motivating force that came from deep within – a talent for survival and for living for the day. His strength was perseverance, and he had learnt it in Australia, Hong Kong and Bangkok, where he had seen people live on a day-to-day basis. He had seen men and women setting up tables on the pavement in Bangkok where they cooked and served steaming meals until they were moved on. A mobile restaurant for a day was a quick way of making enough money to live for a week in some parts of the East. He had picked up this hopeful attitude to life as he battled on alone in the world of advertising, and he had learnt a truth which often doesn't come to people until late in life – that perseverance and single-mindedness can get you almost anything, and if there is talent to go with it, then you'll make it to the top.

When others thought the game was lost, Ted could see it as only beginning. He had learned to live in the present, and by rising early and concentrating on the day in hand, he lost very few opportunities in life. This attitude set him well ahead of most of his Irish counterparts and his ability to disregard developments which would have knocked others off course was his strength.

Rumours of one kind or another about Ted Flynn's personal or business life would be dispersed by his appearance at a race meeting, a banquet or an important conference, where he would play the role of a person intensely involved in what was going on, and this would so confuse his opponents that they would eventually wake up to the fact that by even discussing his antics they were wasting their own living time and opportunities. Stories about him were legion, but always led nowhere as current ones were replaced by new ones, and Ted's courting of well-placed people nearly always brought him home the bacon. Just as his star seemed to be falling, social columns would murmur of a new and interesting departure in his personal or business life. As long as 'they' were talking about him he mattered, and he danced backwards and forwards over the line between acceptable and unacceptable social and business behaviour until people lost track of whatever he was at.

His marriage to Rita had ensured that his home back-drop and his future would be looked after – as long as he kept the money coming in.

He could pose as an expert in any area for a short time, from opera to horse breeding, but he always moved on hastily before he was put to the test. He kept three suits in a wardrobe in his office, all of them cleaned and pressed and ready for unexpected occasions. A black tie lay in his desk drawer so that he could appear at a funeral at short notice.

Ted was generous when it came to colleagues attending seminars or business exhibitions. He insisted on the company paying for flight, accommodation and fees, if he thought attendance on the part of one of the directors or senior staff at a course would enhance the image of the agency and the quality of its service. On one occasion he sent Cas to Boston for three months to do an intensive advertising and marketing study programme, which stood Cas and the agency in good stead. Such courses were frequently mentioned in conversation with clients, and he cautioned people that no one was ever to run down any they had attended, because that would make the investment instantly useless.

Wherever he was he created a world around him, and people were drawn to Ted Flynn's company by his sheer electricity and motivation. They felt they would pick up his optimism and fresh approach to life, and so he was rarely at a loss for company of a superficial kind.

CHAPTER 6

Cas wanted a good row with Martin and he intended to have a proper showdown. Ted had been dropping heavy hints lately that they might be in danger of losing Baby Faire and Arkwright & Dobson, two accounts on which Ted himself acted as Account Director. There was no doubting Ted's genuine concern, but try as he might, Cas couldn't get together a proper meeting to discuss the matter. Cas knew that since Martin wasn't pressing Ted for a knock-down, drag-out session, he must be familiar with the details – whatever they were. He was convinced that everything had been thrashed out at an informal meeting in the fishing lodge in Leitrim, and that Ted and Martin, and Liz had met there to discuss the agency's fortunes in private. He found this unacceptable and intended to tell Martin so, and then tackle Ted about it.

Cas went across to Martin's office and put his head around the door.

'Are you free? I need to talk to you – in private.'

'Sure.' Martin squinted at Cas through a plume of smoke. 'But not right now.' He glanced at his watch. 'I have a meeting ten minutes ago.'

'Phone me when you get back, whatever the time,' said Cas.

'Sounds serious.'

'It is.'

'I'll be back about six, we'll thrash it out then.'

At 7.30 Martin came into Cas's office. 'Sorry I'm late. As usual the meeting need only have lasted five minutes, but it took four hours.' He sat down heavily opposite Cas and lit a cigarette. 'I've got a blinding headache.'

Cas leaned across his desk. 'Explain to me why you and Ted were closeted in Ballyowney Lodge along with Liz discussing agency plans without my being invited along. And what the hell is happening with Arkwright & Dobson and Baby Faire? And why haven't I been told what's going on?'

'Hold it, Cas, no need to blow a gasket. Ted is entitled to invite me fishing if he wants to, and I'm entitled to accept.'

'I never heard of you with a fishing rod in your hand before. Come off it, Martin, I'm sick of you playing a double game between me and Ted. Fishing? Fishing for what?'

'I resent that.' Martin's voice rose. 'I'll do what I shaggin' well like, Cas. If Ted wants to discuss things with me then that's all right with me. Go and bawl him out, not me.'

Cas stopped short in his tracks. He realised he was going over the top.

'Okay, okay, okay, but you have to realise that I can't be kicked around by you and Ted. One minute I'm in on everything, and the next you're running the place without me.'

There was a low, long sideboard against the wall underneath a large oil painting by Cas. Cas went over, opened one of the doors and took out a bottle of Black Bush, two glasses, a siphon of soda, and ice from a small fridge. He held up the ice. Martin nodded. Cas fixed two monster drinks and served one to Martin.

'Cas, face it. Ted is keeping you away from the big accounts, not me. While he needs your face of integrity to give the agency cred, he's terrified you'll up and away and bring some of the better clients with you. But look, we've been over this ground a hundred times before, in a hundred different ways. I'm not telling you anything new. Remember when you met Doug Lucas in the Stephen's Green Club, and he asked you to pitch for the Barton Flour Mills advertising, because he was so impressed with you personally – what did Ted do? Because Doug was only the Managing Director of Bartons, Ted immediately contacted Uel Elton, the Chairman, for God's sake, to upstage you. Then Ted claimed he was responsible for getting the business, even though he hadn't even known the account was on the move!'

'It still rankles. But what about this meeting in Leitrim?'

'What about it?' Martin sipped his whiskey.

'What was discussed?'

'Baby Faire and A&D. There's a problem.'

'I know there's a problem, but what problem?'

'I can't talk about it.'

'For Christ's sake, why not?'

'I just can't. Your name was mentioned.'

'Apropos of what?'

'I can't go into it. You'll have to talk to Ted – and that's flat.' Martin traced the pattern in the circular rug in front on Cas's desk with the toe of his shoe. Cas knew he would get nothing further out of Martin.

'I'm getting tired of all this. Sometimes you're on my side and other times you're on Ted's.'

'It's not a case of sides. You know I'd back you every time. But in the end this agency is a one-man-band. Oh, I know there are – what – twenty-nine, thirty people working here, all contributing mightily to the success of the agency. But Ted's the Flynn in Flynn & Malby. He's the one the clients think has all the ideas. It's nonsense of course, but then he's an ideas man, an account director, a copywriter, a presenter. He has the drive, the charisma, the spark, the salesmanship, and he does know a hell of a lot about advertising and marketing. He's also a messer and a shit of Everest proportions.' He laughed in spite of himself.

'Aye, there's the rub,' said Cas. He was cooler now. 'But all – well most – Irish agencies are one-man-bands, or very close to it. Just look around. They've gone through the forties, fifties and sixties with the original founder or his son still clinging on to power and cuddling their shares, but they don't seem to be out of register like we are. That's not to say we aren't doing a damn good job. But wait 'til the eighties. I predict that in ten or fifteen years' time, UK agencies, or even the Americans, will have bought into the Irish ones. Then there'll be some stiff competition. There's no room for an agency which confines itself just to the home market. And there'll be new products coming from abroad, and that'll mean more advertising and more advertising money about. In the meantime ...?'

'In the meantime we make as much money as we can, one way or another.'

'Is that your ambition?' Cas sipped his drink and studied Martin.

'Yep. I'd like to have old money. Anybody's old money.'

'Well, at least you're honest.'

Martin leaned forward.

'Look Cas. Cop on. You're as far out as The Baily. You haven't even woken up to what we're all about in our different ways. I'll be honest with you ...'

The whiskey was having a sudden effect on Martin and Cas realised that he already had had a good few drinks before he arrived.

'The rest of us came from what the analysts call deprived homes, in quotes. You didn't. If you did, the way this agency operates would be as plain as the nose on your face. Look at us. Ted, Liz and myself. We'll never be secure, no matter how much money we make or how many smart social occasions we attend. Why do you think that the Giraffe is so determined that the agency wins awards? More to the point, why do you think he's always forcing himself on to committees for this and that? New business? Not the root cause. No, he needs to go on feeling accepted each time the certainty of it wears off. And all this crap about his being elected King of Dalkey. The bastard would get himself on the Council of State if it was a guarantee that his feelings of inferiority would go away, once and for all. And Liz's the same. She pulled herself up by her bootstraps here, and without Ted she'd never have done it. Mind you she's a bright woman, but she has no real confidence. Limited, very, very limited. Without the designer gowns and the cosmetics she wouldn't be able for the social whirl. And she needs Ted to get her through it all. She won't always need him, but she has done until now. They need each other to face the world and fool the natives. They boost one another because they've nothing to hide when they're together. Both have come a long, long way, believe me, and they needed one another to do that. There they are, hob-nobbing with politicians, poncing around with the smart and international fashionable sets ...'

'And you?'

'I never made a secret of my background. You know all about it. But you're different.'

'What's so great about mine? Middle class, that's all.'

'That's just it. You're so certain of what you are. Christ, pure middle-class is right. No fears about your background. No hang-ups about your education. Nothing to hide. You don't have to worry that the mask will slip one day.'

'Oh come off it ...'

'I mean it. It's time you did a bit of clear thinking. You're an artist, Cas, and you should have stayed one and not allowed yourself to be siphoned off by Ted Flynn into the administration side of the agency. You were a brilliant creative man in your previous agency, and a great account executive when you joined Flynn & Malby, but Mr Manipulator needed your honest face to give him the freedom to do as he liked. So he made you MD – end of story.' A long cigarette ash fell to the floor.

'He manipulates everyone, even you, Martin.'

'Maybe. Maybe. I've to survive in my own way and I've lots of commitments to meet. More than you. I'm a bit older than you and I've gathered plenty of liabilities.'

'Tina from Twylight Productions, for example?'

Martin poured himself another whiskey, spilling soda on the carpet. 'She wasn't supposed to get pregnant. A deceitful girl. You can tell she's deceitful – her boobs are too close together. But that's another day's discussion. Anyway, we're talking about you.' He raised his glass. 'It was a great move on Ted's part to divorce you from your real talent and nab you for the job of MD after stunning you with expense accounts and a dizzy social life attached to the business. Flying schedule instead of charter when you go on holidays. Anyone's head would have been turned if they were as absolutely, utterly and completely devoid of street sense as you are. You were putty in his hands. That was a real Ted stroke. Keep you away from the clients. There you are, ordering shirts from Tysons every time you need a swanky new one for a function. And you have your personal account in the Shelbourne Hotel. You let yourself be seduced by it all, and then he had you where he wanted you, out front to confuse the punters who might be on to him. Jesus, Cas, you're a painter and a damn fine one at that.' He gestured towards Cas's painting with his glass. 'You could live by your work. I couldn't. I may be Creative Director around here, but I need the likes of Ted to keep the money coming my way. But you'd need to work your arse off to succeed, talent or no talent. You know there's no short cut to the arts. Talent's a shaggin' burden if you don't use it, and that what's wrong with you, mate. That's why you can't see straight. You're loaded with it, and you're not using it. Whether you have it in you to do so or not is something I don't know. No one knows but you. Remember, a person is only young once, but they can stay immature forever.' Martin changed tack abruptly. 'Do you trust Paul Bennett?'

'What?'

'Oh, forget it. I need a coffee.' Martin put the unfinished drink down on Cas's desk, turned and made his way unsteadily towards the door. 'See you.' He closed the door after him with exaggerated gentleness. Martin would be glad to see Cas out of the agency.

* * *

Ted continued to affect disinterest in Rita's project by not even referring to it, and she suddenly realised that his petulance was actually affording her full privacy, and she stopped minding one way or the other. Each morning when Ted and the family had left for town, Rita did her few household chores, left instructions for her cleaning woman, and then dressed smartly and drove down to The Teashop. She bought three daily newspapers on the way and arranged them in the rack inside the door before she did anything else. So much did she enjoy her little private kingdom that she was occasionally taken by surprise when an early customer came in. Whatever the weather, Rita enjoyed the view from her bow-fronted window, even on a stormy morning, and it was an ill wind that blew no good, as customers came in as a respite from poor weather, looking for a pot of coffee and somewhere to chat.

She was building a regular trade already. Tessa Bennett hadn't returned, but she would surely come back, and older women had taken to dropping in on their morning walk from the hotel further along the seafront. One man who looked about 30 came in a few times, obviously breaking a run to judge by his gear and runners. He never got into conversation but preferred to take a newspaper and read it while he breakfasted on brown bread, marmalade and coffee. He looked interesting – didn't wear a wedding ring and had a Scottish accent.

One morning, when her male visitor was sitting there deep in his paper, the door opened and Tessa Bennett came in. Rita went to welcome her and the man in the corner looked up. He smiled wanly at Tessa and gave a little flick of his hand in mock salute.

'Hello stranger,' he said. Intrigued, Rita nodded briefly at both of them before slipping to the back of the shop to watch the proceedings. Tessa was taken by surprise at meeting this man, although she obviously knew him. She had blushed and she hadn't quite known how to cope with Rita and the man at the same time, smiling at her and giving the man a hurried greeting.

'Hello,' said Tessa.

'How are you?' said Roddy.

'Fine.'

'Will you join me?'

'Is this one of your stop-off places?'

'Yes. I'm a regular. Tessa, sit down.' He was taking control of the conversation.

'I know Rita. Do you know Rita Flynn, the proprietor?'

'I just know her from coming in.' He pulled out a chair and gestured to her to sit down. She sat at an angle, not putting her legs under the table.

'May I order something for you?' Roddy asked.

'Just coffee. I'm in a bit of a hurry.'

Roddy waved to Rita. 'And another coffee please.'

Rita had the distinct impression that there was tension between these two. Well, well, well. Life was full of surprises and anyway, trysting was good for business – but Tessa Bennett! Now who would have thought she had another dimension to her.

'You never turned up at the obelisk,' Roddy said quietly.

'No.'

'Why not?'

'Don't be silly. You know I couldn't.'

'Why?'

Tessa just shook her head. She had no intention of either apologising or explaining herself to this annoying man.

He tried again. 'Where have you been? I haven't seen you around Dalkey or the Vico, or anywhere.'

'I've been running alright, but I was trying out other places.'

'Practising for the Olympics in secret?' Roddy sat back in his chair, his normal confidence returning. Tessa smiled in spite of herself.

'I thought you might be avoiding me,' he said. 'At least I hoped so. It means I'm important enough to avoid. Is that why I haven't seen you since the lunch at The Aristocrat?'

'Sorry. I intended to thank you for that, but I've been extremely busy, between one thing and another.' She couldn't bring herself to mention either her husband or the children, and in this she felt she was betraying them somehow. Roddy would use it against her, she was convinced. He would turn any family talk back on her in some way.

'Of course you have. Tell you what. I'll pay for your coffee, if you agree to meet me here again some morning. Bargain?'

Tessa laughed lightly. 'I'll drop in some time.'

'This day week?'

'Perhaps, I'll think about it.' She finished her coffee, smiled over at Rita and said goodbye to Roddy, who was sitting back relaxed, watching her with pleasure. Damn, she thought. I've gone and committed myself in some way to this irritating man, all over again.

A week slipped by and Tessa found herself thinking quite a lot about Roddy. Paul was home some of the evenings, but she was preoccupied and didn't seem to mind now when he buried his head in files. He was certainly hatching something, but as he so rarely talked agency business with her, it didn't seem to matter. When she met other agency couples, the wives seemed up to the minute about which agency had acquired or lost what account, but she preferred to hear amusing anecdotes about Liz and Ted, Ted and Rita, Cas and his girlfriends, Martin and his conquests, or stories such as the ill-fated Blobby-Nose campaign.

Tessa was a family person and always liked to get back to Waterford to her own people. She spent much time phoning her sisters and discussing families, and she greatly appreciated the facility of going down with the children for holidays and short breaks. Later on, when the children would be more grown up, she would be able to leave them with their cousins for a couple of weeks, and Paul and she could do interesting trips together. Everyone wanted to come to Dublin, and Paul never seemed to mind this traffic, since the visitors always brought nice pickings from their farms in the form of meat cuts for the freezer, new-laid eggs, and after harvest sacks of potatoes would be put on the train for collection, and, in season, a salmon or two from the brown rivers of Waterford always found their way to Bennetts' address by train or other means. The new house in Bulloch hadn't much in the way of extra accommodation, but they had found a nice guest-house nearby where they could put people up, and have them down to the house for meals.

Normally Tessa would be working out these combinations and permutations, but just now her mind was far from family visits. She was toying with the idea of meeting Roddy Ogilvie just one more time. He was really entertaining, and his line of chat was deliciously unsettling. One more meeting wouldn't do any harm, she convinced herself, loathe to give up the new dimension she had found in herself, and in denial about the real attraction.

'So you came to see me after all?' Roddy Ogilvie stood in front of Tessa's table in The Teashop.

Thank God Rita's not here this morning, she thought. A bit of luck really, that the place was being minded by a young woman instead. He stood there, arms on hips and feet apart.

'I just dropped in,' Tessa answered. She looked up at him and his penetrating gaze seemed to strike to her very soul. A thrill ran through her, giving her pains in her calves, as if a slight electric shock was going through them. She wriggled her feet on the floor to rid herself of the feeling, but the tingling persisted. Roddy sat down immediately at her table, without asking if he could, and she looked at him under her eyelashes like a schoolgirl.

He caught her look and held it, and caught her hand and held that too.

'You have beautiful hands – for a hard-working, downtrodden housewife, that is?' He was teasing her already. Tessa freed her hand, but the feeling of his caressing fingers remained. She wanted to say something, but she couldn't think of anything to say.

'Tessa,' he said abruptly. 'I want to take you out on a date. I'm not playing hide-and-seek with you any more. Come for a drive and lunch with me tomorrow. Please.'

'Roddy, I can't. You know I can't. I have the children to collect – and other commitments.' He had called her a housewife, and she relaxed about mentioning the children.

'I'll have you back safely, well before four o'clock, believe me. I have to be on duty at the restaurant at that time, and if the boss isn't punctual, how can he expect the staff to be on time.' He motioned to the waitress and ordered coffee and toast.

Tessa said nothing for a moment. Then: 'Couldn't we just be friends in a casual way? You know – just friends.' She stared out at the passing traffic.

Roddy put out his hand and gently turned her face towards him. 'We'll leave early, about half-past ten, and I'll drive you to a beautiful little restaurant in the Wicklow mountains. I've read about it and I've been waiting to see what they're doing up there. Apparently they do wonderful things with wild game. That's settled then?'

Tessa had already lost the struggle. She had lost it earlier that morning when she put on a new casual outfit and made up with great care – in case she met Roddy Ogilvie.

'Alright, I'll come.' She was surprised at how easy it was to accept his invitation. 'If you promise to have me back in Dalkey by a quarter to four, I'll come – but no dressing up, mind you. I'll be dressed casually,' she said brusquely. Roddy was amused at her seeming illogicality, but the thought that dressing too glamourously might draw attention to what she was doing had suddenly grown out of proportion in Tessa's mind.

'Cinders, you can come dressed either in rags or a ballgown, whatever you like,' he teased, 'as long as you say you're coming with me tomorrow.'

'I'll come.'

They finished their coffee and Tessa left first, promising to meet him at the corner of Ulverton and Harbour Road at half-past ten the next morning. As she walked along the seafront, she was still saying to herself that it was only a fun outing and that this time would be the last. She certainly could never tell Paul about this invitation. He would be terribly knocked about by such a trip into the unknown on her part, and he could never have understood why she would agree to go. Sometimes a woman has an undercurrent of feeling which, if not conducted into the flow of her marriage, can pull her away from it dangerously, but this was not the kind of thing that Paul Bennett could grasp. He would never have done anything of the kind, himself, and it would never occur to him that Tessa might do so.

* * *

Paul Bennett felt that the time was right for an in-depth chat with Cas Maitland. Even before he had done his Master's degree, using 'The State of Advertising in Ireland' as a basis for his thesis, he intended to leave Flynn & Malby and start up his own advertising agency. Every move he had made since then had been with that objective in mind. Finance would be no great problem. While he had no real money himself, Tessa's favourite uncle was a wealthy businessman with interests all over Waterford and Cork, and he was good for a substantial loan. He could also borrow a fair sum from the bank, if his father went guarantor, which he knew he would. There were several clients with Flynn & Malby who were on the brink of leaving the agency, and with the right approach and pressure, they could be persuaded to place their business with his new agency. One ingredient was missing: Cas. He wanted Cas as his partner. He knew if he were to dislodge some of the bigger accounts from Flynn & Malby, he would need to have Cas on board. But would Cas join him? Cas often sounded off about Ted, and by now he must really have had enough of him, but still, he was very much an F&M man.

It was early afternoon and as it was an exceptionally sunny day, Cas decided to walk to Fitzwilliam Lawn Tennis Club from the office. Paul was a member there and Cas had agreed to meet him in the members' bar. Paul had phoned him from the club and said he needed to talk to him urgently and privately, not at the agency, but on neutral ground. Could he make it? What the hell, they were both due an afternoon off anyway.

He went through the main door and up the thickly carpeted staircase to the bar, where Paul was sitting at a window table, watching two elderly members playing slow-motion tennis. As it was afternoon, the place was practically empty.

'Ah, the man himself,' said Paul waving to Cas. 'Pull up a pew and sit yourself down. What's your poison?'

'Gin and tonic, thanks Paul.'

Paul went to the bar for the drink and ordered a pint for himself. He brought them back to the table. 'I was feeling like a small boy mitching from school,' said Paul, 'but now that you're here I'm legit.'

'Well, spit it all out. What's on your mind, and why the neutral territory? What's so urgent?'

'I know you're strapped for time with the Giraffe and Martin away again, but this is important.'

'Business or ....'

'Both in a way, but mostly business. Did you ever think of leaving Flynn & Malby, Cas?'

'Every hour on the hour.'

'No. I'm serious,' said Paul.

'Look Paul, what's this all about?'

Paul studied his pint.

'Okay, here it is.' He paused and then rushed on. 'I'm thinking of setting up – no, I'm going to set up my own shop and I want you to join me as a partner. Fifty, fifty. I've been talking to Bruce Bellingham and Tim Cranby and I think they are about to take their accounts away from the agency. Western Distillers' new business is also iffy. I think I could persuade them to give their business – to a new agency – mine – ours – if you join me. I'll be frank with you, Cas. I could definitely get the business if you were part of the set-up. I know that.' Cas was amazed that Paul was privy to what were obviously still confidential plans on the part of the clients, particularly Western Distillers. How did he do it?

'Paul, you know I should really stand up and go at this point, or go and phone Ted and tell him what you're up to, and then try my damnedest to persuade Bruce Bellingham and Tim Cranby to change their minds.'

'No point. They're disenchanted with Flynn & Malby – at least they are with Ted. No, Cas. Think seriously about it. You and I would make a formidable team, you know that.'

'But I've no money, Paul. Setting up an advertising agency needs big bucks.'

'That's my end of it. I can raise the cash no bother. Here, look at this.' He passed a file to Cas to examine. Cas couldn't help smiling when he saw, roughly printed on the file, the words, 'Bennett and Maitland Advertising Limited'. He leafed through the contents slowly. Included, and neatly laid out were the possible maximum and minimum budgets for Baby Faire, Arkwright & Dobson, Allied Oils and several accounts handled by other agencies. It showed commissions and service fees, as well as special fees and production charges, salaries, rent and so on, and approximate gross and nett profit over five years. It was all spelt out. Cas looked up, startled.

'This is a massive piece of work. Is it accurate?'

'Spot on.'

Cas stood up and went over to the window and stared out. Paul's proposal was the most tempting offer he had ever had. Initially he had nursed the possibility of having his own agency, where he could run things entirely his way, and handle the clients exactly as he pleased. He knew he could give them an excellent service, crisp and creative, and forward-thinking. He could produce the best advertising campaigns they could get in Ireland, rooted in careful marketing, backed by thorough qualitative and quantitative research. Clever and punchy sponsored radio programmes. Visually stunning television commercials, with the product as the hero for maximum impact. Imaginative and persuasive newspaper advertisements in black and white and full colour – wildly avant-garde. Glossy magazine advertisements with unrivalled pulling power. Dramatic roadside hoardings ... but he couldn't do it if it meant demolishing Flynn & Malby. And it would do just that, if he took their key clients away.

His attitude towards Ted might be ambivalent, but to start his own agency from the ashes of another, if he were the one to light the fire in the first place, would be just sharp business practice. Perhaps he wasn't cynical enough, or ruthless enough. Perhaps it was because he didn't see truth as something which came in various shades. Perhaps it was because he viewed 'being pragmatic' – one of Paul's favourite phrases – as half-brother to unprincipled. Whatever the reasons, it would have to be no.

He came back and sat down heavily beside an expectant Paul.

'No, Paul, I won't join you. As Managing Director of Flynn & Malby it's out. See it in the round. I'm not your man. I'm in far too deep with F&M. It's too late for my personal break-away. I could still join another agency – but setting up on my own, or in partnership, on their ashes would not be right for me. There you have it.'

A bitterly disappointed Paul sat back and looked long at Cas. He could see for himself that he had chosen the wrong man.

'It was worth a try, Cas.'

'No, Paul. It wasn't. It could never have been.'

They finished up their drinks and by mutual consent went out of the bar and downstairs, talking of other things. They parted in the sunshine and went their separate ways.

CHAPTER 7

The morning dawned clear and bright and Tessa was awake to see it. Inwardly greatly excited, she lay beside Paul, waiting for the day to come up, until she could bear it no longer. She tiptoed out to take a shower before the family and spent a good hour in the bathroom, washing and blow-drying her hair, and giving herself a facial to look her very best for meeting Roddy Ogilvie. She'd leave him with a lasting memory of her, she decided. Then she manicured her nails and felt she was ready for the world, and not afraid of any man in shoe leather. Paul stumbled out of bed and met her coming out of the bathroom as he was going in.

'What has you running around at this hour?' he mumbled.

'Oh, I've loads to do, and I thought I would be in better form if I paid some attention to my appearance first. I have to call up to the school about the possibility of organising PE classes, and sporting facilities for the older ones.'

'Precious little in the way of sporting facilities for us when we were under ten, if I remember rightly' he said. 'We just kicked a ball around the place.'

'Times change,' she said and went past him into the kitchen. The early start had been a good idea. No real discussions at this hour of the day.

Paul said over breakfast that he would be a bit late that evening.

'Are you planning to move the Shelbourne from one side of the Green to the other? I've rarely known you preoccupied for such a long time.'

'Business developments,' said Paul. 'Or lack of them.' I've to meet a friend of mine from another agency to talk over a possible deal. I had someone in mind but he bowed out. I have to find a substitute. Must rush.'

Tessa hadn't the slightest idea what he was talking about. He kissed her on the cheek, hardly pausing in his stride to do so, and the car swung out of Bulloch Harbour and up Harbour Road without Paul losing a beat. In a strange way it acted to remove the guilt in Tessa. If Paul was so busy with his life, she had a right to hers. And what was wrong with having lunch with someone, anyway?

The children picked up her heightened mood and chatted all the way to school.

'Are you going somewhere today, Mummy? You smell nice.' Stephanie said, with the straight aim of the very young.

'I'm looking nice, and smelling nice because I'm bringing you two to school.'

'You don't always look like that in the morning, Mummy.' Tessa laughed. She was in too good a humour to care. She kissed them both as they got out of the car, and said she'd be there at five to hear all about the music class. As they ran into the school she felt suddenly proud of them and of herself. Two lovely children, and a nice home, and if she did have a too-busy husband, she was obviously still very attractive. Roddy Ogilvie's attention had proved that to her.

Instead of meeting at the top of the road as arranged, Roddy walked down to the harbour to take a look at Tessa's house from the outside. He found it tasteful, in fact absolutely charming with bay windows looking across the harbour, and suddenly he wished he lived in a house like that, with a woman like Tessa, and some stability in his life. He banished the thoughts from his mind.

When Tessa returned, she saw him standing at the end of the pier, his back to her. Her heart missed a beat. This exciting man was waiting for her. She walked silently up behind him, put her hand on his shoulder and gave him a pretend push, pulling him back from the brink all in one movement. Startled, he swung around.

'Tessa!'

'What are you doing down here?' She was smiling. 'I thought we were to meet at the top of the road.'

'Sorry – am I being indiscreet?'

'No, it's alright.' Tessa was in playful mood and bent on enjoying the outing.

Roddy responded. 'It's a lovely harbour, lovely and serene like yourself.' He turned everything to advantage.

'Oh, on occasions things can get quite stormy here,' she said, enjoying herself already in the same vein.

'I'll bet. Come on. We're off.'

'Look, I have to slip into the house to get my bag. Will you come in for a minute?' He nodded, and walked companionably with her along the short distance to the house and followed her inside. He stood in the front room and took it all in. The Bennetts seemed to have money or the promise of it, and their taste was excellent. A minute or two later they were out of the house and walking up to Roddy's car, with the day stretching before them.

They pulled out on to the dual carriageway which would lead them past the small Sugar Loaf mountain and up into the Wicklow Hills. As it was fine and sunny, Roddy let down the top of the Fiat 124 Convertible. Until then they had been talking naturally and animatedly, but now with the summer breeze blowing in their faces, they just smiled at each other occasionally enjoying the exhilaration of the morning drive. After some miles, Roddy pulled the car into the side of the road so that they could go for a stroll through the fields on Callary Bog and get up an appetite for an early lunch. They were completely at ease, side by side, with no contact but their conversation, and Tessa felt on top of the world.

The old-fashioned, tavern-style restaurant Roddy had picked out was situated near Roundwood, high in the mountains, and they were welcomed by the proprietor, who served game as the 'chef's recommendation'. The warm friendly atmosphere and the wine relaxed them, and Roddy enjoyed the meal so much that he decided to talk to the chef afterwards with a view to serving something similar in The Aristocrat.

'We'll go for a drive after all this,' said Roddy, 'I promise I'll have you home in time. I booked the lunch early so that we could have more time afterwards and it's only half past one now. We've plenty of time. Come on.' As usual he was completely in control, and now revelling in his well-planned excursion, he moved on to the next phase. He had been very entertaining right through lunch, and Tessa had found herself sparking off him and gaining a new confidence as he amused her with anecdotes from his culinary past. Her own contributions were well beyond her usual form.

'Alright, let's drive for a little, while we digest that delicious meal,' Tessa said. 'When I'm with you I seem to spend all my time guzzling food and fattening myself up, or else I'm running to stay slim.' They both laughed. 'An ominous pattern is forming.'

'Nonsense, you're as slender as a reed. People like you fascinate me – a lotus blossom who can put away a fine lunch – if you'll excuse the mixed metaphors.'

They strolled across to the car and Roddy held the door while Tessa slipped in gracefully. All this talk of lotus blossoms was having its effect. He turned purposefully into the hills, apparently knowing his route and driving with care along the narrow roads.

'I want to show you somewhere special,' he said after a while. 'It's down by Lough Dan and must be one of the most strikingly beautiful places I know. I was shown it the first week I was in Ireland, and the calm there is amazing. That great, deep mountain lake has a solemnity about it that can't be described. You probably know the area, anyway, but I can show it to you from a wonderful vantage point.'

'We've come up here once or twice. The Guinness family have a house near the far shore at Lugnaquillia and they use the little beach you can see from this side. I remember it, alright.'

Having driven for some time, Roddy turned off the road and down a grassy track which ran a further mile. The lake came into view on the right, and Tessa assumed Roddy had found a special viewing point and looked forward to it. She was therefore quite surprised when they came to a solitary cottage beautifully placed on a height over the lake. Roddy stopped the car, got out and opened the cottage gate.

'Come on and see for yourself,' he said, and Tessa felt she had no option but to follow him. A little alarmed at the smoothness of the arrangements, she told herself she would just admire the view and then ask Roddy to head straight back for Dalkey.

'I've rented this little place for my quiet times,' he said. 'A neighbour is going to keep an eye on it and light the fire for me regularly. I'm very pleased about it.' Inside, Tessa looked about her. It was a real country cottage with a wide hearth, but on one side a large, plate-glass window had been set into the wall, to allow for a breathtaking view of the lake below, deep brown peaty waters, with the sun skimming over the surface, and a lone bird gliding across it. In the distance, the creamy-coloured half moon beach sparkled brightly making a picture in itself, with a small red boat on one side of it. This cottage was pure magic, the way it was sited. The fire glowed in the hearth and Roddy turned around slowly and looked deeply into Tessa's eyes, drawing her gaze from the lake to his. Then with a rush of electricity, he reached across and gathered her in his arms, and kissed her firmly and strongly. Taken unawares by the swiftness of his movements, she responded in spite of herself, and then he kissed her again, with the enquiring excitement of a man urgently bent on making love.

Tessa disentangled herself from Roddy's embrace and turned towards the window of the cottage, looking down into the deep waters of the lake. Her hands were flat on the table and her body was angled forward, as she stared with unseeing eyes, her senses blurred with excitement.

There was something she must think about, but what was it? Faded shapes of Paul and the children danced will-o'-the-wisp through her consciousness, but they were so insubstantial that her mind failed to engage properly. She felt strangely young, heady with anticipation.

Roddy went over to a cupboard and took out a large odd-shaped bottle and two small glasses. He filled them to the brim. 'Here, try this.'

She turned, folding her arms in a useless last-ditch defensive gesture, but her face, luminous in the soft angled shadows of the cottage, betrayed her true feelings.

'I don't know. What is it? I'm still enjoying the effects of the wine at lunch.'

'It's Austrian.' Roddy, holding out the glass, was smiling and watching her closely. 'Do you good. Swig it back.' His Scottish burr was more pronounced. She accepted the glass and took a few sips of the thickish, sweet, fruity liquid. She felt a pleasantly mellow sensation. Roddy came over to her and placed his hands on her shoulders. He stroked her neck and cupped her head in his hands. Then he leaned towards her and brushed her lips with a whisper of a kiss.

Tessa could feel his body against hers, tensed like a coiled spring. With an almost inaudible groan, she laid her head on his chest, and the last drop of resistance drained from her as Roddy put his head down and buried his face in her fresh and fragrant hair.

Barely conscious of their decision, they moved towards the bedroom with its low, slanting ceiling. The pine bed had a well-washed patchwork duvet, and a candle stood askew in its enamel holder on the bedside locker. There was a slight scent of lavender. As they sat on the edge of the bed, Roddy gently removed Tessa's polo-neck cotton top. She could feel his open lips soft against her skin as he kissed her shoulders and then her breasts. She was spinning, spinning, spinning like a child on a fairground chair-o-plane. He opened the buttons on his shirt and Tessa slid her hand around his chest. She could smell the pleasant muskiness of him.

'You have a group of freckles on your chest like the constellation, The Great Bear,' she said softly.

Roddy gave a low chuckle.

'I am the Great Bear.' Suddenly the dam burst and they were both carried away on a wave of uncontrollable, all-consuming passion.

Roddy was strangely quiet as they drove back, perplexity showing on his face. He was so used to being successful with women that it hadn't occurred to him that he might, just might, feel a little more strongly for this pretty mother of two, safely settled in her married life. He didn't want to leave her back to her life, he wanted to keep her for himself. He should have looked out for a single woman, he told himself ruefully, mildly irritated at the thought of handing Tessa back to her husband and children. Looking at her out of the corner of his eye as they drove over the hills and dropped down towards the sea and Dalkey, he found her beautiful rather than pretty in her newly found confidence as a responsive lover. Now she had real colour and sparkle. She had obviously not thought this adventure through at all, and like most women, had been putting more thought into the delicious moments in the pursuit. He must see her again. She interested him greatly as a sexual partner and her quick wit and easy conversation attracted him further. She seemed to have a kind of innocence which was something new, different from the worldly-wise girls he had known until now. He liked that. But he must keep things uncomplicated at all costs. It was too early to dwell on this kind of thing, and so he began to hum a tune to distract himself. Tessa sat there beside him, hands entwined, peaceful, beautiful and smiling.

'I'll let you out at the end of Convent Road. It wouldn't do to compromise you in front of the neighbours! It wasn't a particularly good idea for me to come strolling by your house this morning.'

'Yes do. I can't believe I'm taking all this so calmly, but I am for now. Until I get my thoughts together.'

'You were wonderful this afternoon, Tessa. I'll be in touch. I'm looking forward to it already.' He stopped the Fiat and let Tessa out. 'Now, I'm gone!' he said with a big smile and drove away.

Tessa stood there for a moment, and then walked briskly along, wondering what in the name of God would come next.

* * *

Cas had taken the day off. He had been working extra hard, not getting home until after twelve at night, so he planned to sleep late and then drive to the Sugar Loaf mountain, to do some sketching. With his drawing pads, pencils and water colours, he set off in expectation of an enjoyable and relaxing day, away from life, love, and agency complications.

Paul Bennett's suggestion that they both leave Flynn & Malby and set up their own agency had come as a shock. He liked Paul well enough, but always felt he was a bit of a gambler with other people's goods. What Paul had said was true: clients were becoming dangerously disenchanted with Ted Flynn. Ted could be erratic, unctuous and untruthful, but he was immensely talented and able – deep down Cas supposed he must like the man!

Cas remembered the time when he joined the agency. He had come as an artist, and within a few months Ted had put him in charge of a number of important clients, and he had been delighted by the sudden promotion to Account Executive.

Then Ted had entrusted him with the task of finding out why clients were not paying their bills. At that time the agency had no staff accountant, just one book-keeper. It didn't take Cas long to discover that the reason for non-payment was that clients were not being invoiced. After some probing, it emerged that the overworked and under-enthusiastic book-keeper was producing the invoices and statements late or incomplete every month, and in a panic hid them in an out-house in the back garden pretending that they had been despatched. Cas had been asked to make the necessary staff changes to deal with this. Around that time Eric Timmerman joined the agency too, he recalled.

Eric Timmerman was a graphic designer newly arrived from Holland. He had come directly to the agency and requested a meeting with the Art Director, and even though he was told that Martin O'Neill was unavailable for some hours, if not all day, had insisted on waiting for as long as it took to get an interview. Eventually Martin, feeling sorry for him, agreed to view his portfolio of work. The quality was first-rate, and Timmerman knew it, and Martin immediately entrusted him with a large assignment on a freelance basis. Eric was back within 48 hours with the job completed, and the work was of such high quality that Martin offered him a permanent position with the agency right away. Eric Timmerman started work as a senior artist with Flynn & Malby the following day.

It was shortly afterwards that Ted came into his office one morning at about half past six. He hadn't slept well, and had decided to capitalise on it by coming in and getting some work moved on. He was only at his desk a short while when what seemed to be the smell of cooking bacon assailed his nostrils, and a curious and disbelieving Ted made his way downstairs, nose twitching, until he reached the basement of the house which had been the kitchen area long ago, when the house was a private residence, and was now the Production Department. The trail led to the scullery at the back, where the block clerk's printing blocks, plates, stereotypes and matrices were pigeon-holed. He opened the door to find a frying pan on a gas ring, with rashers and sausages spitting and sizzling busily. Nearby were black and white puddings, a carton of eggs and a pot of coffee. Over an old-fashioned sink, to one side, was a hose pipe fixed into what Ted had thought to be a defunct old geyser. Hissing steam, it was now pumping hot water through the hose, which ran across the floor, out the door and down the garden path. Intrigued, Ted followed the hose to the bottom of the garden where he found a naked Eric Timmerman whistling as he soaped himself generously all over, and rinsed himself methodically under the end of the hose, which had been attached to a tree.

Eric was not at all fazed when he turned around and saw Ted, but greeted him with a 'Luffly morning, Mr Flynn,' and went on rinsing his toes carefully.

Ted, taken aback, could only reply, 'Looks like rain.'

Later that day it emerged that Eric's unusual washing and breakfasting arrangements were due to the fact that he had no fixed address. It was discovered that he was sleeping in an old station wagon which he parked nightly in a quiet place along the Grand Canal, in the company of his dog, Adolph, whom he dressed, for no reason that could be explained, in an old pair of Y-fronts. Martin undertook the job of finding Eric and Adolph a suitable place to live, as they agreed that they should hold on to Eric, come what may, so good was his work as an artist.

'He may be an eccentric,' Cas had said, 'but he's gifted. Keep him, but for God's sake keep him away from the clients.'

He isn't the only eccentric, thought Cas. There's Birdie Malby.

When Frank Malby died, Ted offered his widow a job in Flynn & Malby, partly out of concern and partly to keep an eye on her. Birdie was without any business know-how, and had little experience of the world in general. From the time she left school until her marriage to Frank, she had looked after her elderly parents, almost to the exclusion of everything else. She had met Frank in the church choir. An unspectacular, dumpy woman, she wore her hair bleached and permed close to her head in what looked like a 1920s Hollywood-starlet style.

She had two major weaknesses. One was chain-smoking Albany cigarettes, and the other – in which her parents, and also Frank had indulged her – was jewellery. Earrings and bangles, rings, brooches and bracelets, pins, lockets and necklaces, pendants and chains were worn in profusion. Gold cascaded down her front, with beads of all descriptions abseiling over her bosom. On her wrist she wore, among other ornamentations, a charm bracelet composed of a multiplicity of trinkets garnered over the years. Everywhere she went, the rattling noise of this adornment preceded her.

'Just like the bells of Alpine cows,' Ted had remarked.

'Marley's ghost,' suggested Martin.

Unqualified for any agency post, Ted put her in charge of 'vouchers'. This meant that her job was to select the pages from the newspapers and magazines containing clients' advertisements, which were later sent to clients with invoices, as proof that the advertisements had appeared as ordered. She also took cuttings of advertisements and pasted them into a book called 'the guard book'. This, the lowliest task in any agency, was time-consuming, though not onerous, and should have kept her busy, but unfortunately Birdie found enough time on her hands to interfere in other departments. The staff, knowing that she was part-owner of the agency, could hardly object. Things came to a head one morning when Ted, unable to get an answer to telephone calls to the Production Department, with all extensions constantly engaged, went downstairs and found all the production staff on their knees reciting the Rosary, led by Birdie. All telephones had been taken off the hooks. Cas smiled to himself when he recalled the look on Ted's face. Ted was stumped as to what he should do about the situation, when fate took a hand. Birdie's mother died suddenly and she asked Ted if he could see his way to releasing her, so that she could look after her very elderly father, which she now saw as her bounden duty. With a great show of reluctance he agreed. Active agency life for Birdie mercifully came to a close.

Cas spent the day happily working in water-colours, far from the agency. Sometimes he wondered what he was doing in an agency at all. He had gone so quickly from Commercial Artist to Account Executive, to Director, to Managing Director, and here he was at 28, not sure where he was going in life, and too much in the control of others. So many agency people would have queued to get his position in a leading agency, so why wasn't he delighted with himself?

* * *

For once Paul was home in good time for dinner. He seemed to pick up Tessa's elation, although she went to great lengths to conceal it, and he said that it was too long since they had been out together. He had been told that a good new restaurant had opened in Dalkey, The Aristocrat – had she heard about it? Maybe they'd go at the weekend. If she arranged for a sitter for the Saturday night, they could try it out.

Tessa appreciated Paul's return of interest in her as a wife, but to her horror it was coming at a time when she was least interested in him, with her mind fixed on Roddy and the memory of his muscled body against her.

As she tidied up after dinner, her heart was back in the cottage and she found herself wondering how soon she would go there again, she, who had gone on the outing as a farewell to Roddy Ogilvie. Now she had opened up feelings within herself, and it was going to be terribly difficult, if not impossible to keep them under control. She had convinced herself that it would be fun to flirt a little, and instead she had responded to a rush of passion, of which she hadn't thought herself capable. Other women could presumably cope with such an adventure, and regard it as a bonus to their already established life, but she was not so sure that she would be one of them. She jerked back to reality. She mustn't think of Roddy now. He had said he would be in touch very soon, and she certainly wouldn't be doing a Casablanca by coming into his restaurant. Of all the gin-joints, in all the towns in all the world .... She'd tell Paul she'd do the booking, and then that she couldn't get a reservation, and book somewhere else.

Surprisingly, Paul wanted to talk to her about the agency, and she had some difficulty in following his conversation. It was about possible developments outside of Flynn & Malby, which might lead to greater things for them as a couple. Tessa knew well that Paul had a streak of the adventurer deep within him, and on principle she didn't take him seriously when he talked big, as he was doing now. She had backed him in the risk of taking on the heavy mortgage for their new home, because it was what she really wanted herself, and she felt her family would bail her out if a crisis ever arose about payments, but this new speculation didn't appeal to her, so she paid little attention. She knew he put her lack of interest down to the fact that he had been so uncommunicative for so long about his work, and that he had resolved to let her in on things a bit more in future. When he asked her to make love to him later that night, she was confused and not a little guilty, and she told him she had back pain, but that she would make it up to him soon.

A few days went by without Tessa hearing from Roddy. She began to feel nervous, but eventually he phoned and she was there to answer it. The waiting was at an end. He explained he had had to fly over to Scotland unexpectedly, and he naturally hadn't wanted to contact her in the evenings. In her heart she felt he could have contacted her from Scotland or wherever, but overcome with relief at his call she let it go. He proposed another outing to the cottage, and, with an intoxicating sensation and not a little guilt, Tessa agreed.

But there had been no trip to Scotland for Roddy Ogilvie; he was an experienced man, and he wanted to keep the upper hand in this new liaison. He was well used to making women wait for his attentions, so that they would not become secure and demanding too soon, and spoil the element of chase for him, and he could easily have telephoned Tessa since their outing to Lough Dan.

They went off to the cottage again, and Tessa fell deeply in love. It was an overcast day and the lake below the window in the cottage looked black and sad, and she held herself close to Roddy as they gazed down at it, and wondered how deep it was. As before, their lovemaking was unsuppressed and magical. They were to go back to 'their' cottage three or four more times, and Tessa felt herself swept into a love-trap from which she might never escape.

Each night she waited until Paul slipped into his customary deep slumber before quietly getting up again. She would make herself a cup of tea and sit in the living-room studying the sea and the way it eddied and flowed into the harbour and filled it up, constantly renewing everything. She loved to see the boats rising, or dropping, and in this private time she sought to come to terms with what she was doing. At night she told herself that this liaison would have to stop immediately. What would Paul do, if he were to find out? What if the children were inadvertently to learn of it? Had anyone ever seen her get into the car with Roddy? Hardly. No one knew her around Bulloch as yet. Maybe she was just frightening herself, and the early hours of the morning lent themselves to such thinking. When day would dawn, whether she was back in bed, or still sitting around the house, she felt she couldn't possibly give up this delicious romantic involvement, even though it was so powerful that it threatened to submerge her.

She was sitting at the back of the living-room one night, with a record of Carole King's, 'It might as well rain until September', playing softly to keep her company, when she heard the noise of an envelope being stuffed through the letter box in the hall. At first she thought she was mistaken. Who would be at their door at that ungodly hour? She finished her tea and then tip-toed out to the hall curiously to see a long white envelope in the box. She pulled it towards her and saw it bore uneven printed letters cut from a newspaper. It simply said, 'Bitch'. She took it up with distaste, knowing she would be compelled to open it, and fearing to do so. She sat down again, shivering with fright. A folded page opened to reveal three lines of disgusting and offensive words, which made her stomach churn with fear. It referred to her friendship with Roddy in nauseous terms. But who could have sent her this repulsive note? She peered out the side of the window terrified, forcing herself to search the area with her eyes. The harbour was deserted. All hope of sleep banished, she put the note at the back of her writing case, and returned to bed to lie there, tossing nervously.

* * *

It was afternoon when Pat Grehan shuffled up the Vico Road towards White Rock, clutching a plastic supermarket bag containing bits of bread and half a bottle of tea. His shoes were too tight. The busybodies from the St Vincent de Paul had given them to him two days previously and they were too small for him. They didn't care. They just handed out things to make themselves feel good. They kept calling to his bed-sitter, asking him if he was alright. Was he lonely? Of course he was lonely. What the hell did they expect from a man of his years. Why did they think he walked around Dalkey all day looking at things, the stupid buggers. He had seen that young one who lived at Bulloch Harbour running around making a spectacle of herself. And she a married woman with children. He had seen them and he had taken note. He knew what she was up to with her fancy man from Dalkey. He had seen them together at the harbour. Laughing. And the man had gone into her house and then they had driven away together. His eyes were red-flecked with anger. He had a woman himself once. But she died. Good riddance. These bitches were all the same, disgusting, filthy creatures. Always with men.

Pat Grehan took the path from the main road down to White Rock beach. Half way down he veered left and continued over the hill towards Decko's cave, so called because Decko Kavanagh, an old sailor who came to Dalkey in 1914 had lived there. Pat spent a lot of time in the cave, imagining some connection with the notorious beggar, long since dead. He had read about Decko somewhere many years ago, and had found the cave and made it his own. Now it was overgrown and few knew of its existence.

Not far from the cave was a vantage point from which Pat regularly watched the women coming down to the bathing place reserved for them. Some swam with nothing on – the temptresses! Did Decko Kavanagh crouch there too, he wondered, watching those evil women. He ate some bread and drank some tea and then went to the back of the cave and rolled back a stone. From a hole he took out a tin box containing paper, envelopes, old newspapers, glue and rusty scissors.

* * *

Saturday was a good day for Ted. Normally he went into his office which he felt was an oasis of calm, unlike the pulsating centre of tension it proved to be throughout the working week. Today he had much to occupy him, and he felt anything but calm.

He tilted his high-backed swivel-chair and placed his feet on the desk, and, with his hands behind his head, contemplated the disaster that would befall the agency if Bruce Bellingham were to take the Arkwright & Dobson account away, and they lost Baby Faire as well. And the Western Distillers business they had pitched for might also go elsewhere. First thing on Monday morning he'd call Cas in and sort out this rumour that Bruce Bellingham and Tim Cranby were going to set up Cas in his own agency, maybe with Paul Bennett. He suspected Paul as being the driving force, but he would certainly find the Judas.

First he must contact Bruce and Tim in their homes, even though it was Saturday morning. His watch said nine forty-five, but he would wait until ten o'clock before making the calls. If he could see them that day, so much the better, but he was prepared to go out to their homes any time over the weekend if necessary. He would use every ploy he had to convince them to stay with Flynn & Malby, and promise them anything at all to keep their business. He would tell them what they wanted to hear. Better service? Maybe a cut in the twelve and a half per cent commission? Maybe a reduced service fee? Jim Reilly would be very angry. Typical accountant. He claimed that all commissions were eaten up by the high costs of running an agency, and that agencies only survived on the five per cent extra service fee charged to clients – that's where the profit lay. And, of course, it was against the rules of the Institute of Advertising Practitioners in Ireland to rebate commissions. He didn't care, he'd do whatever was necessary short-term, to keep the agency afloat. And to hell with the begrudgers!

He looked around his office affectionately. He loved this room which had been a Georgian drawing-room in the days of gracious eighteenth-century Dublin. This was his real home, not Dalkey where he and Rita lived virtually separate lives. He thought briefly of her teashop venture, and of how he had ignored the whole matter. Rita looked cheerful enough these days, so she couldn't have been making too many mistakes. He'd check it out later, when all these agency troubles were solved.

He looked down at the neatly tended back garden from the long window and marvelled at how far he had come in life. His eyes roved across the impressive white marble Adam fireplace, and the accumulation of silver ornaments on its mantelpiece, the paintings by contemporary artists which he had had chosen for him and, likewise, the small collection of leather-bound books, the deep pile carpet and the attractive lamps supplied by a designer, an ambience which had helped soothe many a prospective client. His eyes rested on the two exquisitely carved desks, both valuable antiques, his large and impressive, the one Liz used smaller and more discreet, positioned near the folding doors which led to the boardroom.

He'd get a specially carved plaque to hang on the wall, if he were elected – when he was elected – King of Dalkey. It was all great fun, of course, this honorary title nonsense, but it did carry a certain amount of prestige. And it would be a great slap in the face to all those Dalkeyites for a poor boy from Black's Lane to be chosen as their King! Even if it was a make-believe one. He had talked to all the right people and he had called in a few favours here and there. He was nearly certain he could pull it off.

It was an excellent idea to revive the eighteenth-century mock ceremony. Norman Judd had made a great King and so had Noel Purcell before him. He'd do better. He opened the bottom drawer in his desk and took out a file. Liz and the others would think him a complete fool to be bothering with this hokum. Certainly Rita and the children would! He didn't care. He wanted this honour. He took a sheet of paper from the file and read the full impressive title: King of Dalkey, Emperor of the Muglins, Prince of the Holy Island of Magee, Barton of Bulloch, Seigneur of Sandycove, Defender of the Faith and Respector of All Others, Elector of Lambay and Ireland's Eye and Sovereign of the most Illustrious Order of the Lobster and Periwinkle.' He would need a very large plaque indeed.

He started when the phone rang.

'Hello, yes?'

'Hello, is that you Ted? I thought I'd find you in the office. Do you ever go home?'

'No rest for the virtuous. Is that you, Derry?' Derry O'Dowd was Managing Director of a small firm called the Diamond Tobacco Company, which sold pipe tobacco and imported Dutch cheroots. Flynn & Malby handled their modest advertising budget.

'It is. I'd like to see you Ted, It's important.'

'Sure. Let me look at my diary. Wednesday is okay. No, on second thoughts, how about Thursday afternoon?'

'No, Ted, when I say important, I mean very. It means more business for you.'

'Good, we can always do with more business.'

'Big business,' said Derry. Ted felt a familiar tingle of excitement.

'How big?'

'As big as it gets.'

'Derry, name the time you want us to meet, and I'll clear the decks.'

'Today. This afternoon. Your office, three o'clock.'

'Okay, done.'

'And Ted ... I'm phoning you at the weekend because this is top-secret. Don't breathe a word that we're meeting. And I mean, not to anyone. Not your staff, or even your directors – for the moment. This is important.'

'Sure, sure. See you at three, then.' Ted could hardly wait to find out what Derry O'Dowd was going to reveal.

In spite of O'Dowd's stipulation of confidentiality, he phoned Liz right away and begged her to cancel her Saturday arrangements and come straight into the office. He needed her, and he needed her badly. Then he telephoned the homes of Bellingham and Cranby, but Bruce had gone to London and wouldn't be back until Wednesday, and Tim had left for the day. Damn. Now he would have to wait until next week to contact them, Maybe he'd see them at the Marketing Society meeting on Wednesday night, when an eminent American from Harvard Business School was to be the guest lecturer. As members of the Society, neither of them would miss a talk like that.

Instead of his usual visit to the Horseshoe Bar, Ted asked Liz to bring him in a sandwich, so that he could wait for Derry O'Dowd and collect his thoughts. O'Dowd arrived at three sharp, and on the way upstairs to his office, Ted explained that Liz, who knew all the agency business, would have to be there as his confidential secretary. Once they were seated, Ted leaned back in his chair, eyes alert, tongue playing with his loose tooth, listening intently to Derry, with Liz immobile in the corner.

The story unfolded quickly. B. K. & W. Ridgeway, the English cigarette company, were planning to launch a new cigarette on the British market, but first they wanted to test-market it in Ireland through the Diamond Tobacco Company. Ted already knew that Diamond was partly owned by Ridgeway. Now a national launch was being planned for Ireland and Flynn & Malby were being asked to handle the advertising. The budget would be the biggest ever in these islands for such a project – a cigarette brand introductory campaign. Fantastic, thought Ted, just what the agency needed. Thank God!

O'Dowd filled him in fully. Ridgeway had decided not to ask any other advertising agency to pitch for the account for one reason only – secrecy. Secrecy, said Derry, was paramount, because industrial espionage was rife in the cigarette industry, and if another company got wind of what was happening, they would bring out a similar cigarette in advance of Ridgeway to sabotage the venture. This is why they wanted the test market carried out in Ireland. The cigarette would be different to any other currently available. Ted was leaning forward, elbows on the desk, fingers playing with a silver ornamental fish. This could save the agency.

CHAPTER 8

Tessa brooded as to whether or not she would tell Roddy about the insulting note. Would it make him apprehensive about continuing to see her? She was now totally in his thrall and unwilling to do or say anything which would change the course of their affair, and she was completely overlooking her own situation. Wife and mother she might be, but so infatuated was she by this Scottish newcomer who had walked into her sheltered world and taken her over, mind and body, that she couldn't bear the friendship to end abruptly. She was too scared to show her insecurity to Roddy as she couldn't gauge how he would react to it. Instead, she convinced herself that it was a case of mistaken identity, that the sender of the horrible, filthy note had somebody else in mind. No names had been mentioned. She didn't know anyone in Dalkey, after all, and maybe other people living around had been the target of a similar crackpot action. She couldn't ask around. After much reflection, she convinced herself that it would be better to put the whole thing out of her mind and mention it to no one.

Tessa's love affair with Roddy had gone into a new phase. She could feel the difference, and surmised that he was actually falling in love for the first time in his life – falling in love with a woman, instead of just using her body for his satisfaction. As a new emotion, that would have frightened him not a little, an emotion that he couldn't completely dominate, a new and uncomfortable feeling for him.

Yes, Roddy was changing. At first he had seemed to her to be self-centred and astute in his approach to life, and this was acted out in his lovemaking, but as time went on, he talked less of his life in the restaurant and more of his early years in Scotland, sometimes recounting events of growing up in a poor part of Glasgow. He seemed to be bonding with her, with another person, and probably for the first time in his life, like an emotionally damaged child.

Roddy knew that Tessa was not reading him correctly. If she could have seen into his mind she would have found a man who compartmentalised his life, business and emotional. He was bonding with her alright, but only in as far as he needed the relaxation of communication to pace himself as her lover, and the warmth he was drawing out of her was something he regarded as a bonus to their lovemaking. A new and enjoyable dimension for him. He would never have been rough with her, knowing that he would lose more than he would gain if he were. While Tessa rejoiced in the change in him, it was not anything as deep as she believed. Roddy knew this and found it irrelevant to the joyous, satisfying liaison.

* * *

When she had been in business for some time, Rita felt she could do with permanent assistance, so that she would be less tied to the enterprise. The Teashop was open from half-past nine in the morning to half-past four in the afternoon, but it was obvious that good money could be made by marginally extending the hours. She could do with a little freedom, now that it was up and running, and proving to be a spectacular earner. It was around that time that a French woman approached her, a regular customer, and asked if she needed assistance in the afternoons. She wore a beret which clung to the side of her head without any visible means of support, and her mouth was shaped for pouting.

'I would be most interested, Mrs Flynn. I know about the business, as my father has a restaurant in Lyon,' was her introduction to the conversation. Rita pursued the idea with her, and decided to take her on a month's trial, having interviewed her fully and found that she had grown up in the business. It transpired the young French woman was now married to a very wealthy Irishman, who had a good deal of property. Rita liked the idea, and so they made arrangements accordingly. The woman's name was Lisette D'Ambly.

Lisette also explained that she was a teacher in the École d'Anglais de Dublin, which had opened in nearby Glenageary. Plans were afoot to keep the school open all year round, and Lisette intended to continue teaching there, but would also like to work in The Teashop, as it was patronised by so many of the foreign students. Until it had opened, the students had had nowhere to go for good quality snacks and to relax and talk English among themselves.

When a good business relationship had been established between Rita Flynn and Lisette, the French woman put a further proposal to her.

'Mrs Flynn, I'm wondering if you would think of taking over any more space in this building. I went upstairs one day to see the view from the top window, and there are two empty floors there. Have you thought about it?'

'Well, one thing at a time, Lisette,' Rita answered. 'I only wondered if the landlord had plans for the storeys above, in case anything detrimental to the business would be involved with other lettings. Why do you ask?'

'I thought that maybe the catering service could be extended to other foreign students in the area, a sort of club, if we could find space for them. I mean, they could have their coffee upstairs, along with supervised conversation classes. They wouldn't be in the way of the regular customers and business would expand. What do you think?'

Rita was quite knocked out by the forward thinking of the woman, and decided to take it slowly, and to come back to Lisette on the subject. A club for continental students! Rita Flynn would certainly be going places with that. Lisette D'Ambly had further thoughts.

'You see, Mrs Flynn, the view takes in Joyce's Tower, and there are many American students in Dublin studying the works of James Joyce. I feel sure that a trade catering for them could also be developed. So many of them come out here to visit the tower, as it is, now that it has been converted into a museum. You've been there, of course?' Lisette raised her eyebrows.

Rita gave a half-laugh. 'No, I've never been inside. That confirms me as a true Dub.'

'Oh, it is wonderful,' enthused Lisette. 'It was Michael Scott's idea to turn the old Martello Tower into a museum. It was built originally to keep my invading ancestors out.' She smiled. 'So many people helped with the conversion, even John Huston, the American film director, donated a thousand dollars.'

'It's certainly a marvellous attraction.'

'Wouldn't it be exciting,' said Lisette, 'if a Joycean school could also be developed, say on the top floor of your building here, catered for by The Teashop? I must admit I have an ulterior motive. You see my 'usband is a Joycean scholar and he lectures on Joyce part-time.'

Rita was very excited by these proposals, though she didn't show it. What would Ted think if he knew how well she was doing? The venture had remained a no-go area between them, so she'd just work this out first. He would have to be told in due course, as there were limits even to dealing with a man like Ted.

Delighted with the initial reception of her business ideas, Lisette D'Ambly was happy enough to wait until Rita felt like further discussion.

* * *

The sumptuous dinner had been Chloe's treat. The waiter in the Hibernian Hotel poured out coffee and checked if anyone wanted an after-dinner drink. Barry opted for a port, and Cas nodded for one too. Both of them settled back and waited for Chloe to speak. Chloe lit a cigarette, leaned forward and tracing her finger around the rim of her coffee cup, started to explain her idea.

'You know I work in Hollywood in movie production. I say in movie production rather than as a movie producer, because I've been very much an associate until now. My plan is to set up a movie production company in Ireland and I want you guys to join me in the venture.' She smiled winningly at them.

'Well now ...,' said Barry, and stopped.

'You want to make films in Ireland?' said Cas.

'Yes. One. I've quite a bit of experience in putting together the bits and pieces necessary to make a movie. In fact I'm pretty damn good at it. Apart from distribution the main ingredients are finance, finance and finance.'

'But we haven't got that sort of money,' said Barry bleakly. Chloe laughed.

'No, I can raise the wampum to make the movie, in fact I've raised fifty per cent already. I've all the contacts I need Stateside. What I want from you guys is to help me set up an Irish production company which will organise things here and also buy into part of the movie. The movie must be made in Ireland. And – this is the second prong of my plan – the company will also make television commercials for the Irish market. That's where Cas comes in, with all his contacts in the advertising business.' She fondled the back of Cas's hand lovingly. Cas's eyes shone. He was doubly thrilled at the possibility of being involved in film-making and at Chloe's attention. 'So I want to make a movie and I want to make TV commercials in Ireland. And I need your help, okay?'

'You were very tight-lipped about your plans until now,' said Barry. 'Why so?'

'I needed to be sure I could get the full financial backing to make the movie. I'm determined this venture will be a success.'

Barry said he just knew that whatever Chloe turned her hand to would be a rip-roaring success.

Cas sipped his port and tried to look at things analytically. 'Let's take things one at a time,' he said. 'First the commercials. It takes a special kind of knowledge and creative talent to make television commercials.'

'Sure. I've spent a lot of time headquartering in an office on Madison Avenue in New York working my butt off doing just that before I went to Hollywood. I know the score.'

'Certainly there's plenty of room for a good TV production company here,' said Cas. 'And I can introduce you to all the right people alright. I just wonder if advertising agencies will give their business to a production company which includes me, the MD of a rival agency? They're a suspicious lot, you know.'

Chloe ran her hand up his arm and rested it on his shoulder.

'Simple. You just make the contacts for me – us – and then take a back seat. You see, I need both of you guys operating here in Ireland. I'll be shuttling back and forth between Ireland and the US of A, raising the extra greenbacks for the movie, and getting re-writes of the script.'

'Re-writes!' Barry exclaimed. 'You're that far advanced?'

'Yeah. The basic script is already written. No script, no backers.'

'What's this film about anyway?' asked Cas.

'Yeats. W.B. His life story. Or at least part of it. His involvement with the Gore-Booths, Eva and her sister Constance, that's Countess Markievicz. His visits to their home, Lissadell in County Sligo.' She lit another cigarette and let a ribbon of smoke spiral slowly past her face. Clearly she was captivated by the great poet and Cas suspected that the making of the film was one of Chloe's obsessions.

'I love the poem he wrote about Lissadell and the two girls, "The light of evening, Lissadell, great windows open to the south, two girls in silk kimonos, both beautiful, one a gazelle".' She gestured with her cigarette. 'Plenty of shots of the enchanting Irish countryside, including Drumcliff where Yeats is buried, "under bare Ben Bulben's head". I went there with Laura when we were on vacation in the west. What was his epitaph? Something like, "Cast a cold eye on life, on death. Horseman, pass by!" Yes, that's it, I think.' In fact, Chloe was well acquainted with Yeats's work. 'Coole, the house in County Galway where Lady Gregory invited Yeats, Æ and Edward Martyn to discuss the founding of the Abbey Theatre. Coole isn't there any more, but we'll mock it up somehow. Yeats the Senator. And of course, Maud Gonne McBride, who was the inspiration for most of his love poems. It will be a wonderful love story. Great fun to cast. I'm working on getting the right sympathetic director. We'll shoot most of the interiors at Ardmore Studios in Bray – or the National Film Studios of Ireland as it's called now that your RTE has bought it over and intends to revamp it. I've been there on a recce and it's perfect. Huston, Boorman and Kubrick have all made films there successfully. Nerve-tingling isn't it? Well gentlemen of the jury, what say you all, what is your verdict?'

'Chloe O'Leary, you take my breath away,' said Cas.

'You leave me breathless too,' Barry concurred. 'Here, let's order more port.'

Chloe was glowing with excitement. She leaned down and took two copies of a summary of her plans out of her brief-case and handed them each a copy. Barry shook his head at the efficiency of it all. He and Cas flicked through the document and noted that her proposals had been laid out in some detail. Chloe suggested Cas and Barry each take a 24 per cent stake in the new company and that she take 52 per cent. She would be away from Ireland on a regular basis, of course, at the beginning, so they would need to appoint someone to run the company, but they could deal with that matter some other time.

They sat around the table and chatted eagerly about this fascinating new business venture. Cas wondered where in the name of God he'd get the money to invest, so that he could be close to his precious Chloe.

* * *

'Dad, it's Rita. How are you, love? You're well? Great, great. Listen Dad, I want to drop over and fill you in on my business life since I saw you last. Things are bounding on and I'd love to have a good chin-wag with you, and get advice here and there.'

Down the years Rita and her widowed father had kept their friendship, and although he was older now, and no longer in business, he still had a good hard head, and she valued his advice. It was some time since he had made over part of the proceeds of the sale of his garage to her, and it was thanks to his astute investment that her private money had increased significantly. And she'd had the sense to follow his counsel and not to spend it until now. She felt due for a good general chat.

She found him content in his small house, from which he had never moved down the years. He wouldn't have dreamt of it, cherishing his friends and neighbours, and Rita was happy that he had so much company, living as he did on the other side of the city.

At the end of a long visit she had some exciting news to absorb. Her father told her about a commercial property which he had bought years ago in Drumcondra, a nice secret he had kept down the years. That was his nature. He had been mulling over what to do with it off and on, and now, in the light of her new business development, he had reached a decision.

'Rita, my little love, I was thinking of leaving you that load of bricks and mortar in my will, but I've a better idea. Wouldn't it be a fine thing for you, if you owned the building where you have your teashop, and where you are now thinking of setting up this school, or club, or whatever it is. Well, I could sell Drumcondra, and buy that premises for you if it's available, and give you the benefit of it while I'm alive, and here to see you enjoy it.' Rita was ecstatic. What a brilliant plan. 'Though it's a pity Ted is so against your business venture, Rita,' her father said, taking off his glasses, hawing on them and polishing them slowly.

'Well, he's not so much against it as totally disinterested.'

'I'm sad that you two have drifted apart so much in recent times.'

'Oh, with the family no longer needing the structure they once depended on, now that they are going about their own lives, it was inevitable,' said Rita. 'And Ted's crazy social ambitions don't really fool anyone.'

He shook his head sadly.

'He's left you behind in lots of ways. You know, Ted wasn't my first choice for you, love, but the two of you got on together better than anyone would have guessed, in the early days. You were so sure that he was the man for you, and I respected that.'

'Dad, I'm not going to tell Ted about your offer.' She came over and sat on the arm of his chair, like she used to do as a child.

'You must do what you think best,' he said, clasping his hands and rotating one thumb around the other.

'It's not that Ted would ask me for money, or anything like that, it's just that he would find it hard, knowing that I had substantial money of my own now. His horizons are so wide, and getting wider and wider. Where it will all end, I don't know.'

'Well, it means that if anything really bad comes about – and please God it won't – at least you would be able to look after yourself, and live well.' He looked up at her and patted her on the arm. 'You're a wise girl, Rita – you take after your old man.'

'Thanks Da, you're a trooper.'

'You've a lovely family and a good home, just play it wisely and everything will stay nicely in place.' Rita hugged her father and stayed the whole evening with him.

A short time later, the two sales were effected and Rita Flynn became the owner of the building in which The Teashop was housed. She was absolutely thrilled with herself and her big secret.

* * *

It was early Monday morning when Ted asked Liz to see if Cas was available in an hour's time. He could wait no longer. He wanted to confront him with the rumour that Bruce Bellingham and Tim Cranby were going to offer him their advertising accounts, if he set up on his own. And was Paul Bennett involved? Ted's face was strained and taut with worry. Liz checked and found that Cas was in his office and available as required. Ted had weighed up the thought of contacting Cas over the weekend, or inviting him for a drink or lunch at his club, but decided that the more formal approach would be better.

'Will I make myself scarce?' asked Liz, 'and leave you to it?'

'No,' said Ted, 'I want you here to take notes. But sit over at your desk and do it on the quiet. Anyway, you're a director, you should be present. I want Martin to be here too.'

'And Jim?'

'No, I'll leave Jim out. He's inclined to back Cas on everything. Anyway, he has an important meeting with the bank.'

Liz phoned Martin and arranged for him to be available, then she placed two chairs in front of Ted's desk.

At ten o'clock Cas put his head around the door and said, 'Ready for the meeting?'

Liz smiled and waved him in. Martin was already sitting impassively in front of Ted's desk in a personal fog of cigarette smoke.

'Well, what's the meeting for?' asked Cas lightly, when he had settled himself. He had the distinct gnawing feeling that he was the reason for it.

Ted leaned across his desk and arranged and re-arranged paper clips in a small silver tray. He didn't look at Cas. 'I'll come straight to the point,' he said in a tight voice. 'Cas, are you leaving the agency to set up on your own, and taking some of our clients with you?'

There was a long silence and Liz could hear the clock on the mantelpiece ticking, and a lone wood pigeon's hooting call from the tree in the back garden.

'No.'

Ted darted a look. 'I heard differently'.

Liz was sitting motionless at her desk, staring at a blank sheet of paper, her ears pricked. Martin was putting out a cigarette, vigorously sweeping the ash to one side of the ashtray with the stub.

'I'm not leaving the agency. I'm not starting on my own. I'm not taking any clients away.'

'What about Paul Bennett?'

'What about Paul?'

'Come on, Cas' said Martin, 'Ted thinks Paul is behind all this, even though it was your name that was mentioned.'

'Mentioned by whom?'

'That's irrelevant,' said Ted.

Martin lit a cigarette.

'Look Cas, you're Managing Director of the agency. Surely your loyalties, your responsibilities, lie with us, the firm, not with Paul who's only an employee. If Paul is involved, then stop shielding him.'

Cas moved heavily in his chair. He hated the thought of telling on Paul, revealing the plans Paul had so eagerly confided in him, but he had accepted the directorship of Flynn & Malby, and with it the responsibilities which it brought. He also resented being interrogated by Martin in this fashion. 'Yes, Paul was planning to open his own agency, but only if I joined him. I'm not going to, so the whole scheme is off, QED.' He added, 'In fact, it was never on.'

Ted looked hard at him. 'Can I have your word on that?'

'Yes,' said Cas.

'Are you sure Paul won't go it alone?' queried Martin.

'Quite sure,' said Cas.

'Paul will have to go, of course,' said Martin. 'We can't have that shyster around. Give him a month's notice. Better still, give him a month's salary in lieu, and run him out of here.'

'No,' said Cas. 'The plan's off and nothing has happened. Everything is as it was. Paul is a good executive. Can we not keep him on? There's no real harm done.'

'Forget it,' said Ted harshly, 'we'll deal with Bennett another day. I'll have to keep him on a leash, though, until I regain control of the accounts he's working on.' Then, suddenly, Ted was smiling, as he stood up and came around his desk. He put his arm around Cas and squeezed his shoulder. He knew how valuable Cas was to F&M. 'I always knew you were onside, Cas, and that Bennett was the fly in the ointment.' He swung around. 'Liz? Get on to my club and book a table for lunch for four – you're included – and we'll have a small celebration.'

'Will I make it five, and include Jim?'

'Yes, indeed,' said Ted expansively.

Cas and Martin protested that they already had appointments, but Ted would not be put off and insisted on a celebratory lunch. Ted might be feeling good but his problems weren't over yet.

* * *

It was half past five and the girls from the accounts department were leaving the agency on the dot, neither a second too early nor a second too late. They had stopped for a last-minute chat on the steps when Pam emerged and joined them, as they stood there, laughing and admiring a pair of new lavender-coloured thigh-boots, which one of the girls had just bought. Cas emerged from the hall-door and came out onto the steps. He exchanged a few pleasant words with them, and was walking away when Pam, on the spur of the moment, caught his arm and asked if he was going straight home to Sandycove, and would he give her a lift. Her old Simca was being serviced and she had no car.

'Yes, of course, Pam', said Cas a little stiffly, as he had been avoiding her over the last few weeks. They sat into his car and Pam chatted away amiably about office matters as they drove towards Sandycove. He was acutely aware of her feminine presence, and of the air of electric tension in the car. Cas knew that he must talk to her about Chloe, and it was suddenly important to him that she understand that he was in love with Chloe, and that Pam's and his time together had ended. He had a strange feeling she knew already. He felt a knot in his stomach as he thought how he must be hurting her, and that when he put it into words, he knew he would injure her even more. He hated that. He would do anything not to wound her. But he had delayed too long already about sorting it out. She would hardly wish him well .... They were nearing Sandycove when he said, 'Would you like a drink in Fitzgeralds?'

'No. No thank you.'

'Come on. Are you tied up for the evening?'

'No.'

'Well, come on then,' he coaxed gently. 'I want to talk to you about something.'

'Talk away.'

'Just one,' said Cas, and pulled the car into the pavement.

'No. I'll get out here and walk the rest of the way.' Pam was adamant. She was totally regretting her impulsive request for a lift.

'Alright. I'll drive on.' Cas drove to the gate of the house where they both had apartments and stopped the car.

'Thanks for the lift,' Pam said, as she went to open the door.

Cas leaned forward and put his hand over hers to stop her getting out.

'Please Pam, I must talk to you.'

She sat back in her seat with a sigh. 'Okay, fire ahead.'

'Pam, I want to talk to you about us. I know I've been neglecting you lately, and treating you unfairly – and I'm sorry, but well, we're still good friends. I mean, we've been more than friends – but things have changed.' Pam polished a speck of dust off the windscreen. 'Circumstances have changed. Things have moved on. We'll always be friends of course. But you see, I've met someone. Someone special. I think I've fallen in love. I know I have. Her name is Chloe O'Leary. She's American.'

Pam sat looking straight in front of her. She didn't move and she didn't speak. Then after a while, she said softly, 'I had a feeling – more than that, I knew. I called to your flat several times. You were out,' she added unnecessarily. Tears were blinding her as she opened her handbag and rummaged for keys. She could never find anything in this bloody handbag when she wanted to. She found the keys and fumbled as she took one off the ring. Without looking at Cas she dropped it on his lap. Then, with her head averted, she said, 'I wish you luck.' She grabbed the handle and flung the door open and jumped out.

Cas called, 'Pam d'Or, look, I'm sorry....'

'Go to hell.'

She rushed to the door of her apartment with the keys in her hand, opened the door, went in and slammed it behind her.

* * *

Tessa was now faced with a severe dilemma, one she now had brought on herself. Should she terminate this crazy and totally inappropriate love affair on which she had embarked, or should she tell Roddy she would never see him again? They both lived in Dalkey and they might meet casually in the main street or elsewhere, but she would keep moving if they did. One option was as tortuous as the other.

To stop seeing Roddy would actually break her heart. She felt she was being loved as a woman, and she was flowering under the influence of his attention. She believed, in spite of that crackpot letter, that she had been absolutely discreet in her meetings, and she had worked out a strategy by which she met Roddy on 'The Cat's Ladder', a narrow and nearly endless flight of stone steps leading from the Vico Road upwards to Torca Road on the hill. The top of the steps was facing Torca Cottage, where George Bernard Shaw spent his youthful summers, and either she or Roddy would park their car there, while the other car stayed below on the Vico Road at the foot of this funny and overgrown vertical passageway. They would wait for one another on one of the stone steps about half way down, and then stand locked in a loving embrace, before driving off in one car or the other to their love nest at Lough Dan.

Paul was busier than ever and Tessa felt increasingly marginalised in their joint life. He had promised to tell her about his new business developments, but the moment never seemed right, and with Roddy absorbing her thoughts, she had a feeling that she wanted to push back such information, since it would commit her to ongoing interest in something for which she might have no room in her life.

The big question was forming in her mind: did she want to go on living with Paul in the face of her love for Roddy? Roddy seemed to be striving to come out of his locked affections and reach out to her, and something approaching the maternal was aroused in Tessa, as she felt him try to find her as a person, and not just as a woman with whom he was having an affair. Roddy had not asked her to make her life with him, but they might get to the point where he would. And she would have to think this overpowering question through, well in advance.

To do so would mean giving up the lovely home at Bulloch Harbour which she had so excitedly furnished with Paul, in her pre-Roddy days. And what would be the effect on the two happy children, two youngsters who were so unquestioningly used to their parents and their home? Of course it would bewilder and upset them. And where would they live? There were plenty of properties to rent in the area .... At that point she would snap back into reality and common sense, her future still a confused stream of thoughts. Her stress levels were certainly rising, though good grooming, extra attention to the children, and affecting a lighter manner than usual when she was with Paul, helped to conceal her state of mind from him. Still the emphasis in her life was definitely changing.

* * *

When Pam heard that Cas had fallen for the American girl, Chloe, her heart almost broke apart. For years she had loved him, joked with him, even moved into the flat above his to be near him, shared intimate times with him and seen him through rougher times. She appreciated what the real Cas was all about. She knew he was a particularly good artist, and it was she who always made him come back to painting. In fact, he had quite a collection of good work built up, among it one painting which was very special to her.

It was the half-finished painting of Pam herself, done in oils and suggesting a good likeness. The previous winter Cas had painted it over a period of weeks, and while he hadn't finished it, he was beginning to catch her essence. They had been planning to have a few more sittings so that he could finish it off.

Now she knew she was beaten, and although she loved him dearly, she also knew it was time to go, to leave his life before she acquired full doormat status, and became incapable of making a life of her own. She secretly felt she could not fall for anyone else. She didn't want anyone else. She told herself she never would.

The big difficulty was that they were working in the same agency. She would have to 'set her face like flint and go up to Jerusalem', for this would be her personal crucifixion. She would have to leave the agency, but she would leave a great piece of herself behind her when she did. Pam loved her job and did it well, but now she would have to adopt an alternative plan and look around carefully first, so that she wouldn't be making a wrong move in her search for a solution. She'd leave Flynn & Malby alright, but in the proper way. And in the meantime, she'd avoid Cas as much as possible and look for somewhere else to live. She felt as if walls were crushing in on her on all sides, but she was not without courage and knew that given time she would stick it out and rearrange her life, painful as it would be. She had never had a firm agreement with Cas about their eventually leading their lives together.

He might be head over heels in love with this Chloe woman, but Pam knew that he was not fully aware of the suffering he was causing her personally.

She quietly moved out of her apartment when she knew Cas was away on business.

* * *

The following Sunday morning Pam parked the car at the end of Torca Road and set off alone along the Green Lane, a route she and Cas had so often taken to get fresh air and enjoy the view, or even to cure a hangover. Parallel with the Vico Road, this route cut into the hillside, starting with a leafy green tunnel floored with pine needles, until it emerged into a dramatic view of the coast down as far as Wicklow Head. This was a view she and Cas had enjoyed together, even when the rain pock-marked the sea and gathered in droplets on their eyebrows. The morning was fine and the sun quickly burnt off the mist on the water, leaving Dalkey Island looking impossibly green against the turquoise water, set in the morning light. The smell of the dew-damp ferns warmed by the sun reached her and Pam sat down on one of the benches along the path, swept by a wave of stinging loneliness.

Their loose and cosy arrangement meant that she and Cas had taken one another for granted, and now she would have to pay the price for it. Cas in love with an American woman? Tears gathered at the corners of her eyes and she hastily blew her nose. A pair were coming into view from the leafy tunnel and her emotionally upset imagination made her think for a moment that it was Cas and his new love. Of course not, but all the same the man was dark-haired and about Cas's height. Surely Cas would never do their walk with anyone else – or would he? Men probably didn't think in the same way as women about these things.

Pam continued her climb upwards until she reached the pine grove where the path divided. She took the track leading across to the Telegraph Tower and as she reached it a little boy ran past her, calling excitedly to his father, 'Daddy, Daddy, I can see the whole world from here,' as the panorama of Dublin city on one side and Dun Laoghaire and Dalkey in front of her met her weary gaze. She studied it all, remembering with great pain how she and Cas had so often stood there to take in the view of what the child had called, 'the whole world', and how her whole world had shrunk down to just herself and her job at Flynn & Malby.

CHAPTER 9

The annual television advertising awards festival week at Kinsale came around in due course, and Pam decided that even though Cas would be there, she would go along in her own right. Advertising was her world too, and the fun in Kinsale each year was famous. She would be mixing and mingling, and needn't spend any time near Cas; in fact it would be a good move to buy a few new clothes and go along with the gang to get her confidence back. And so she booked herself into Actons Hotel when she was making a booking for Martin. Kinsale would be the right place for making contacts with a view to going elsewhere, but if she were to breathe a syllable about leaving Flynn & Malby, the word would go around in minutes and it might affect her plans. Of one thing she was quite sure: she needed a complete change of day-to-day life.

The wining and dining in Kinsale at the festival was legendary, and on the first evening, at the Lord Mayor of Cork's reception, Pam circulated with everyone else. On previous occasions she had made it a point to talk to older women who came with their husbands, but who could feel left out when everyone else was talking shop. At the welcome party she found herself beside Mrs Bruce Bellingham. She'd do her little bit of public relations for the agency, by chatting to Ruth Bellingham, a nice but rather shy woman, expensively and tastefully dressed, who looked as if she could do with some attention. She'd start with her.

Ruth Bellingham had all the best qualities of an Englishwoman, and Bruce had spotted them on first sight when they had met in the home of a friend in London, when she was in her early twenties. Ruth and Bruce had married quickly so that he could bring her back to Ireland as his bride and start married life in the family home, 'Winchester', in Dalkey. They had three daughters, none of whom was interested in going into the business. Ruth was an active person, working with the Red Cross, a member of the board of trustees of Monkstown Hospital, and a contributor to St Patrick's Church of Ireland parish activities in Dalkey, as well as being a woman who kept a beautiful home and garden. Bruce liked it that way. She knew that Ted Flynn, of Flynn & Malby, lived in Dalkey, but they hadn't become too friendly with him in case it affected Bruce's business relationship, and when Flynn invited Bruce and herself to parties and receptions they always declined.

After initial exchanges the conversation passed to general subjects, and Ruth Bellingham told her that she was on the lookout for the right person to run a small company which operated holiday lettings in Tuscany to an English and Irish clientele. She talked of having an older sister living in Siena who had been running the company for years, but now felt it was getting too much for her. Ruth chatted on and on and Pam let her.

'More a way of life than a job, really,' said Ruth. 'It has to be the right person doing it, otherwise it could lead to spoiled holidays and disappointments, not to mention uncertain profits. My sister made a real profession of it. But then, being married to an Italian has given her a solid basis from which to manage the business, and plenty of time to be with her husband.'

Pam listened intently. Fleetingly, she thought how lovely it would be to live in Tuscany with her beloved Cas, doing a job like that. He was half Italian anyway, and would probably take to it easily. Then she cast this wishful thinking abruptly from her mind.

As others joined them and Pam and Ruth Bellingham were being separated, Pam said she would contact the older woman if she thought of anyone suitable for the position outlined, although finding someone prepared to up stumps and go off to Tuscany wouldn't be easy.

She saw Ted in the thick of things with an executive from Keating Advertising, a man known for having the talent to make an interesting story boring. Ted was leaning forward smiling, with his head cocked on one side in listening mode, but his eyes were combing the room for somebody more important to chat up. Pam gave him a wide berth. She knew one of the Giraffe's tricks when he wanted to circulate was to grab any acquaintance passing by and say, 'Oh, here's someone I'd really like you to meet!' He would then introduce them to one another, and with an 'Excuse me a second,' move on swiftly to more distinguished company.

Surprisingly, Cas had not come down to Kinsale after all. Maybe he was somewhere wonderful with his new love. Pam couldn't let herself think about it, and Martin carefully avoided mentioning him to her, knowing that she must be feeling the break deeply. For all his acquired slickness, Martin could be quicker than most to detect real hurt, and would strive to avoid adding to it. Now she forced herself to circulate freely and she gave the appearance of really having a good time. She was popular with men and enjoyed their company.

When the evening was over and Pam had returned to her room, she sat down on the side of the bed and faced up to the thought that maybe, just maybe, this job in Tuscany would be the right thing for her. Could she really leave agency life and start afresh in a new country, with a new lifestyle? Would it suit her, or was she thinking along these lines as a possible method of running away from her present situation? The more she thought of it, the more she saw its possibilities, and she was glad she had taken Ruth Bellingham's card.

Could she say to herself, to hell with Cas, and go off and enjoy a new phase in her life? And it needn't be forever, need it? People had taken career breaks before, and would again. She wouldn't discuss it with anyone until she had sorted it out fully in her own mind. And there was the sudden thought that Ruth Bellingham might find someone else who was perfectly suited to the job, and she, Pam, wouldn't be in the running for it at all, someone who would have fluent Italian, a pleasant manner, no ties and a good head for business. Maybe she should make a move on this – and quickly.

She wondered what Cas was doing back in Dublin ....

* * *

Cas thought about Chloe. He wished he could get her on her own. The trouble was that now that Laura Burbridge-Otis had faded from the picture, Barry was spending more and more time with Chloe. Barry's job allowed him to schedule his work so that he could meet her during the day, while Cas could only meet her during the evenings – and even then, Barry was always around. They had become a trio since Chloe talked to them about her film and TV idea, and he was torn between the excitement of a new venture and wanting to keep Chloe to himself.

Funny that two offers to go into business should occur at the same time, one from Paul and the other from Chloe.

Paul had claimed that he could raise all the finance necessary to open a new advertising agency, and Barry had offered to lend him the money for Chloe's venture, which she wanted to call Golden Eagle Productions Limited. Cas could pay him back from profits over a period of time, Barry had optimistically and generously suggested. Now that Barry's aunt Vi had died and left him all her money, Barry was a moderately wealthy man, and, among other things, this would leave him free to resign from his position with the pharmaceutical company and take over the management of the Golden Eagle business. Barry was ambitious. With Barry as manager, and Chloe as main shareholder, both of them would, inevitably, be calling the shots. But what the heck, he, Cas only regarded the new business as a sideline anyway, as he wasn't investing any personal money.

Two days later Cas got the opportunity to meet Chloe on her own. Barry was helping his father with stock-taking. Cas brought Chloe to dinner in the fashionable Mirabeau restaurant in Sandycove, and back to his apartment for a night-cap.

'What do you want to drink?' asked Cas, when Chloe and he were settled back at the apartment. 'I've got brandy, Crème de Menthe, Cointreau, and a little whiskey.'

'You choose something for me,' she replied. She was wearing a simple oriental-style dress of the palest green, with a high collar, no sleeves and slits up the sides, and as she sat on a high stool at the bar counter smoking a cigarette, her dress fell back, revealing long, shapely legs. The lounge was lit with pools of light from lamps strategically placed around the room and one of them highlighted the golden threads in her red-brown hair.

'Tell you what I'd really like, Cas,' she said. 'A coffee, if you have real coffee, that is – not instant.'

'Yes, I have some very good coffee, as it happens.' As he made the coffee and set it out on the bar counter, they continued their dinner conversation about their plans for Golden Eagle Productions.

'Know what?' He stood with his elbows on the counter and his chin cupped in his hands.

'What?'

'I think Barry should be persuaded to give up his job and look after the Golden Eagle business full time when we get going.' He looked at her and smiled. He knew that was what she wanted.

'I agree,' said Chloe quickly. She stretched out and took his hand in hers. 'You wouldn't mind, would you?'

'Of course not. Barry's the man for the job. He's reliable. I'm too tied up. And you won't be in Ireland most of the time.'

'Yes, he's a reliable guy – and then some.' The way she said it caused Cas to dart a glance at her. Just then a Nat King Cole record clicked into place on the record-player.

When I fall in love, it will be forever –

Or I'll never fall in love' –

'Oh, I love Nat King Cole!' exclaimed Chloe.

'In a restless world like this is –

Love is ended before it's begun –

And too many moonlight kisses –'

'Dance?' asked Cas. She stood up, smoothed her dress and tenderly put her arms around him.

'Seem to cool in the warmth of the sun – '

They moved around the room, swaying gently to the rhythm of the music.

'When I give my heart, it will be completely –'

The soft pressure of her breasts and the heady waft of her perfume sent a thrill through Cas.

'Or I'll never give my heart –'

Now her stomach was against his and their thighs touched. They moved in unison, her head on his shoulder.

'And the moment that I feel –

That you feel that way too –

He lifted her chin and looked at her.

'Is when I fall in love – with you.'

Her eyes were wide and bright and her lips moist. As he bent down and kissed her, she gave a little shudder and responded hungrily. Then she put her hands on each side of his face and kissed him again, her tongue darting with passion. She fumbled with his shirt buttons, opened them and ran her hands over his chest and around him, and held him tightly to her. He found the top of her zip at the back of her dress and opened it fully. With a wriggle, the dress was on the floor. She stepped free of it. They kissed again, this time with abandon. Swiftly he drew her towards the bedroom. They were inside and within seconds they were naked. Light from a street lamp which slanted through the window cast a golden glow on their bodies. They threw themselves on the bed in a ferment of need. All that night they made love with a wild intimacy and left no curve of their eager bodies uncharted, and with a greedy intensity that brought from every small touch and caress, an explosion of satisfaction.

Cas woke up suddenly to find Chloe standing in front of the mirror. She was holding a mug.

'I heated up some coffee for myself.'

She smiled and turned around. Cas propped himself up on one elbow.

'Where are you going, Chloe? What's happening?'

She was wearing his belted raincoat with epaulettes and a floppy collar. It looked stunning on her.

'Sorry, I borrowed one of your raincoats. I couldn't go back to the hotel wearing evening clothes. People would think I'd stayed out all night.' she laughed.

'Don't go. I was planning to take the day off. I was going to phone in.' Cas was out of bed and winding the bedspread around himself. 'But you can't go now ....'

'Must go,' she said crisply. 'I have an appointment. I've ordered a cab.'

'For God's sake, Chloe, you can't go. What about ...? I mean, well, what about us? I love you! You know that. More than anyone else in the whole world.'

'Come off it, Cas, you know last night was just a once off. "Love is a romantic designation for a most ordinary biological process. A lot of nonsense is talked about it"– as Greta Garbo said.' The hall-door bell rang. 'My cab. Must go. I'll be late.' Chloe blew him a kiss and slipped out the bedroom door.

Cas sat down on the bed, his mind a torrent of confused and conflicting thoughts. He heard the hall-door click closed.

* * *

The room at the Shelbourne Hotel began to fill up slowly. In one part of it there were rows of chairs set out, with a green baize-covered table at the top of the room for the guest-speaker and officials; at the other end white cloths covered tables arranged with a light buffet supper and a pay-bar. The Marketing Society was about to hold one of its regular lectures.

A group of advertising executives from various agencies stood together on the landing outside, gossiping and telling stories. Jack Wallace, a senior accountant executive with O'Carrolls Advertising Agency regaled them with the story of one of their clients who imported a popular line of cosmetics from Britain, which included an anti-perspirant stick.

'Unfortunately', said Jack, 'the plastic containers for the deodorant sticks were unsuitable for sale here. They may have been alright for the dimmies in the UK, but not for the literal Irish. To show how to get the stick above the rim of the container, the British had printed on it in large letters the legend, "Push up bottom".' Ted Flynn's guffaw, a specially cultivated response for sallies on social occasions, could be heard above the laughter of the others. Privately, when he was really amused, Ted shook in silent laughter.

Out of the corner of his eye, Ted saw Bruce Bellingham arrive with the evening's speaker, the American marketing guru, Professor Chuck Flesk. He had him firmly in tow, and was shepherding him carefully into the room. Ted detached himself and followed slowly, nodding and smiling, and giving little hand signals to people he knew. He noticed that Tim Cranby of Baby Faire was already there, sitting in the front row, deep in conversation with the marketing manager of one of the beer-brewing companies. He caught Tim's eye and waved. Tim waved back. Bruce Bellingham had taken his seat at the top table by now, beside Professor Flesk and two members of the committee. Cas was sitting over near the window, talking quietly to his counterpart from another agency.

Ted went up to the top of the room, shook hands with Chuck Flesk across the table, said a few words to Bruce, who smiled thinly and nodded back, and then took a seat in the front row. He folded his arms and waited for the proceedings to commence. He didn't feel his usual ebullient self, but he was damned if he'd let people see it. As soon as the lecture was over, he would try and buttonhole Bruce and Tim, separately, although it mightn't be possible as they were close friends, and would probably gravitate towards each other immediately the lecture was over.

Tim did join Bruce and Chuck Flesk after the session, and several others. Soon afterwards, Ted came over and said, 'Excuse me Bruce, but may I speak to you privately for a minute?'

With a frown, Bruce broke away from the group. 'Yes, Ted?'

'I've heard a rumour.'

'What rumour?'

'About the Arkwright & Dobson account. That you're going to take it away from us.' Ted's voice was uneven.

'Ted, this is no place for a business discussion. We'll have lunch during the week and talk it through. Have your secretary call mine.' He held Ted by the elbow and his voice was as smooth as silk.

'Well, what's new?' asked Tim Cranby as he drifted over, drink in hand. 'Damn good lecture, don't you think?'

Ted looked up. 'Tim, I'm glad you're here. I was telling Bruce that I had heard a rumour that we are about to lose the A&D account. And I heard the same about Baby Faire. If it's true, I'm ruined.'

Bruce and Tim exchanged glances.

'Look, both of you are more friends than business colleagues. Surely, I can appeal to you to have second thoughts, if it's true. Without your business, Flynn & Malby will go under,' he said huskily. He then went on to offer them a better financial deal. And yes, on the servicing side he realised that he himself was to blame. Really, he had too much on his plate. But he would bow out of the day-to-day handling of their accounts. He had a new account executive in mind – a real go-getter – he would appoint him as the new contact man. And the agency had the potential to expand. They were in line for some new, exciting business. That meant more staff.

They would add on several extra, top-flight, creative people. A tighter ship all round. He was at his most persuasive, but he knew he was fighting a losing battle. Blast them to hell!

'You've known for some time, Ted, that we weren't satisfied with the service we were getting from you,' said Tim. 'There was the budget over-run, and that appalling television commercial which was transmitted, even though we turned it down, and the series of magazine advertisements which appeared with last year's prices. And there were other blunders. On each occasion we dealt with you personally, Ted.' He lit a cheroot with the snap of a small silver lighter.

Ted knew that not all the mistakes had been on his side. They were both bloody difficult clients to deal with anyway.

'We had a similar catalogue of disasters,' said Bruce. 'But look Ted,' he added, 'as I said earlier, this is neither the time nor the place to discuss the matter. We'll get together later this week. Okay?'

'Cas Maitland is not leaving Flynn & Malby, he's staying with us,' Ted said suddenly. 'I know the two of you were planning to set him up in business with Paul Bennett.' Now he was throwing caution to the winds.

'Oh,' said Bruce, his eyebrows raised.

'So Cas is staying with you, is he? My, my. Bennett will never make it on his own, that's for sure,' said Tim.

'He'll never make it anywhere,' snarled Ted in a quicksilver change of mood. 'I'll see to that, as long as I have breath in my body.'

'Look Ted,' said Tim Cranby, with a sigh. 'It's too late, even though Cas is staying with you. You may take it that as far as Baby Faire is concerned, we will be asking some other agencies to pitch for the business. Ideally, we had hoped that Cas Maitland and Paul Bennett would form their own agency, and we'd give them the account.

But if that's not on, well, we'll just have to go elsewhere. Sorry Ted, but that's the way it is.' Tim turned away and went to the bar for another drink.

Bruce Bellingham added, 'I'm sorry too, Ted. You insisted on forcing the pace tonight. But I suppose the answer is the same in the end.'

Ted went down to the hotel lobby, and turned into where the public telephones were housed. He placed a call, and lifted the receiver.

'Liz?'

'Yes?'

'It's me. We've lost the two accounts.' He could hardly speak, and there were tears in his eyes.

'Christ!' Liz was well aware of what this meant for the agency. 'This means we could fold.'

'Yes.'

'What can we do?'

'Nothing. There's nothing we can do. Our only hope is that we can keep going until the money starts coming in from the Ridgeway cigarette launch, but we may not have enough money in the kitty to do that. I think I'll have to raise the finance from somewhere to bridge the gap. God knows how! Nothing can be done tonight. I'll have to talk to Jim Reilly in the morning and see what he thinks. I'll see you early in the office, okay?'

'Good night Ted. It's pretty bad.'

'Good night, Liz.'

Liz knew that Ted's handling of the A&D, and the Baby Faire accounts had been sloppy, but she also knew that that wasn't the only reason why Bruce Bellingham and Tim Cranby were taking their business away from F&M.

Some time ago Tim had confided in Ted, over lunch in Ted's club, that his new young lady friend, Clare Madden, was looking for a job around town. Tim, whose wife obviously knew nothing of Clare's part in her husband's life, had set Clare up in a flat in Baggot Street, where he dropped in on a fairly regular basis. Clare had been finding the days extremely boring and had asked Tim if he could give her a job in Baby Faire, but, as Tim had pointed out, this was out of the question. He had not asked Ted about job openings outright, but Ted, ever anxious to impress, had immediately suggested Flynn & Malby as the answer to his problem. Not to worry, he had said, magnanimously, he could offer her a position. Ask her to contact him next Monday.

The following Monday, when Clare came around to Flynn & Malby to start her new 'job' – Liz knew exactly what would happen – and it did. Ted was in London, and no one knew anything about these arrangements. Liz explained the situation to Cas, who exploded and pointed out that there were no vacancies in the agency, and anyway, what were Clare's qualifications? None, apparently. Later, after a verbal tussle with Ted over the phone, Cas manufactured a job for her in desperation. It was 'Head of Messenger Services', which simply meant that she told the messenger boys where to go and when. Clare was happy enough with her non-job, but when Tim Cranby heard that she had been given such a menial post, he was furious. Clare insisted on staying on, and regaled the messenger boys with stories about herself and Cranby. Relations between Baby Faire and Flynn & Malby had become strained, and when Clare eventually left to go to England with a young printers' rep, Tim Cranby blamed Ted.

A not dissimilar situation had occurred with Bruce Bellingham's youngest daughter. On being given a job as a junior in the art department in Flynn & Malby by Ted and against Cas's wishes, making tea and cleaning water jars, she had adopted a bohemian lifestyle favoured by some of the artists. Despite her mother's pleas, she had dyed her hair blue and green, and taken to hanging around with a rather aimless crowd in the Pembroke Bar, adding to her father's fury, who hadn't been aware of the status of his daughter in the agency. The relationship between the two clients and the agency had become soured as a result of these two misjudgements on the part of Ted.

* * *

The sexual chemistry between Sally Worth, telephone switch operator and receptionist at Flynn & Malby, and Karl Cunningham, the most junior accountant executive in the agency, was palpable. Cas noted it with amusement as he went downstairs to the reception room. Karl, now fully rehabilitated after his regrettable Blobby Nose affair, was leaning across the desk, whispering something to an adoring Sally, and when he saw Cas he straightened up.

Sally beamed at Cas. 'I put the gentleman from the furniture company in the reception room, Mr Maitland.'

Cas sighed. Only two weeks ago, on the recommendation of the board, he had signed a contract with this company to supply a range of new office and viewing theatre furniture to the agency. Then Jim Reilly had come to him and asked if it would be possible to fudge the delivery indefinitely, as new figures indicated that overheads were beginning to run out of control.

The reception room was situated up one flight of stairs from the hallway, on the return landing, and was expensively furnished with a thick amber-coloured carpet, off-white squashy leather chairs, and a large, low, square-legged, pale-wood table topped with a grand antique Chinese vase full of fresh blooms. A glass case of national and international awards won by the agency dominated the attractive seating area, and visitors were usually given enough time to examine them while they waited. Sally Worth's reception desk was located outside the room in front of a tall elegant stained glass window through which the sunlight slanted dramatically.

Sally Worth had three claims to fame: one, she was young, carefree and exceedingly pretty, with an enchanting smile; two, she insisted on answering all incoming calls in a monotone with a long-winded, 'Good morning-Flynn-and-Malby-Advertising-Limited-this-is-Sally-Worth-speaking-may-I-help-you?'; and three, she wore microscopically short skirts so that when she went ahead of clients to bring them up the short flight of stairs to the boardroom, her knickers were always on prominent display. And Sally knew it.

Everyone was fond of Karl. Young, happy-go-lucky with a passion for body-building, he was absolutely without guile, and the clients liked him for his enthusiasm and dedication to his job. Karl's father was dead and with six years between himself and his two small brothers, he was the head of the family and the apple of his mother's eye.

'May I talk to you for a moment?' Karl asked Cas.

'Sure. Fire ahead.'

'Remember I'm going to Cork this weekend to make a presentation to Swift and Byrne? Paul and I are doing it.'

'Oh yes, I've seen the layouts and story-boards. They're very good. You'll have no trouble. Swift and Byrne will buy them all right.'

'The trouble is, I've no car. My banger is in being fixed and the garage won't have it ready until Monday.'

'So, what about the train?'

'I have to bring a lot of equipment and there's no way I can carry it all. I need a car and I was wondering if I could borrow one.'

'What about Paul's car?'

'Paul has to go to Waterford first and he's coming to Cork on Monday for the meeting. I want to go down on Sunday and set up everything beforehand.'

'You'd better hire a car then,' said Cas. 'See Jim Reilly and tell him I said it's okay.'

'Great. I'll do that. I fancy myself driving a Rolls Royce.'

Cas gave a snorting laugh. 'Better hire a Mini.' He stopped for a moment. 'Nothing larger, mind,' he said, remembering Jim Reilly's worries about escalating costs.

'Okay,' said Karl. 'The bare Mini-mum.' He winked at Sally behind Cas's back and went off to make his arrangements.

Glanmire village. The last time Karl had visited Cork had been with Cas, and they had stopped in Glanmire for a drink. Remembering, he turned the Mini left over the little stone bridge which crossed the Glashaboy river, and parked. He had driven quite fast down from Dublin, with only a brief stop for a sandwich, and now he could do justice to a G and T. There was only one customer in the Groves pub when he entered, and Karl gave a friendly nod as he ordered from the bar. He rolled his shoulders to relieve the tension of the journey.

There was now only a short distance to Cork city, and it was twilight when he resumed his drive, refreshed and in top form, if slightly light-headed from two large gin and tonics. He began to sing, 'She'll be Comin' Round The Mountain When She Comes', for the tenth time – this time in falsetto. 'She'll be wearin' Ted's pyjamas when she comes ... .'

He suddenly had a heightened awareness of his surroundings, and as he drove along, he took in, with startling clarity, the low wall on the left-hand side of the road running along by the river, the shallow water and the mud flats with the sea-gulls dotted on them. On the right, the grotto of the Blessed Virgin Mary, with 'I Am The Immaculate Conception' in large lettering. The Vienna Woods Hotel. Bet the staff there could tell some tales. He giggled. The red car coming towards him was travelling at an outrageous speed for some God-unknown reason, and it took the curve with tyres squealing on the wrong side of the road. Karl bellowed and pulled the steering-wheel left to avoid a head-on collision. His car hit the low wall with a screech of rending metal, its side and front crumpling like a squashed cigarette packet. In slow motion, it somersaulted and thudded, right side up, into the muddy river. There was silence. Karl Cunningham's body was folded awkwardly inside the wreckage.

* * *

Cas woke with a start, sensing that the phone had been ringing for some time. He had been sleeping deeply. Who could it be at this time of night?

'Hello?'

'Cas, it's me, Liz.'

'Liz, What's wrong? Is there something wrong?' Cas was fully awake now.

'Yes, there is, Cas. It's very bad news. There's been an accident.'

'Des?'

'No.'

'Not Ted?'

'No. It's Karl. He's been in a car crash.'

'Oh my God. Is he badly injured?'

'Oh Cas. It's terrible. He's dead.' Liz was crying.

'Dear God, Liz, are you sure? Has it been confirmed?'

'Yes. He was taken to the Regional Hospital in Cork. He was dead on arrival. Apparently the car was crushed like an eggshell. The Gardaí contacted Ted. The name Flynn & Malby was all over the reports and layouts in the back of the car. They traced Ted to his home. They want him to confirm the identity of the body so that they can contact Karl's mother. Ted phoned a few minutes ago, he's leaving shortly for Dublin Airport. He arranged to take the quarter to seven flight to Cork.'

'This is appalling Liz, I can hardly believe it.' Both were badly shocked and they talked disbelievingly for several minutes.

'There's nothing we can do for the moment until Ted gets back from Cork,' said Cas, eventually.

'I suppose you're right. Ted will be back later in the day.'

'Liz, I'll see you in the office, early.'

'Yes Cas,' she sighed. 'I'll see you later.'

Cas was badly shaken. He went to the kitchen and made himself a pot of tea. The horrible thought had occurred to him that if Karl had been driving a larger, more robust car, and not a Mini, he might have stood a better chance of coming out of the crash alive. Oh my God, was he partially responsible for Karl's death? The observation cut through him like a knife. Niggling about expense when he should have been putting the safety of an employee first. Damn, damn, damn!

Money was being spent on all the wrong things in Flynn & Malby. Like Christmas presents. Every year, Ted insisted on sending expensive gifts to all the clients. Brandy, whiskey, sides of smoked salmon, cigars went to chairmen, managing directors, advertising managers and top executives, as well as to all the 'right' people in the media. And elsewhere. Bouquets of flowers for all the wives. It cost a fortune. And here he had been, paring back on the essentials!

Liz and Cas were in Ted's office when Ted arrived back from Cork. He came in ashen-faced, and sat down at his desk. Liz gave him a coffee.

'What happened?' she asked gently.

'Terrible.' He heaved a sigh. 'The car was a complete write-off. He died instantly.'

Cas poured himself another coffee to keep his emotions in check, and he noticed that Ted had tears in his eyes.

'You know, I employed him as soon as I saw him. I knew he had potential,' Ted said. 'Straight out of school. A very bright young man. Then all those night classes.' He shook his head. 'I'll have to go and see his mother, but I hate the thought of it. How can I face her?'

'I'll go with you,' offered Cas, 'if it'll help.'

Ted looked up. 'Would you Cas? I'd be grateful.'

'Shouldn't someone tell Sally?' asked Liz.

'Yes,' said Cas, 'I'll do that.'

'There's too much drinking!' Ted exploded.

'It's the time we live in. It's all part of the advertising business – apparently,' said Liz tartly. 'Everyone in advertising appears to be living on their nerves. Living on the edge. Moving faster and faster. Analysing, inventing, creating, selling. Working frantically, playing frantically. It's part of the advertising persona to be larger than life, it seems. To exaggerate everything, to see the world through a magnifying glass.'

Two days later, driving home from the funeral, Cas confided his thoughts about the Mini contributing to Karl's death to Celine Dunphy, and she tried in vain to persuade him that his worry was irrational, but Cas felt a sudden urge to leave the tinsel world of advertising.

Sally Worth never came back to work in Flynn & Malby, and some months later she left Ireland to take up a job in a solicitor's office in Leicester, with a flat on the Narboro Road. She had grown up overnight.

* * *

The more she thought about it, the more Pam realised that this could be the best move she would ever make. If she got it, this job in Tuscany could be a godsend. She had some idea of the salary and conditions attached and they seemed fantastic. And there would be further possibilities of earning if she were on the spot, teaching English as a foreign language. Ruth had said that a car went with the job. And Tuscany of all places! Tuscany, with its wonderful scenery, history and not least, its range of wines. Maybe she could cater for passing guests to a limited extent, if the farmhouse base Ruth's sister had used was suitable. And maybe in some strange way, Cas would come back to her, and he would come out and stay with her. Immediately, she realised that this was foolish thinking. Her relationship with Cas was well and truly over, and this was the very reason why she was considering going abroad. Strange how the human mind refused to accept the inevitable when the heart was involved, but sought to get around obstacles, no matter how pointless the exercise.

Pam got business-like, as she well could do. She invited Ruth Bellingham to have lunch with her and said she would seriously consider the proposal for herself, if Ruth would consider her for the job – phrasing which made them both laugh and got the discussion off to a good start. She told her how she was looking for a post in another agency, and was even considering a career break, and the reason for moving, and Ruth liked her for being so straightforward and said she would contact her sister immediately. The recommendation would be one hundred per cent positive, even after such a short acquaintance. They agreed that the topic would not be discussed with anyone in the agency world.

When Pam was called for interview to London, with air tickets and spending cash supplied, she felt she was on to a winner. It didn't take long for her to work out an interesting arrangement with Ruth's sister, and a starting date. Now Pam could take her courage in her hands and resign from Flynn & Malby.

The crowd at the agency was amazed that Pam D'Or should even consider a move. As Martin's secretary she had always been part of the furniture. When she said, with a laugh, that she would keep her cards close to her chest about her plans, in true agency fashion they made her a really funny, gigantic going-away card, showing her ample bosom and a minute hand of cards held against it.

Cas was flummoxed, he felt as if a cold breeze had blown his way. He'd grown accustomed to her face and when she had moved abruptly out of the flat above his, she had taken something of him with her. He told himself that it was for the best, and now that she was leaving the agency as well, he presumed he would see her from time to time in the advertising world, for surely she would be snapped up elsewhere. I'll miss Pam D'Or, he thought, I'll miss her very much, but did she have to take the Chloe thing so badly?

CHAPTER 10

Cas set about overcoming his disappointment over Chloe in true male fashion – absorbing himself in work and refusing to think about her, except in terms of business. Chloe had made it clear that her night with him would never be repeated. She was not in love with him. He took up his paint brushes once more, and worked every weekend, finishing studies of Sandycove and surrounding area, and driving out into the country to start new paintings. His creativity flourished under stress, and he surprised himself by producing some really fine work. A good painter knows when he has achieved excellence, and Cas found himself wishing that he could turn back the wheel of life and work full-time as an artist.

Among his paintings he came on the study of Pam, which he had started some 18 months before, in the days when she floated in and out of his apartment, and constituted a cheery backdrop to his bachelor life. The portrait was beginning to look very good, when he stacked it to one side in favour of other developments. Now, with a week's leave to fill up, he put it up on the easel and looked at it hard and long. Yes, he would finish it. As she had been firm in having no further contact with him, he didn't dare ask her to come back and sit once more, and instead, he cleaned his brushes and set himself the task of finishing it from memory.

Once he began to paint, a curious thing happened to him. He found that he felt constrained to put everything into it which formed the essence of the woman, and he painted as he had never painted a portrait before, in a sort of trance, with total absorption and empathy for the subject. Working late and skipping meals, the more he worked at it, the more he demanded of himself, and soon Pam was gazing at him out of the canvas, her countenance lighting up the corner of the room. He was painting it with love, and he didn't know it. He was actually falling in love with the woman who loved him deeply, who had never distressed him, and who overlooked his male transgressions – the woman he had now lost.

There had been no word of Pam or what she was doing, once she left the agency. At her going-away party she had been grabbed and kissed by everyone, including Cas, but she had not shown, even by the flicker of an eye, that she felt anything for him, and she had left in a taxi for a destination unknown, so that they had all ragged her about her new MI5 lifestyle. Pam was now her own woman.

Some time later, Cas was phoned by a member of the TABS committee, the body which looks after people in the advertising business who have fallen on hard times. The committee was planning an auction to raise funds and he was asked if he had any paintings which he could offer. He gave three recently finished ones, and noted the date of the auction, as these functions were always good fun as well as being good occasions on which to renew contacts in the industry.

Cas went along with Martin and a few of the Flynn & Malby brigade, and in the course of the evening he saw Pam slipping into the hall, looking very smart. She seemed to have lost weight, and her hair was different, and she certainly didn't seem to be looking for his company, surrounded as she was by other people in the business. In fact he had trouble getting her attention, but he waylaid her at the end of the night, as there was something he wanted to say to her.

Cas desperately wanted Pam to see the portrait he had painted of her. Something was driving him to show it to her, and now she would be leaving to live abroad – that much he knew – if he couldn't get her to come out and look at it before she left, then she would probably never see it. He knew it was good, and he wanted the subject to see it.

As she was about to leave, Cas caught her by the arm.

'Pam, wait. Have you a second?'

'A second?'

'A minute.'

'What for?'

'I just want to ask you something. Look Pam, it's important.'

'Important to whom?'

'To me. But please, do me one last favour.'

'Cas, I don't owe you any favours.'

'Yes, I know. It's just that I wanted to show you something, and if I don't arrange it tonight, it'll never happen.'

His woebegone face touched Pam's heart. He looked like a forlorn little boy, standing there in his smart suit, not really one of the hard-nosed advertising types, seeming somewhat at sea. Where was Chloe, she wondered? No matter how much Pam had tried to put Cas out of her mind, it hadn't really worked. But she certainly wasn't going to show him that she still cared.

'What is it?' she said finally, curiosity winning over attitude.

'I've finished the portrait – of you. It's the best thing I've ever done. Let me show it to you, Pam. I want you to see it.'

'Where is it, in your office?'

'No, in the flat.'

'Isn't your flat rather crowded out with American beauties, just at the moment?'

'Pam, look, Chloe and I ... we're not seeing one another ... anymore ... there's nothing going on there ... there won't be ... ever ....'

'It's nothing to do with me, Cas,' she said frostily, but she felt a fluttering in her stomach.

'We've severed connections.'

'Severed? Sounds painful.'

'Will you come and see the painting? Please?'

'Alright. I'll take a quick peek at it, to please you. But it'll have to be tomorrow, because I'm going abroad in a fortnight's time.'

'That soon?'

'That soon. I've endless appointments before I go. How about tomorrow? For half an hour. Say, half six to seven?'

'Perfect. Thanks, Pam.'

'See you then,' she said and moved away. He stood back and watched her retreating figure. So used to presuming that she had all the time in the world for him, he now found himself grateful to be squeezed in for half an hour. The new Pam was completely mesmerising Cas.

Cas made sure to be back at his flat by five o'clock. He felt desperately nervous as he tidied the place. Here he was preparing for Pam's visit, the same Pam who, not so long ago, had a key to his flat and came in and out as she pleased. It had been Pam who straightened things out when they got out of hand, who tidied the flat and cleared out the fridge.

At exactly half-past six a taxi stopped outside his flat, and out stepped Pam. She had been in two minds about coming, fearing that it would upset her emotionally. Even though Cas had claimed that his infatuation with Chloe was over, she remained to be convinced. He had looked so downcast, and for some reason, positively appealing, that she had decided against phoning to put him off. Why was she always soft-hearted, she asked herself. She needed to get more skills and confidence in handling men.

Cas came out to meet her, and brought her in carefully, as if she had never been there before. Pam glanced around the lounge and although it was only a short time since she had been there, it seemed an eternity. Nothing had changed. The selection of Nat King Cole records was stacked carelessly beside the record-player, and the thick, glass sweet jar containing loose change was standing on the centre table. The door to his studio was firmly closed. Why was she so nervous? When Cas spoke, she could tell he was also very much on edge.

'Would you like a drink?'

'Yes, please. White wine, if you have it.'

'Yes, I have. There's some in the fridge.'

Cas took an already-opened bottle from the fridge and poured out two glasses.

'Well, where is this all-to-be-revealed portrait? I'm really curious about it. I never thought you'd finish it, by the way.'

'I didn't either. I came on it recently and found I just had to. Unfinished business.'

Pam sipped her drink and looked at him. 'What do you mean, unfinished business?'

'I don't know. It was just something incomplete. Something I could rectify if I set about it. So I did. I'm dying to show you the result.'

'I'm curious to see it.'

She followed Cas into the studio where the picture stood propped up on an easel, with a large piece of cloth draped over it. Cas took off the covering and stepped back to watch Pam's reaction.

There was silence in the room as Pam looked at the painting. She was stunned. She felt her throat constricting and tears beginning to well up. It was a remarkable likeness of herself, but the face had a sensitivity which was almost other-worldly. She was overcome, as the portrait looked back at her with a depth and a range of feelings that was truly astonishing. Biting her lip in an effort to control her emotions, she knew, without a doubt, that she was looking at not just a fine portrait of herself, but a work of outstanding quality and beauty.

'Cas, it is so beautiful.' Her voice was barely audible. Cas was grinning from ear to ear. 'Like it?'

'Oh it's amazing. How did you complete it without me? I mean, it wasn't half done when we left off and forgot it.' He moved over beside her and they stood together looking at the painting.

'I completed it from memory – from the memories you gave me over a long, long time. You're going away now, probably forever, and I had to have something of you. I'm only glad that I asked you to sit for the portrait in the first place, otherwise I wouldn't have it now.'

'Does it matter that much?'

'Oh yes.'

'I wouldn't have thought that finishing this picture would have been all that important to you – in the light of recent events. You know, you're completely free to make your choices in life, Cas.'

He turned and scanned her face. 'Pam, the thing with Chloe is over – absolutely.'

Pam made no reply.

As he brought her back into the lounge and went to replenish her glass, Pam's mind was racing. It was really all over with Chloe. She could tell.

'No more wine for me thanks,' she said, putting her hand over her glass. 'I said I only had half an hour for my visit, and now that I've seen the painting, I think I should be on my way. Let's keep our goodbyes short.'

'You don't want to make it arrivederci?'

'Oh you never know in life. We may run into each other thirty years from now, and have difficulty putting names on one another.' Pam was trying to be facetious, so that Cas would not guess about the rising emotion within her. She leaned over and picked up her handbag as a preliminary to her departure.

Cas was aghast. She was really walking out of his life, out of the life she had bounced in and out of so readily, and she seemed not to have the slightest regret. How easily he had let her go, how completely Chloe had swamped his affections.

He no longer had anything to lose, because he believed he had lost it all. With an effort born of desperation he blurted out what he really felt in his heart, but which his mind had somehow kept blanketed away.

'Don't go Pam. Don't go. I want you more than anyone in the world. Nothing's ever given me the happiness you have – the fun, the friendship.'

Pam stood looking at him as if he might disappear at any moment, so changed was he. She had known that bringing her out to see the portrait was important to him, but now she saw another Cas, just as he had seen another Pam.

'Cas, what are you saying?'

'I'm asking you to marry me.'

'What? Do you mean that?'

'Yes. Pam, will you marry me?' His voice was strong and determined. Pam felt light-headed. She was going away to make a fresh start in life, a move triggered by Cas, and now here he was begging her to marry him. She decided to keep her head in the new situation.

'This is a big surprise – I don't know what to think. You want to marry me?'

'Yes.'

Pam was playing for time and her mind was racing ahead. She loved Cas dearly and couldn't see herself ever settling for anyone else.

'I'll stay a while Cas. Pour me another glass of wine. You have a lot of ground to make up, you know.'

The white stippled ceiling confirmed that she was in Cas's bed. She snuggled down under the bed-clothes and recalled with a leap of joy that last night Cas had proposed marriage.

Mrs Marco Caspar Maitland. Mrs Pamela Maitland. Mrs Pamela O'Regan-Maitland. Plain Pam Maitland. She tried out the various possibilities. 'Hello, is that Mrs Maitland?' 'Yes, this is Mrs Maitland.' 'Good morning Mrs Maitland.' She sat up, pulled the bedspread around her and wriggled her toes with pleasure.

'Tie a yellow ribbon round the old oak tree ....' Cas was outside making heavy weather of the current hit song and there was an encouraging clink of crockery. She slipped out of bed and gathered the bed-spread like a cloak and gazed out the window where the early morning offered the makings of a splendid day. She felt filled with happiness as she coaxed her hair into obedience at the mirror.

'Morning, construction worker,' Cas greeted her. He was scooping scrambled eggs out of a saucepan onto two hot plates. He poured them out coffee.

'Here, that'll put hair on your chest.' He looked up at her admiringly.

'Tie a yellow ribbon round the old oak tree – that's a quare way for a girl to get her message to her man. What's wrong with the telephone system in America, I wonder?' said Pam.

Cas laughed. 'I've got a plan,' he said. 'When we finish here, we'll go up the mountains to Glencree, and have a long walk in the fresh air. We could have lunch in Enniscree Lodge – and then play it by ear. What say you?'

'Sounds perfect.'

He put his arms around her and hugged her tightly. Then he said, 'I love you, d'you hear me? Come on, breakfast is getting cold.'

A long breakfast, a drive over to Pam's flat and a change into walking gear followed, and then they drove slowly to Glencree, enjoying the heightened awareness of each other's proximity. Cas stopped the car at a gate where the field sloped down the valley, and they climbed over it and set off on a path which led to a river. The beautiful views of Glencree Valley and the Sugar Loaf Mountain added to their joy. With arms around one another, it wasn't easy to make anything but slow progress.

'I suppose I'll have to give up any notion of going away,' said Pam. She was thinking half out loud. 'Now that I'm going to be Mrs Maitland, I'll have to cancel all arrangements.' She squeezed his arm. Then she began to tell him all about her Italian job, and how she had planned to make a complete break with Ireland. And how she had been looking forward to living and working in romantic, sunny Tuscany.

As if on cue, the sky clouded over gently and a light rain began to fall. She kissed him fondly on the cheek. 'But getting married to you comes first. If only I could do both. If there was some way the two of us could live in Tuscany, now wouldn't that be game, set and match?'

They cut short their walk and returned to the car and on to Enniscree Lodge. The shower became heavier and they dashed from the car to the lobby when they arrived. They made their way to the bar, where they had the place practically to themselves, and taking their drinks over to a window they sat close together looking at the changing light on the hills opposite as the rain cleared. Cas took Pam's hand. His eyes were shining.

'There is,' he said.

'There is what?

'There is a way for us to live in Tuscany. Don't let go of that new job. I'll simply resign from Flynn & Malby and we'll go together. Couldn't be simpler.'

'You can't do that!'

'Oh but I can. In a funny way the thought of leaving the agency has been in my head for some time. Two things triggered it, really. Paul Bennett's suggestion that we start out on our own really unsettled me. Then there was Karl Cunningham's death. That shook me to the core. You see, I've run my course with F&M. It's time I moved on and did what I've always wanted to do with my life – and that's paint.'

'Oh Cas, could that be possible? Tuscany is the most perfect place in the world to paint!'

'My mother would be delighted to hear I'm going to live in Italy. She has some property in Arezzo she intends to leave me, and when she hears I'm getting married and going to live in Tuscany, she'll be a happy woman.'

They transferred to the dining-room with its sensational view of the valley. Now that the shower had passed, the landscape was illuminated as if by theatrical lighting. Scudding clouds, alternately darkened and brightened the hillsides of patchwork fir trees, giving a strange sense of movement to the countryside.

They chatted on, Cas wondering how Ted would take it when he told him he was leaving. He almost looked forward to telling him. He would give F&M a month's notice, although he might get away with less. He would cash in his shares and ask Ted for a settlement – at least a year's salary. And would Barry be interested in taking over the lease of his pad in Sandycove? They could get married quietly – in Rome. Pam responded delightedly to this. Yes, a wedding in the Irish College in Rome, and a car trip up to Tuscany where they could settle down as a married pair. Just perfect. Life had suddenly offered them a cornucopia.

* * *

The staff at Flynn & Malby was edgy. Everyone was used to the interminable meetings which are the stuff of every advertising agency: board meetings, executive conferences, creative meetings, production meetings, brain-storming sessions, client-agency meetings, client presentations, new business presentations, plannings, briefings, sort-out sessions – on and on it went. Still, this time they knew that the spate of directors' meetings was of greater significance than usual. Something was in the air.

Representatives of the agency's firm of accountants arrived daily and were barely in the reception area, before being whisked up to the boardroom amid whispered exchanges. Jim Reilly, normally laid back, was scuttling in and out of the meetings with files and papers. Ted was lacking his usual over-the-top bonhomie, and Cas, Martin and Liz were uncommunicative. Something was definitely afoot when a jewellery-bedecked Birdie Malby was seen frequently. A constant supply of coffee and sandwiches was available and, on several occasions, lunch was laid on in the board-room, so that discussions could continue uninterrupted. From time to time, one of them would emerge for a respite, white-faced, with tired eyes and an acrid smell of smoke clinging to their clothes. There was a strong rumour among the staff that one of the larger English agencies was going to buy into, or take over, Flynn & Malby.

Despite the upheaval his departure from the agency would involve, Cas was determined to do his best to secure the future of Flynn & Malby. He hoped that the worst of the crisis would be over before he told Ted of his intentions to leave.

Ted knew that all the meetings in the world wouldn't solve his problem. Yes, they had succeeded in drastically pruning back most of the excessive expenditure. Expenses were astronomical, particularly in the television department. Jim Reilly was always saying that. All the same, television was relatively new in Ireland and, to a large extent, they were only learning their craft and feeling their way. Some staff would have to go, of course, particularly in the art department, and he, Ted, would have to cut back on his personal expenses. All this, and more, had been agreed over the last few days, but it still wasn't enough. An injection of funds was essential, and it was Ted's company after all, so in the end it was up to him to provide the necessary cash. Somehow, somewhere, he had to find the extra capital to keep the agency afloat. None of the other directors said they had money to invest, not even Birdie Malby who had added to his woes, by indicating that she was anxious to sell her shares. He begged her to postpone the idea until he got the agency back to profitability and could afford to buy them himself. Then he would happily do so.

There must be some action he could take to help him weather the storm. The bank was being downright unhelpful, dithering over his request for increased facilities and demanding more and more figures from Jim Reilly, until in the end they had said ... No. The last thing Ted wanted was to allow in an outside investor who would want to take over the company, and he, Ted Flynn would be relegated to the position of a minor shareholder in his own company. An outsider would want control. No, damn it, even if such an animal existed, and with the agency in such a parlous state it was doubtful, he wanted to go it alone. He would have to find the money himself, but how, and where? The new Ridgeway Cigarette would help, but had it come in time?

* * *

Now Tessa's affair took a different turn. She was bonding so closely with Roddy during their frequent drives and visits to the cottage, that she felt she just couldn't break off the affair. The damage to her own psyche came second in her mind, and it was a case of her becoming 'addicted' to Roddy without knowing it. At other times it seemed perfectly clear to her that the affair would have to stop – more likely abruptly, as there was no way of tailing it off.

She planned to talk it out with him on their next trip to the cottage, which was set for a couple of days later, and this gave her a temporary respite from contemplation of the trough of sorrow ahead, should she have to stop seeing him once and for all.

On the night before their tryst, Tessa couldn't sleep at all, and finally she slipped from the bedroom into the living-room and made herself reasonably comfortable on the sofa, with music playing softly and a clandestine glass of wine on the little table beside her, to calm her nerves. Sitting there sipping, and turning the pages of a magazine, she heard a scratching noise at the hall-door, the same noise as on the night the obscene note had been pushed through. She froze. Not another? Surely not. It must be a nocturnal cat brushing by the door in hope of some shred of unexpected good fortune. She stole over to the window as a small figure, well concealed in a hooded anorak, skulked away from the gate and was quickly lost in the darkness of the harbour background. It was a return visit from her correspondent all right.

She slipped out into the hall, dreading the envelope which must surely be lying waiting for her. What if Paul were to get to it first and open it. What would he find inside – a repeat of what had gone before – or worse? She lifted it up and went back into the living-room, tearing it open as she went. The page was folded over once again, and the word 'WHORE' met her frightened gaze. She trembled all over as she read the words following it – a foul message. Then she closed her eyes briefly, hoping, childlike, that when she opened them, she would have been mistaken. Following on the previous note, it was definitely intended for her. And whoever was writing the notes was shadowing her affair with Roddy. She knew it now, without a doubt. Maybe Roddy could help her find out who it was. She would absolutely have to tell him this time.

Pat Grehan hurried up the steep road from Bulloch Harbour, anger and relief swopping places in his twisted mind. That would show that vile woman that she couldn't play around with people's affections. They were all depraved in the end. If her husband found the note first, she would be in for a roasting. He told himself he wasn't sorry.

She had spoiled his days watching her come and go, from his seat at the end of the harbour pier. There she was, deceiving her own family. Each time she returned from the school with her children, he had seen her talking to them as they went into their home. Sometimes with the weekly shopping. Other times, when she had taken them for a walk, and they had come back squawking and gabbling together like demented seagulls. And all those times she had slipped past him on the Vico Road, running like an animal, with her hair tied back, and her brazen young face looking out across the bay. She would never have noticed him, of course. He was invisible. He might as well be dead. Like old Decko Kavanagh. But he had seen her each time she met that man. By jingo, he had discovered their meeting place on The Cat's Ladder. One day he would wait somewhere along it and give her the fright of her life. He'd do that soon, he told himself, as he shuffled back to his miserable patch and went to bed half-dressed and tired out. As he fell asleep, he told himself he was satisfied with his act of justice and revenge.

* * *

The last piece of dismantled bed was being removed from the Shelbourne Hotel bedroom when Cas walked in and laid his files on a chair. He checked that the telephone was working, and then waited for the hotel staff to bring in chairs and tables and set them up in the near-empty room. This would be the secret 'studio' of Flynn & Malby for as long as it took to produce the Ridgeway cigarette campaign. The agency's financial problems had been left on hold while this campaign was being put together.

Ted and Liz arrived together, and Martin a little later. They had used the side entrance to the hotel or come through the kitchens, and had gone directly up to the room without crossing to reception or passing through the lobby. Liz had booked the room days ago, and arranged for a typewriter and general office equipment to be supplied by the hotel. Among other things, Cas had brought advertising rate cards for all the media –

including newspapers, magazines, posters, radio and television. Martin had pads of flimsy paper for layouts and storyboards, and a supply of paints and coloured pencils sneaked from the agency art department. All relevant files were in Ted's brief case.

'From now on, I think we should refer to this campaign as "Project 106,"' said Cas half-seriously.

'Why Project 106?' asked Martin.

'Because that's the number of the room.' There was light laughter.

'Good idea,' said Ted. 'Project 106 it is.'

'I feel like a spy – no, more like a criminal,' said Liz.

'I feel like a fool,' said Martin. 'Why are we doing this to ourselves, when we have a well-paid and perfectly good staff to do the job? Is all this cloak and dagger stuff really necessary?'

Martin was just being difficult, he already knew the answer, which they had discussed at length at a board meeting.

'Absolutely necessary,' said Ted. 'Derry O'Dowd insists. Nobody, but nobody is to know about this campaign except ourselves. We are the entire creative team.' He glanced at his watch. 'Derry should be here with the Ridgeway marketing wallah, Lionel Parsons in about 15 minutes to brief us. They're coming direct from the airport.'

'So, let's get these tables set up the way we want them and have coffee and tea sent up,' said Cas.

'We need an easel to display our ideas for discussion,' said Ted. 'Liz, would you ask the hotel if they have such a thing?'

When O'Dowd and Parsons arrived, there were handshakes all round, and some gentle banter before they got down to business.

'Sorry about the cramped quarters,' said Ted, 'this is the best we could do.'

Lionel Parsons, who lacked any subtlety replied, 'I expect it's adequate as long as your activities remain secret and are successful. That's all that matters to me.'

The men took off their jackets and Lionel Parsons went across to the easel which had been set up with a flip-chart, uncapped a felt-tipped pen and began to write. The F&M team sat back to listen intently to his briefing and to make notes.

They were greatly impressed with his presentation of the Ridgeway marketing strategy as it unfolded. He gave them the market share of all the cigarette brands on the British and Irish markets, and then concentrated on Ireland. The plan was simple. As they could see, most smokers preferred plain cigarettes – that is, untipped, but a growing number were shifting slowly from plain to tipped. He said the research showed that plain cigarette smokers didn't really like tipped cigarettes because they were too bland, but, nevertheless, they wanted to change to them for 'perceived health reasons.' Lionel pursed his lips and waved a dismissive hand. Ridgeway's plan was to position a very strong, tipped cigarette on the market, which would give the same satisfaction as a plain one, and persuade plain cigarette smokers to change over to it, particularly the smokers of their rivals' brands of plain cigarettes. To do this, they had produced a prototype, tipped cigarette which was fatter and stronger than any other on the market. He handed around samples. They were called 'Commodore.' Many names had been researched, and this was the one found most acceptable, and with the greatest impact. He showed them the newly designed packet. It would be launched in Ireland through the Diamond Tobacco Company, and Ridgeway was confident of a huge success. When he mentioned the size of the advertising budget, Ted couldn't prevent an audible intake of breath.

Fresh coffee was ordered and they began to work out the mechanics of the campaign. It was agreed that finished artwork for posters, newspapers and magazines would be produced in Holland, as well as the plates for colour advertisements. To do it in Ireland or Britain would be far too risky. Television commercials would be shot in America, where Flynn & Malby had good contacts. All media bookings would be made in the name of Allied Oils to throw people off the scent. That would be okay, Liz said, until Allied Oils got to hear of it, then all hell would break loose.

'We'll cross that bridge when we come to it,' was Ted's dismissive comment, ignoring the long-term problems that would result.

'I'd like to have a good piece of music on the soundtrack of the television commercial,' said Lionel, capping and uncapping a very expensive Waterman fountain-pen. 'A jingle – something which would become associated with Commodore cigarettes in the same way as that superb jingle for Coca-Cola. "I'd like to Buy the World a Coke!" '

'Which was transmogrified into, "I'd like to Teach the World to Sing",' said Martin.

'We'll put a team of the best composers of popular music on the job,' said Ted.

'What was the name of that group who sang the song?' asked Lionel. 'I'm sure nobody here knows.' He gave a shadow of a smile.

'The New Seekers,' said Martin. 'They had a big hit with it on both sides of the Atlantic. The original artists were the Hillside Singers.'

'I'm impressed,' said Lionel, softening for the first time. 'I'd like to use The New Seekers for our jingle.'

Cas darted Martin an amused look.

'I didn't know you were such an expert on popular music,' he said.

'One of my least controversial pastimes.'

'We'll have to be careful, though,' said Ted, 'to strike the right note ...'

'If you'll pardon the pun,' said Cas.

Ted frowned. 'Remember the "Lonely Man Theme" tune for Strand Cigarettes,' he continued. 'And we know what happened to Strand. Extinct.'

'Anytime I think of Strand Cigarettes, shivers run up and down my spine,' said Lionel. 'But it was the complete advertising campaign which was duff, not just the jingle.'

'"You're never alone with a Strand". What a dire slogan,' said Cas.

'Yes,' said Lionel. 'Dire is the word.'

'The "Lonely Man Theme" was probably the first chart hit advertising theme tune ever. Cliff Adams recorded it,' said Martin. 'Then Georgie Fame and the Blue Flames did "Get Away" in 1966 for some petrol company – I can't remember which. David Dundas' "Jeans On" and Danny Williams' "Dancin' Easy" also began life as advertising jingles.' They all turned and stared at Martin. He shrugged and made a face. 'Sorry, I just know these things.'

After three hours of intensive discussion and planning, Lionel Parsons and Derry O'Dowd left for the airport and Lionel's flight back to London. As soon as they were gone, Martin jumped up and went out of the room for another cigarette. He had been going in and out intermittently during the meeting as, ironically, he had been banned from smoking by Parsons, because the room in which they were working was so small. Cas went to stretch his legs, and when he came back he suggested they should call it a day. All that week they worked from early morning until late at night putting together a persuasive, exciting and hard-selling campaign for presentation to Ridgeway. This was advertising life at its hottest.

CHAPTER 11

'Oh by the way, I'm getting married.' Barry said it with an exaggerated casualness, when the barman had put two creamy pints in front of them in the Queens. He waited for a reaction.

Cas slapped him on the back. 'Well done. Full marks. Congratulations.' He lifted his pint high. 'Here's to you and – what's her name anyway?' They both laughed.

Cas said, 'Chloe is a wonderful girl. I'm sure you'll be very happy.

'How did you know for sure it was Chloe?'

'Ah, come on, Barry.' Cas was managing the news splendidly, even though it wasn't long since he and Chloe had spent the night together. He wondered if Barry knew. There was no reason why he should. Barry and he had been friends since schooldays and Barry was, as Chloe had recently put it, 'a regular guy.' He now realised that Barry was head over heels in love with Chloe, and he only hoped to God that she felt the same, as he wouldn't like to see her do something similar to Barry as she had done to him. But Barry was different – harder as a person.

Cas was surprised at how swiftly he had got over Chloe, how easily the bubble had burst. There was no doubt she was a very attractive woman and it wasn't long since he had thought himself irredeemably in love with her, but the sudden rush of realisation that Pam was the one – absolutely everything he wanted in a woman as a mate for life – had firmly relegated Chloe to the category in which she had put him, 'just a fling'. Was that a man's way of coping with rejection, he wondered. To downgrade a deeply-felt love to a mere night of passion – well, it was one way of closing the books on an emotional attachment. But anyway, it hadn't really been love. It had been infatuation and never could have reached the dizzy heights of his newly unleashed feelings for Pam. He knew that in his innermost being.

'I'm due for a spot of congratulation, myself,' Cas said and took a deep drink from his pint of stout.

'Hells' bells!'

'No. Wedding bells. And before you ask me – it's Pam O'Regan.'

'Of course it's Pam d'Or, you sod,' said Barry joyfully. 'Everybody knew that one day you and Pam would get shackled.'

'I didn't.'

Barry put an arm around Cas's shoulder. 'Ah, let's face it Maitland, you were never the brightest star in the firmament when it came to women. But my best wishes anyway. Wait till I tell Chloe, she'll be delighted.' Cas winced.

Barry ordered more pints and a bottle of champagne and when they had drunk about an inch and a half of stout from the glasses, Barry topped them up with champagne.

'Black Velvet's your only lady for tonight,' he said. 'It'll have to do as your Hoor du Jour.'

'Let's drink to each other,' said Cas, 'and to our respective ball and chains, or is that balls and chain, or ...'

'And to our new business venture, Golden Eagle, and to the three musty queers, you, me and Chloe,' Barry went on.

'Let's push out the boat now that our ship has come in.'

'I won't be joining you and Chloe in the new business, Barry,' Cas said suddenly. 'Sorry about that.'

'Why not? What are you talking about?'

'Sorry, but I have to pull out.'

'You're joking.'

'No, I won't be here. Pam and I are going abroad. We're going to live in Italy – Tuscany.'

'Bloody hell!'

'Pam has fixed herself up with a great job there and I'm going to paint. We're getting married in Rome.'

'What about Flynn & Malby?'

'I'm resigning, but keep it under wraps for the moment. I'll be leaving behind a trail of blazing bridges.'

'Well hump that for a barrel of pork.'

'Listen Barry, you and Chloe won't really miss me. I know that.'

'No, no, don't get me wrong. I'm glad you two are getting married and I'm in hog heaven you're going to paint full-time. And Italy sounds A1. But we'll miss you alright, as a partner in Golden Eagle and I'll miss you as a friend, believe me. What does Pam think?'

'Pam's over the moon. And I'm looking forward to seeing Ted's face when I tell him I'm leaving. On the other hand he might say good riddance, of course.'

'No Cas, never. I'd say he has relied greatly on you down the years, more than he'd admit, just as I have. Ted Flynn and I are two of a kind, in a way, and we need someone to steady us up, someone like you who doesn't quite know their own value. He'll miss you a lot more than you think, and so will I.' Barry made a face.

It was dark when they emerged from the Queens, ever-so-slightly unsteady and smoking cigars. Cas said, 'Let's go to the Vampire Restaurant for a bite.' Barry giggled. There was talk of a meal in a Chinese restaurant, and as they made their way down Dalkey main street with its darkened shops and special night atmosphere, Cas gave a raucous rendition to the air of, 'They Tried to Tell us We're too Young....' of, 'They Tried to Sell us Egg Fu Yong....' and Barry followed with, 'All Things Blurred and Beautiful'.

They entered a restaurant and when the maître d' had seated them, Cas noticed Terry Brady of RTE and Pad Padmore, an account executive with Keating Advertising having a meal at a table in a corner. Terry was telling Pad a joke and he had him convulsed with laughter, as he gesticulated to emphasise the punch-line. The waiter was uncorking a champagne bottle to follow on from the one upturned in the ice bucket. Terry, seeing Cas, jumped up and came over and insisted that Cas and Barry join him and Pad. When they were reseated and ordering their meal, Barry explained that they were both celebrating their forthcoming nuptials and Terry insisted on ordering a supplementary bottle of champagne.

Everyone got nicely drunk and Terry was back in full flight in his role of raconteur. He had them rocking with insider stories about RTE.

'Also I remember one Christmas,' he went on, 'when we had a slide advertising Paxo Stuffing. The guy doing the voice-over got it mixed up and called out, "Stuff your children and delight your turkey – with Paxo". And then, one Easter, the lads in Telecine laced up a piece of film back-to-front, and the Pope gave his 'Urbi et Orbi' blessing with his left hand.'

'What was that story about the Kish lighthouse?' asked Cas.

'Oh, that was the time the maritime lads were commissioning the new Kish lighthouse, and the plan was to build the foundation on land and tow it out into Dublin Bay and sink it at the designated location. One of the newsreaders – I don't remember which one – was reading a news item about it on the nine o'clock bulletin, and he stumbled over one line with disastrous results, although – or because – he had rehearsed it many times. The line was, "The lighthouse will sit on the shingle"'.

'Well now,' said Cas, 'I heard a slip of the tongue on radio the other day on the part of one of RTE's leading presenters.'

'We call them the VIPs, or very important presenters,' said Terry.

'Well, this VIP was interviewing some fellow who had dated a famous Hollywood star, and he was going on and on about how beautiful her legs were until, eventually, the presenter asked, "That's great, but legs apart, what was she like?"'

Pad Padmore threw back his head and guffawed and as Terry smirked and looked over at Cas, Cas knew he was making a mental note to add this one to his repertoire.

Then Barry dropped his clanger and said, in spite of Cas's warning, 'Cas is leaving Flynn & Malby.'

Cas saw Terry Brady stiffen and Pad, who thought it was some kind of a joke which he hadn't understood, chuckled anyway. Cas froze. Shit! How could Barry be so stupid. An intoxicated Barry sat there mildly making train tracks on the table cloth with a fork. He'd make mincemeat of him when he got him alone, thought Cas.

'Don't mind him, he's talking rubbish,' said Cas, 'he's pissed. Look at him.'

Pad chuckled again and Cas knew he probably wouldn't remember a bit of this in the morning, but Terry was different. Terry would sense the truth behind this exchange, he would know that something was in the air, and Cas knew that on Monday morning within hours, news about him leaving F&M would be around the whole advertising community. He would have to get to Ted first thing, before the story got to him. All the effects of the night's drinking drained from him and he looked at his watch. It was very late and he'd have to go home and get some sleep, or he'd wake up with an unmanageable hangover.

'Cas?'

'Yes, Pad.'

'You're a member of the Advertising Press Club, aren't you?'

'Yes.'

'Well, I could use your help. I'm chairman of the Programme Committee and we could use an extra body. Will you join the committee? Go on, say you will. We're short-handed. You'd make a great addition.' His voice was slurred and Cas knew that Barry's comment hadn't registered.

'You never know your luck,' said Cas. 'I might just do that.'

'We're meeting next Tuesday in the agency viewing theatre at six thirty,' said Pad. 'And I have a treat for afterwards. I've got my hands on three new blue movies.' He giggled. 'There's, "The Man from Manhattan Meets the Queen from Queens on the Staten Island Ferry".' He ticked them off on his fingers. 'And, "Three Little Maids from Night School", and then there's, "The Swedish Nun and the Body Builder from Cricklewood."'

Terry Brady slapped him on the back. 'Good man Pad. You haven't lost it.'

Cas stood up.

'Do you know what time it is?' he said. 'Have you no homes to go to?'

'Good God!' said Terry. 'She-who-must-be-obeyed will go mad that I'm coming in this late again. She'll have a piece of my anatomy lopped off and put in a jar on the mantelpiece if I don't go now.'

Depends on who she-who-must-be-obeyed is, thought Cas. If it's Mrs Terry Brady, you betcha. Probably not if it's the little red-haired PA he saw him with at the Clio Awards Festival.

* * *

Tessa got ready for her meeting with Roddy. This time she didn't put much thought into her appearance. She was too distraught since receiving the note two nights before, and just needed to talk to Roddy straight. She drove to Torca road, as it was her turn to leave the car up there, and then she almost ran down the Cat's Ladder, dropping from slab to slab with youthful precision and fitness. Roddy was waiting for her. He lifted a smiling face, and was puzzled to see the distracted look in her eyes.

'What is it, Tessa?'

'Oh, it's so hard to tell you.'

'What's so hard? Why can't you tell me?'

She turned her face towards the sea.

'Do you want to wait until we are driving along? We could stop somewhere,' he said.

She moved away from him. 'We have to stop seeing one another. It must stop now. Right now, before something terrible happens.'

'What do you mean? What something terrible? Here, sit down.' He gestured and they sat down side by side on the step. Tessa didn't speak but took the envelope out of her pocket and gave it to Roddy. He frowned as he read the note.

'When did you get this?'

'Two nights ago. It was pushed through the letter box.'

'Have you any idea who might do this?'

'No. I saw someone moving away from the door in the dark, but I couldn't see them properly.' She looked at him. 'Somebody is watching us.' Then she added hesitantly, 'It's not the first one.'

'Another one? Why didn't you tell me about it? You should have told me.' His voice had an edge.

'I couldn't. I mean I was afraid to, I ... I didn't want anything unsettling to come between us.'

At once a mask seemed to slip down over his face, as he sat looking at the sheet of paper. He turned away, and Tessa was frightened by his reaction. He had made no move to comfort her, no arm had slipped around her shoulder, and now his body had stiffened as he sat looking ahead, his mouth tight.

'Say something! For God's sake, say something. I've been through hell since I got that note.' Then her nerve broke and she burst out crying, nearly shouting. 'Roddy, I love you so much. You know that. I want to spend the rest of my life with you.'

Roddy didn't answer. She held his arm and forced him to turn around and look at her. Her cheeks were red and glistening with tears. When at last he spoke his voice was casual and his Scottish inflection underscored his words. 'Keep your head. There's a sensible lass. One minute you're telling me our affair is over and the next you're saying you want to spend the rest of your life with me. Steady up. You know that's not possible. You're a married woman. You've two children.'

'Roddy! You're not thinking of me, you're thinking of yourself.'

He shrugged. 'I'm a newcomer to this area, and any scandal would affect my business at The Aristocrat.

You know the kind of people I have as customers, they don't mind reading scandal in the newspaper columns, but they don't want it on their doorstep. And my financial backers in Scotland are very puritanical indeed. I think we should forget today's outing,' he said formally.

Tessa was truly heart-broken. She had turned to Roddy for love and comfort and instead found that a self-centred man, cold and aloof, had replaced the one she had come to know and love.

'Is that all you have to say?' she whispered.

'What can I say? Someone has obviously cottoned to the fact that we're seeing one another, and whoever it is doesn't like it. It wouldn't be your husband, would it?'

Tessa looked at him with horror, fresh tears on her face.

'No. It wouldn't be my bloody husband. He's not the type to send obscene notes, for God's sake.' She was deeply offended by the unkindness of the suggestion. 'I saw someone shuffling away from the door, I told you.'

'You never know. Neither of us is here long enough for a stranger to follow our movements and be outraged by them. He could have got someone to do it for him. Tessa, you're such an innocent.'

She jumped to her feet, her ears pounding with rage. 'Paul is not like that.'

'I think we should call it a day,' said Roddy looking away and brushing some dust off his sleeve. He did it unconsciously, but Tessa saw more in the gesture.

'Look, Tessa, I couldn't care less about the foul-mouthed ramblings of this perverted bastard. But things are getting complicated. And when things get complicated, I don't like it. I don't like it at all. I'm out. I'm gone. If whoever wrote these notes knows about us, you can be sure others will eventually. I don't care if one or two know where I get my sex from, but the fewer the better. I don't like complications. Life has too many of them.'

'Sex? Sex?' Her voice rose and she shook uncontrollably. 'It was more than that. I could tell.'

'Knock if off, you knew what you were at. We had fun. We had great fun. But it was sex. Just sex. Don't try to turn it into some smarmy teenage love-pact. Maybe whore wasn't too wide of the mark.'

She raised her right hand to hit him, but he caught her wrist in mid-air. His face was like carved ivory and his eyes were two small dots. She brought up her left hand and slapped him back-handed across the cheek, the stone in her engagement ring cutting a gash which oozed blood immediately. She broke free and shrank back, and without another word she turned and ran up the steps, sobbing and panting, away from Roddy Ogilvie, leaving the last vestiges of her peace of mind behind her. When she reached the top she stood trembling on the road, and then she stumbled to her car, wrenched open the door, threw herself in and, with her head in her hands, wept. Eventually she sat back exhausted but still trembling and her swollen eyes fell on the commemorative plaque beside the gate of Torca Cottage. The plaque quoted Shaw: 'The men of Ireland are mortal and temporal, but her hills are eternal.' As she drove along Torca Road and down the hill, her head swam and her mind clicked back to the time she had met Roddy on Killiney Hill, and she told herself she would always remember the words of Shaw, and that maybe he hadn't known some of the men of Scotland could be bloody temporal too. She knew now that she would never, ever, tell Roddy that she was pregnant with his child. For the first time in her life she hated someone.

* * *

The early Monday morning sun was stretching across the Merrion Square flower-beds and probing the shrubbery with tentative fingers of light as Cas stood at one of the large windows in the boardroom and watched the day unfold. He went into Ted's office. Ted was unusually late. Liz was busying herself at her desk and had just received a phone call to say that Ted had sat up most of the night worrying, and had overslept as a result.

Oh God. Now, he didn't relish telling Ted he was leaving the agency, particularly at this point in the fortunes of the company. How would he take it? He used Ted's phone to make a call to one of the copy-writers while he waited.

The door opened and Ted came in, slightly breathless. 'Good morning Liz, morning Cas,' he said, trying to sound cheerful. 'I had to park miles away. My usual space was gone, dammit.' He placed his brief-case on the floor beside his desk and sat down. Liz came across to him with a file of mail and a large diary opened at the page with the day's appointments. 'Cas has been waiting to talk to you Ted, before you start into the day. I don't know what it's about, but he says it's important.' She smiled thinly at Cas.

'Fire away,' said Ted, as Liz returned to her desk.

Cas pulled over an arm-chair and sat facing Ted across his desk. There was no doubt that Ted was looking terrible. He had a pale parchment look to his face and there was strain behind his eyes. He smiled wanly and raised his eyebrows questioningly. Cas took a deep breath.

'Ted, I'm leaving Flynn & Malby.' There was a silence and Liz froze. Ted leaned forward and took up the little silver fish from the paper clip tray and fiddled with it.

'Are you serious?' He avoided looking straight at Cas.

'Yes, I'm afraid so.'

'You're not really going to leave us, Cas?' said Liz.

Ted cut across her. 'But you said, in this very room, that you had no intention of leaving!' He was suddenly deeply angry.

'That was different,' said Cas. 'I mean, I have no intention of setting up a new agency, with or without Paul Bennett, and I'm not going to join another agency either.'

'But, you know I told Tim Cranby and Bruce Bellingham you were staying with us, and you'd no intention of leaving.' In spite of all, Ted half hoped he might keep the Baby Faire and A&D accounts, although in his heart he knew it was futile. 'If we can just get over this financial hiccup, the future of the agency will never be better, with the big Ridgeway deal in the bag. Why are you doing this to me?'

'I'm not doing anything to you, Ted. I don't want to let you down, but I won't change my mind either. I can't.' Cas was also full of anguish.

'Is it cash? Is that's what's wrong? You've a very good salary as it is, and your expenses are virtually unlimited. But we'll have to review it if you think ....' Ted came around the desk and put a hand on Cas's shoulder. 'Shares?' Liz darted a look at Ted. He would do anything now to keep Cas, but he might regret his offer of more shares.

'No, Ted, not shares.'

'Have I done something to really upset you, Cas?'

'No. No, well yes, but that's not the reason ...'

'What have I done?' Ted pounced triumphantly.

'Well, you know,' said Cas, 'I've told you often enough when I didn't agree with your way of handling things, but this conversation is going in the wrong direction.'

'Go on,' said Ted in a grimmer tone.

'Well, ever since I became Managing Director, you have manipulated the situation so that I'm no longer in direct contact with the bigger accounts, and I'm bogged down with the day-to-day running of the agency. That's not what the clients want, they've told me, and it's certainly not what I want. And you've interfered in every major policy decision I've made. We've had this conversation many times before, and you wouldn't listen. Anyway, without wanting to moralise, I'm finding this way of life increasingly synthetic as the years go by. I'm only 28, which is young in the business, and I'm thoroughly pissed off with it already.' He hadn't meant to add the last bit.

Ted stuffed his hands in his pockets, hunched his shoulders and went over to the window. Standing in silhouette he said softly, 'Look, I know I'm a bit of an old fool ...' Oh my God, thought Liz, here comes the sales pitch.

'I know I interfere too much, and that, well, I'm inclined to exaggerate a bit, but it's only because this agency means so much to me and I get carried away. You know that, Cas. There's no real harm done. All you have to do is to humour me a little. I suppose basically, I'm a creative person – an ideas man – and I tend to think in superlatives. I'm a bit of a dreamer, unlike you – you're creative too, of course, but you have your feet planted firmly on the ground. You know how much regard I have for you, Cas – we all have – Liz will tell you.' He was being deliberately selective in the way he addressed Cas's remarks.

This is getting completely out of hand, thought Cas.

'Ted, I'm leaving. I'm going to Italy to paint.'

'Jeez! Paint? Nonsense! You'll starve. Nobody bloody well makes money painting.'

'I think I'll manage it alright,' said Cas lightly.

'Look,' said Ted, 'what is so wrong about wanting to keep you with the agency. Surely it is a compliment to you that we think so highly of you?'

'I appreciate that, but ...'

'You've done particularly well in advertising, Cas. You've come a long way from just being another artist. You're now a respected member of the Institute of Advertising Practitioners. A well rounded and successful advertising and marketing man, with enviable management skills. Why have you taken such a turn against the advertising industry?'

'I haven't. Not really...'

'It's a damn fine profession to be in. Agencies have come a long way from being just space-brokers. Much more sophisticated now. Opinions are expertly researched. These are exciting times. And with television, all sorts of highly creative people are finding advertising an outlet for their skills. Quality and standards are improving all the time. Irish agencies are winning awards internationally. There are festivals, university degrees, bursaries ... And don't you realise that in two or three years time Flynn & Malby will be the top agency in the country. With salary increases, bonuses, expenses, more shares and directorships of other companies, you could be a very rich man indeed.'

'I've got to leave now Ted, I must. There comes a D-day in everyone's life – decision day – when you have to make up your mind which way you want to go. I accept it when people do U-turns. It's more intelligent than continuing along the wrong road, regardless. I've always found advertising absorbing and exciting, but in my heart I've wanted to be a full-time painter, and if I don't make the change now I never will. I don't want to be a very rich man.' A pause. 'I'm getting married and I'm going to Tuscany to live and paint.' Ted was silenced. Liz looked up.

'Pam?'

'Yes, Pam,' said Cas. Ted went back around his desk and slumped sulkily into his chair. Cas went on: 'I'll talk to Jim Reilly about selling my shares back to you, and about getting a severance cheque. I thought about a year's salary?' Ted didn't look up. 'I'll leave you now,' said Cas. 'We can talk about the details later.'

Late that night, as he was just about to get into bed, there was a ring at his hall-door. When he opened it, Liz was standing there. 'May I come in?' Completely taken by surprise, Cas motioned her in. This was the first time that Liz Downey had ever called to his apartment, and the number of times they had socialised together, except in large groups, was small. Liz sat down and he offered her a drink, which she accepted. For the next half an hour she tried every possible way to persuade Cas to change his mind about leaving Flynn & Malby. She denied that Ted had sent her, and said it was entirely her own idea, for the sake of the agency, and because she thought so highly of him. Cas began to wonder if Liz was more concerned about her own future in the agency than his. He knew just how calculating she could be. Just before she left, Liz gave him a small package saying it was a wedding gift from herself and Des. Later when he opened it, it contained a finely crafted silver bowl, hallmarked with a crowned harp, and with a little ticket inside it stating: 'Irish Silver 1735'. He fell into bed, putting the agency out of his mind, and thinking about Pam, Tuscany and his future, drifting into a deep and peaceful sleep.

* * *

After the rain, the water was like a looking-glass in the late evening stillness of Bulloch Harbour, and the boats were high on the tide. Paul Bennett sat outside his home on a quay-side seat facing out to sea, and studied the darkening, distant city skyline, which curved comfortingly around the bay to Howth. The puff ball clouds were gold- plated from the last rays of the sinking sun, and the warmth was slowly draining from the day.

He ran his hands roughly across his face, pressing the tips of his fingers against his eyes and his temples. What a bloody awful day it had been. The drinks in the club hadn't helped either. He had gone through so many mood changes from fury to bravado, to surliness, to resignation. My God, but Ted had been savage. Not only had he sacked him, but he had said – no, inferred, Ted was too smart to actually say – that Paul would never get another job in advertising in Ireland. Ever. Ted would see to that. And he would make sure that he never got 'recognition' from the media, and so could never set up his own agency. There had been no witnesses to his threats and Liz had scuttled out of the office as soon as he came in. He had known it was coming for some time. He knew Ted had the full story on the Cranby/ Bellingham plans for a new agency, but he hadn't known that Ted would be quite so black-hearted about it. Then he had had a senseless row with Cas.

What was he going to tell Tessa? What would she say? Would she be furious, totally negative, or sympathetic? He had phoned her several times during the day to try and set the climate for a serious discussion, but she was out each time. Anyway she hadn't known about his plans this last while, so she wouldn't be prepared for discussion of any kind, except good news. He didn't know why, but his mind slid back to the time before he was married when he lived in a ramshackle bachelor pad high on the hill overlooking Killiney Bay, near the Druid's Chair pub. There were exactly 26 steps – plus a broken one – from the road to the door of his flat. He knew it because several times he had climbed them on his hands and knees after a night's roistering, drunkenly reciting the alphabet. He had thrown great parties too. One of his friends had dubbed the flat 'The Memories Club', and it had been known as such thereafter. They were fun times. He stood up and walked over to the house, noticing that there was a light in the bedroom. Tessa must be having an early night. He opened the door and went in, detecting a strange stillness in the house. He went straight to the bedroom and found Tessa sitting up in bed, her hair pulled back in a bandana and her face pale and drawn. An unopened book lay beside her on the bed.

'Hi!'

'Hi.'

'This place is like a morgue. Where are the kids?'

'Over in Foleys. They're staying with their friends for the night. Remember? They've been planning it all week.'

'Oh yeah. Sure, sure, I forgot. I'm going to make some coffee, would you like some – or are you trying to sleep?'

'I'd like a coffee. I'm not able to sleep, although I'm tired out.'

Paul made the coffee and brought two mugs to the bedroom. He went over and sat edgily on the chaise longue under the window.

'I've some bad news, very bad indeed,' Paul said, his voice harsh and tight. Tessa sat motionless except for an occasional sip of coffee, as he recounted the bits and pieces of his failed plans to open his own agency, which she hadn't known about, finishing with his dreadful meeting with Ted. The details tumbled out.

'So I'm up the creek without a paddle – as far as this country is concerned anyway. I'll never get another job in advertising here, and advertising is what I know best. There's a glimmer of hope, though. Keith Oldham – he's the Advertising Manager of Tilley UK – offered me a very good job in advertising a while back. In London.' He shrugged. 'I don't want to approach the old man for obvious reasons, so I'll have to take Keith up on his offer. It means moving to England. We'll have to sell the house.'

He darted a look at Tessa, to find that tears were splashing down her cheeks. He went over and sat close to her on the bed.

'Tess, I'm sorry, I really am,' he said softly. 'I've made a terrible balls-up of everything. I'm sorry. I know this whole thing sounds appalling, and I know how much this house means to you, but if we pull together, we'll manage. The London job is a good one. I'll go there first, and you and the children can follow in a month or two. We'll find schools for them. I'll ...'

Tessa was shaking her head and weeping.

'I'm going back home,' she said, her voice barely audible.

'You don't have to do that, love,' said Paul. 'You can live here with the kids for a few months. We don't have to sell the house immediately. Look, we'll talk this whole thing out in the morning ....'

Tessa was shaking her head again. 'You don't understand. I'm going back to live with my family in Waterford and I'm taking the children. You can see them anytime you want. They're your children and ... Paul, I'm leaving you.' She looked up at him, red-eyed, the agony behind the words etched plainly across her damp and crumpled face. The sight shocked Paul.

'I know I've been a bloody fool, and I haven't managed our life together very well, but ...' Paul was mumbling, still uncomprehending.

'No. No. This has nothing to do with you, or your work, or Flynn & Malby, or London or whatever. This is about me, me, me.' She was slightly hysterical. 'I'm all mixed up. I don't know where I'm going. I can't breathe.

I don't know who I am any more. I need to be on my own. Don't you see, I must have space to think, to work out my life. I feel like a fish out of water. I'm struggling ...' She started to cry again, her nerves completely gone.

Paul could hear the hall clock ticking and a dog barked in the distance. He felt as if he had been punched in the face. His arms shot out and he pulled her limp body to his.

'Please, don't ask me to explain any further. I can't.' She put her head on his shoulder and sobbed uncontrollably.

'How long will you go back to Waterford for?' Paul asked quietly.

'I don't know.'

Silently the tears ran down Paul's face, and mingled with those of Tessa.

Paul woke-up, having dozed off beside his silent, tear-stained wife. His mouth was dry. He had been so confused that he felt a few hours sleep was imperative if he were to tease out the next round in his shattered life. There was silence in the room, and he put out his hand to see if Tessa was alright. There was a space where she had lain. He sat up and put on the bedside light. Probably she had gone to check the kids, or sit by herself downstairs as recently she occasionally did. No, the children were spending the night at Foleys. He felt a sudden stab of concern and got out of bed and went to the top of the stairs.

'Tessa?' He went down. 'Tessa. Tessa, are you there?' His sense of disquiet increased. A chill breeze blew past him from an open front door, and immediately a feeling of sheer horror engulfed him. She would never do anything foolish, for God's sake? But he knew she would! He just knew. He jumped the remaining steps and flung himself out the hall-door. Sweet Jesus, his Tessa! Where had she been in his life over the past months – nowhere really. Why was she suffering so overwhelmingly? She said she was going back to Waterford, but now .... A lamp-post on the far side of the harbour threw a yellow light on to the agitated boats, creaking and chattering, creating confusing shapes in the choppy water. Halyards clinked against metal masts. He ran bare-footed along the quayside, his thin pyjamas no protection against the rising wind.

'Tessa. Tessa. Tessa.' He called her name again and again, willing her to materialise. Lights went on in the house of the local boatman, and a door opened. Then he saw her. She was sitting in a small rowing boat at the mouth of the harbour. Her white nightdress was momentarily highlighted against the blackness of the harbour wall, before a wave took the boat and swept it out into the open sea. He ran to the far side of the quay, trying to shout, but no sound would come from his constricted throat. The heavy sea threw the boat near to the outside of the harbour wall, and jumping down the steps he lunged at the boat as the upsurge brought it closer. But it dropped into a trough, and he missed. A brutal wave slapped him violently across the face and buried him deep in the piercing cold water. Panic and the roaring in his ears petrified his brain. Tessa screamed, a frightened heart-broken shriek which seemed to come from the depths of her body, and then crumpled into a heap on the floor of the tossing boat. Instinctively Paul's arms shot up above his head and clawed the night. His fingers touched and fastened on the rim of the boat, but cold-numbed and wet they slipped as a wave wrenched the boat from his grasp.

Dimly he heard men shouting and a strong beam of light penetrated the darkness, dazzling him. Hands stretched out and dragged him from the water, and he saw someone wrapping a blanket around Tessa. With relief and exhaustion he lapsed into semi-consciousness.

CHAPTER 12

Lisette had been working steadily on her theme of an overseas students club, to be accommodated in the premises of The Teashop. She could see enormous potential for herself in the idea, and felt that it would also be a mutually satisfactory arrangement for Rita. As she had been trained as a teacher, she also envisaged that the club could develop into a full-scale school. There was room for a new one specialising in good spoken English and the teaching of Anglo-Irish literature in south-east Dublin. Six such schools already operated, but they were all in Dublin city.

The American market had hardly been tapped at all, and a meeting with the Department of Education would definitely be her first move. She felt it was a little early to unfold such an ambitious plan to Rita Flynn, and that it would be better to concentrate on the development of the students' club in her negotiations with her. Still, it was an exciting thought, and something which Rita could well be interested in at a later stage. Au pair agencies were on the increase and would generate more people who would go on to study at the new college at Windsor Terrace in Sandycove, and, certainly the club would be the perfect recruiting ground for them. A clever and far-seeing French woman, Lisette D'Ambly was rather pleased with her plans.

* * *

For the first time in his life, Ted Flynn felt very close to being a beaten man. It would take a great deal of money to prevent the collapse of his beleaguered agency, and money was the one thing in short supply, due in no small way to his profligate lifestyle. He had tried his damnedest – and in part succeeded – to get new business to keep the agency afloat and expand it, but careless handling of accounts which were the backbone of the agency, meant that core business had seeped away like water into sand. He knew he was a first-rate salesman, and an excellent advertising man, but when he came to running a company he was, well, less effective. He had always known that. That's why he'd wanted Cas as Managing Director. But he hadn't given him his head as he should have. He could see that now. And Cas was leaving – another blow. Well, if he, Ted Flynn succeeded in saving Flynn & Malby, he would appoint a new MD and take a back seat himself. This time he really meant it. But what was the use, the agency was beyond saving. Almost. There might, just might be one way of getting cash to tide him over, one which he had been reluctant to consider until now. One small chance – Liz. He knew that Liz and Des had a substantial sum of money tucked away. Liz had alluded to it on one or two occasions. If he could get her to invest ... .

When Ted came into his office, Liz was sitting at her desk editing a report which she had prepared for a client.

'Morning.'

'Morning, Lizzy'. He came over to her desk and put his arm lightly around her shoulders. 'You're looking particularly attractive this morning, Lizzy. What have you done to your hair?'

'What do you want?' she grinned as he went over to his desk. 'I must say, you're in much better humour than when you were leaving the office last night. You were so far down in the dumps, you were unreachable.'

Ted sighed.

'I know, but I was thinking, if it wasn't for this blip in the agency's fortunes, life would be so wonderful for us all. It's all out there to enjoy, you know.'

'Blip?' said Liz. 'Dear God, Ted, it's far worse than a blip!'

'Liz, I've been thinking ... you have some money salted away ...'

'Stop right there.' She put up a restraining hand, flat-palmed in Ted's direction. 'You're not seriously going to suggest I lend Flynn & Malby money, Ted?'

'Think about it for a moment, Liz. It could be vastly to your advantage.'

'Absolutely not, Ted. Des and I have the future to think of. We have a lifestyle to maintain. And you've always said that's important. Anything I have has been invested, and there it stays.'

'But Liz, listen ...' He came and sat, companionably on the corner of her desk and put his hand over hers.

'I'll give you a much larger stake in the agency. Birdie Malby wants to sell her shares and I'll see you get some of those. Can't you see – when we get it all straightened out, you'll be the first to benefit – the major beneficiary. You'll be in a commanding position and that will make you financially secure for the rest of your life.' He smiled winningly at her.

'Financially secure? I'm not so sure about that. If the agency can come to the brink of crashing once, it could do so again. No Ted, I'm afraid Des and I are not prepared to take that kind of risk.'

'What's all this "Des and I" stuff? You've always made your own decisions, Liz.'

'The answer is still no. Anyway...' She left her desk and went to a filing cabinet, opened it and pushed in a file. When she turned around, her face stony.

'I was working up to telling you something, Ted, and I might as well say it now. I – we – Des and I have thought this out hard and long ...' She sat down again and folded her hands loosely in her lap and stared at them. 'I want out at this point,' she said slowly. Ted was like a statue. She went on. 'I've been making discreet enquiries, and as a result I've already been head-hunted on a completely confidential basis.'

'Liz, this isn't true.'

'Yes it is. My mind is made up.'

'But Liz ...' His voice was choking.

'Sorry Ted.'

'You can't ...'

'Sorry Ted. I've made my decision.'

Abruptly, the remains of Ted's composure vanished and he raged at Liz. 'Christ! What a betrayal! What a bloody betrayal! You can't walk out on me just like that. First Cas, now you. I can't believe you'd walk out on me now, after all we've built up together.'

There was a soft tap on the door and Hairy Bacon put his head around it and said, 'Ted, could I talk to you about Allied Oils for a minute, if it's convenient?'

'Get out!' Ted roared. 'Just get out!'

Hairy stood there for a moment, stunned, then he retreated.

'I brought you in here when you had nothing,' Ted stormed at her. 'Just a smart nose for business, and a huge ...' he waved both his arms, 'a vast ambition to jump up a fair few steps socially. Now you're deserting me when I most need you.' He thumped his desk and shouted. 'How's that for fucking ingratitude? By God, Liz, but greed is your mistress, and no mistake about it.' He banged his fist on the desk again. Staff who were passing his office door were agog with excitement. 'A rat deserting the shagging sinking ship,' he snarled.

'There's no need to be insulting,' Liz said. 'We're only business partners after all, not married to one another. Look, I think I've made myself clear. No loans, no investment, just a resignation coming in shortly. I need to go where I have security.'

Ted looked at her and was shocked to see a face chiselled out of granite. This was a Liz he hadn't known before.

'I know what I'm worth,' she continued. 'Des has calculated what I expect to take away with me financially, when the money is available – if ever. Remember Ted, you used my brains and my contacts down the years, as well as your own. I've already invested heavily in Flynn & Malby, but everything has a life, and my F&M life has come to an end. I know it. I think we'd better postpone any further discussion for the moment, until you have recovered yourself.'

Liz reached for her handbag and briefcase, and went over to the door, opened it wide, turned and with a face completely devoid of expression said, 'Sorry Ted.' She closed the door softly behind her.

In complete desolation, Ted left his office and went into the adjoining boardroom. He caught a last glimpse of Liz as he stood at the long window and looked down into the street. She would be back in the office as usual tomorrow, but it would be a different Liz. He knew that for certain. He watched her get into her car and drive out of his life.

He looked sadly around his board-room with its fine, expensive furniture and superb paintings, and its familiar scent of cigar smoke, leather, furniture polish and printers' ink. He had spent so many enjoyable hours here, more than he had spent at home, and the key ingredient had been the presence and support of Liz, who could reverse any difficult situation into which he got himself. Then he looked back across Merrion Square, with its leafy pale green lime trees, and the glowing red brick of the Georgian houses piercing the foliage at intervals. Would he really have to leave his beloved agency? He sat down, a lonely figure at the large, polished board-room table, put his head in his hands, and wept.

He drove home later, horrified at the stage he had reached in his business life. How could he keep his large home in Dalkey? He couldn't. It would have to go. It would be necessary to move to a much smaller house. Thank God the children were almost reared. But the shame of it all made him perspire heavily and it struck him that even his Mercedes 280S would no longer be his to drive. He drove past Dun Laoghaire Town Hall, along the seafront past Windsor Terrace and The Teashop without seeing it, turned into Sandycove Avenue West, and on to the main Dalkey road.

It was only at this point that Ted specifically thought of his wife, Rita, the woman who had stayed with him all his married life, devoting herself to building a home for him and their children. He was on his way now to telling her that all her efforts had been wasted, and that she must give up their lovely home. He felt suddenly deeply ashamed that it had taken him this long to start thinking of how she would feel on receipt of the news, so much so that he barely avoided hitting the kerb, he was driving so badly. He passed a weary hand over his forehead as he drove through Dalkey village. And he would never be able to make it up to her. He'd be too old by the time he'd be on his feet again, that is, if he ever did get on his feet again.

Rita was waiting for him when he got in. The children were out, so they had the place to themselves. She knew, when Ted had phoned her to say he would be home, that something was very wrong. He rarely came home for an evening meal these days.

An appetising smell of steak and kidney pie wafted from the cooker in spite of the extractor hood, as Rita busied herself about her large and superbly appointed kitchen, kitted out with every labour-saving device. She had chosen to prepare just the kind of meal which would underline the trouble she always took to do things well at home.

One glance at his face and Rita knew that her husband was in deeper trouble than she had ever seen him in before. He looked devastated, and could only nod to her, as he went across to the drawing-room and poured himself a stiff whiskey.

Ted took his drink with him to the kitchen and sat down on the built-in bench in the adjoining dining area, where Rita had set the table for the two of them. A conical-shaded ceiling lamp hung low over the table, giving Ted's heavily lined face a haunted look.

'Rita, the agency's nearly gone.'

'What do you mean?' She came to the table and poured herself a glass of red wine.

'I mean there's a ninety-nine point nine per cent chance that the agency will fold. We're completely strapped for cash.' He downed his whiskey in one gulp.

Rita brought several hot dishes to the table and started to serve the meal.

'The problem is,' he went on, 'we owe money – big money – left right and centre – to the newspapers, to RTE, to printers, and to a large number of suppliers.

We haven't got the wherewithal to meet our commitments. And at the end of the month they'll all be baying at our door to have their accounts settled. It's started already. There's no way we can pay our bills. And there's every indication that word is getting around that we can't. It looks as if we're sunk.' He poured himself a glass of wine.

'How did it happen?' Rita asked in a flat voice. Ted gestured with his table napkin.

'It's a long and tortuous story. I won't go into details now, but we overstretched ourselves, in so many ways – including money I took out of the company for – well, the cost of running this place, for example – and other things.' He skimmed over his personal excesses. 'The house will have to go. Sorry Rita.'

'Dear God, is there nothing that can be done?'

'No, I've tried everything. The sad thing is, we have a new cigarette account – a big one – with a huge budget, just about to take off ...'

'Will that not help?'

'No, it comes too late to save us. We need a substantial injection of cash now, to tide us over until that account begins to produce revenue. The banks are adamant, they won't advance us another penny without some personal investment. No, I've made every effort to crack this one, but it's no use. I've come to the end of the road, I'm afraid. We'll have to move. The house will have to go – the Mercedes – Jane will have to pull out of college. I don't know what I'll do. There are a lot of people in the advertising industry who don't like me, so I can't expect mercy from that quarter.' He picked at his meal.

'If I know you, you don't want anyone's mercy. But Ted, did you not see this coming? All that lavish living and carry-on had to paid for sometime.'

'I know, I know – at least I know now. The agency was always buoyant. Although Jim Reilly warned us, I never thought ... I'm an advertising man, for God's sake, I'm meant to be optimistic.'

'But surely it's possible to get another investor?'

'No, the way the finances are, it would be the same thing as selling out. And just at the moment there's not an awful lot to sell – except potential, and that's a bit tenuous.' He poured himself another glass of wine and topped up Rita's glass.

'I asked Liz if she wanted to invest.'

'Oh?' Rita was non-commital.

'She declined. In fact she bloody well refused, point blank. What's more, she's leaving the agency.'

'Oh she is, is she? Well now ...' Rita went to the kitchen counter and brought back two Venetian glass dishes of summer fruits and a cut-glass bowl of whipped cream. 'I'm not surprised,' she said softly. 'Liz would only stay around where there's clover. She's not one to support others, she likes to have a good time and make others pay for it. Pardon me if I don't swoon with sorrow or reach for the tissues. I take it she's resigned?'

'Yes, and there's a sizeable financial claim. She has it worked out already. I didn't think Des would let her go that far so soon.'

'Des gave up trying to influence his precious Liz years ago,' said Rita. 'The mystery has always been how he stayed with her, but I suppose the perks made it irresistible. She sure rolled out the red carpet for him, something he could never have done for her on his salary.' Ted was distinctly uncomfortable with Rita's observations.

'I'd rather not discuss Liz, if you don't mind, Rita. It's been a huge shock, particularly with Cas leaving as well. You do know he's leaving don't you? I did tell you?'

'You did, but there were no details.' said Rita. 'He's getting married?'

'Yes.'

'I like Cas very much. You'll miss him as well as Liz.'

'I've worked closely with Liz for so many years that this is a kind of a bereavement in a way.' Rita raised one eyebrow and said nothing. She took the blue and gold, French coffee pot off its stand, and poured two coffees into small matching cups. There was one advantage, she thought. That woman would be out of her life at last, and maybe she could get back the Ted she married all those years ago. He'd always been a rogue, but she was fair enough to admit that she had known that when she married him. She let Ted ramble on, drinking wine, as her mind went into overdrive.

'Look Ted, go into the drawing-room, pour yourself a glass of port and put your feet up. I'll bring in the cheese-board. I got a nice selection of cheeses today in Caviston's in Glasthule.'

Ted stood up to go as bidden, too spent to have a mind of his own. Rita was an extraordinary woman, he thought, shaking his head, to take all this so phlegmatically. Any other woman would have flown into hysterics at the thought of losing everything, but Rita had handled the situation so differently.

Rita moved around the kitchen as Ted sat in the drawing-room slumped in a chair, considering the wreckage of his business life. Later, when she wheeled in the trolley with cheese and more coffee, she found that Ted had nodded off, with an empty port glass on the small table beside him. He hadn't slept properly in weeks, and the wine and exhaustion had got to him.

She didn't want to leave her splendid home in Dalkey. She didn't want to lose the debonair, manipulative Ted whom she, as just plain Rita Doyle, had married. It had always been a tremendous achievement that she had caught and kept him, when he could have gone after anyone else in Dublin at the time. She didn't want to lose this lovely backdrop, just when the family was moving to and fro, in and out, three young people setting up their own lives like spokes at the rim of a wheel, while she remained contentedly at the hub. They would be making their own marriages one day and she wanted to give the wedding receptions here in the house. Later on they would bring back grandchildren. She wanted to keep exactly the life she had. She wanted more of Ted in it, and now that would be possible with the departure of Liz. Could she wave a wand like a fairy queen and save everything for herself, and for this broken man, inside the man she had married?

Rita went back to the kitchen, closed the door and phoned Lisette D'Ambly.

'Lisette? Rita Flynn here. I need to talk to you urgently.'

'Rita, 'allo. What's wrong?'

'Nothing's wrong, Lisette. It's just that I've made a sudden decision to sell The Teashop, and I thought you might want to buy it.'

'Merde, Rita! This is such a surprise for me.'

'Well, I thought I'd give you the opportunity first. I want to sell it lock, stock and barrel, and I know from our conversations that you would be interested. Isn't that right?'

'Oh yes, very much so. The entire business?'

'Yes, including the building. I own that too. I bought it recently. I want to make a quick sale, so the price should be acceptable.' She named it.

'Rita this is most exciting news. But is everything alright with you? Has anything happened?'

'Oh, I'm fine, thank you. But circumstances have changed.'

'Well, I am very interested, yes, very interested. When may I talk to you about it? Soon, yes?'

'Tomorrow. Do you think you could get sufficient backing to take it on immediately?'

'Yes I do. I shall talk to my 'usband. I am sure he will back me. I told you once he was in property. Leave it with me. I shall make a few calls in the morning and come back to you very quickly. I think I can make a success of this project.'

'Wonderful, Lisette. That's great. You'll contact me tomorrow then?'

'Yes. Au revoir, Rita, A demain, au revoir.'

When Rita went back to the drawing-room, Ted was still asleep. The light had faded and the room was quite dark, so she drew the curtains and turned on one side light, then she went over to where he sat, and, standing behind his chair, stroked his forehead with her fingertips, as she had done in the early days. Ted stirred and opened his eyes.

'No further discussions this evening, Ted,' she said softly. 'You're tired out, and I have to absorb all this. I'm in shock too. Just leave it all till tomorrow and we'll talk again. We'll go through it all then.' She continued to massage around his temples lightly until she heard him snoring gently.

The following day Lisette phoned in high excitement, to say that her husband would indeed put up the money, and she agreed to meet Rita that afternoon in the offices of Rita's obliging solicitors in Dalkey, to sign a preliminary agreement. They would come together the day after, when she would hand over the bank drafts, and dot the i's and cross the t's.

Well pleased with herself, actually delighted, Rita went about her home, lovingly putting small things in order, as she waited for Ted to come home. She didn't want to let this treasure slip through her hands, and would take no chances on a reversal, in what she considered to be her good fortune. But she would insist on keeping the financial power in a resuscitated Flynn & Malby. A rising tide was lifting all the boats once more.

When Ted crept in that evening, looking forlorn and limp, Rita poured him a drink and asked him to sit down and listen well to what she had to say. She told him her plan, and how she could offer to keep the company afloat. Of one thing she had no doubt, and she made sure he realised it. She convinced him that she believed fully in the man she had married, and she had no hesitation whatever in believing that he would make a success of his business the second time around. He was the same old Ted. Always would be. He'd never change, and he'd always talk people into giving him their business. He was the most talented man in advertising, in Ireland.

Ted listened, first in disbelieving silence, and then in full admiration for his wife, faith in himself slowly returning. As he put his arms around her, Rita knew they had started a new life together.

The following day, on her return from the solicitor's office, Rita got out of her car and let herself in to the house. It was late afternoon and the place was stifling. All the windows must have been closed. She was feeling hot and sticky, but very happy. It wasn't euphoria, it was more a sense of gladness and contentment that the business with Lisette had gone well. Three of them had been ranged against her: Lisette, her Irish husband and his accountant, but she had managed – even if she had to reduce her asking figure slightly at the last minute. It was okay, the deal was done and she would have a significant sum to invest in Flynn & Malby, enough to make the banks reconsider their decision.

Rita threw open the bedroom windows and let the sultry, late afternoon air circulate. She kicked off her shoes, and slipped out of her blouse and skirt without taking her eyes off the stunning view of Killiney bay. The cloudless sky made the foam-fringed sea look almost uniformly blue, like a royal cloak trimmed with ermine. Far out, a dicing speed-boat made a jagged tear in the surface, and the beach at White Rock, alternatively sandy and stony, was dotted with the remaining family groups, where small children ran excitedly in and out of the waves.

She loved this view of the sea in its many moods: serene, cool, inviting in summer, grey-green during rain, cruel and turbulent in winter – always unpredictable. I never want to leave this house, she thought. When I do, it will be feet first.

Then she had an idea: a swim! I know, I'll have a swim, I haven't had one for ages. But first she must phone that new restaurant in Dalkey village. What was the name of it? The Aristocrat. She would book a table for two. Ted would enjoy a celebratory night out. She rang him to check that he was available and he was delighted with the plan. She made the arrangements from the bedroom telephone extension and then phoned her hairdresser for an early appointment. She stepped into the adjoining dressing room and found her black one-piece bathing suit in a drawer. She stripped off and was about to pull it on when she caught a glimpse of herself in the full-length mirror. With hands on hips and head tilted, she appraised her naked body. Not bad. Not fantastic, but not bad either – although she had eaten a little too much for lunch! She put on her swimsuit and flip flops and wrapped herself in a generous white towelling robe. Humming an unrecognisable tune, she threw a bright red, expensively monogrammed beach towel over one shoulder and set off for the Vico ladies' private bathing place. At this time of the day it would be uncrowded, probably deserted. She had only to cross the Vico road and walk a hundred yards or so to reach it.

Pat Grehan shifted position in the long grass on the hill overlooking the Vico ladies' private bathing place.

He wanted a better view of the woman in the white robe as she descended the steps from the road to the rocky shore. There was no one else swimming and he kept his moist eyes riveted on her, wondering if she was wearing a bathing suit under her wrap. Occasionally women swam nude, he knew. He saw her drop a red towel on the rock platform, then the robe, and then he was disappointed to see she was wearing a swimsuit after all. He watched as she dipped her foot in the water, and then edged tentatively down the few steps to the sea from the platform. She lowered herself into the sea and swam jerkily out from the shore using the breast-stroke and keeping her chin awkwardly above water.

Pat Grehan watched the woman swim around for a while and then he began to lose interest. As he stood up to go, he saw her wave in his direction. He dropped to his knees in fright. He scanned the hillside to see if she was waving at someone else, but there was no one around. She waved again. Now she was lying on her back, and one of her legs was thrashing in the water. She waved both arms. Cramp. She had a cramp! She was calling out now, a distant cry for help, but there was no one to hear it but himself. What could he do? He was no use. He could do nothing. He couldn't swim. Nothing to do with him.

He turned and scrambled up the hillside, slipping and clawing at the grass. He must get out of here. If she drowned the police would be involved, and they would want to know what he was doing here. They had warned him several times before, when he had been fancying he was Decko Kavanagh, the man who used to live in the cave half way down the hill. Sweating and out of breath, he got to the top of the hill and fell out on to the road, nearly knocking down a young man, who was walking briskly by.

'Oi? What are you at?' said the young man.

Pat Grehan stared at him and then pointed down the hillside to the sea. 'Down there ... a woman ... drowning ...' The man looked at him for a second, then he ran, scrambling and slithering down the steps to the bathing place. When he reached it, all he could see was a white robe, sandals, a bright red towel lying on the platform, and an expressionless sea lapping against the rocks.

* * *

Driving through Dalkey, Ted fiddled with the car radio. He wanted livelier music, in tune with his buoyant mood.

Both doors of the Garda car were open and a Garda was coming out of the hall-door and replacing his cap, as Ted swung into the driveway and crunched to a halt on the gravel. The Garda came over to him. He was about 24. 'Mr Flynn?'

'Yes?'

'I'm sorry ...'

* * *

The taxi swung into the Piazza San Giovanni in Laterano, near the centre of Rome, and then down a small side street, stopping with a jerk outside the high-walled Irish College. A few words through the intercom and the gates parted automatically. As Cas and Pam stepped from the hot, bright sunlight into the shady coolness of the flagged hallway, they were cordially greeted by the guest master, and a student took their luggage to their rooms. They were shown into a large, ornate reception room with a high painted and gilded ceiling, and gold chairs upholstered in red. Another student brought them coffee, which smelt as coffee should. Pam noticed that everyone was smiling and she felt relaxed and happy.

When they were settled in, one of the priests outlined the programme arranged for them. This evening they would dine in a little family-owned ristorante, off the Via di San Giovanni. And they would spend the night here in the College and tomorrow they would be married in the College oratory. There would be a small post-wedding reception and then, as Cas had arranged, they would take a taxi to the Hotel Bernini in the Piazza Navona, for their wedding night.

Cas and Pam spent the remainder of the day checking the details of their wedding. The following morning the ceremony was joyful, and profoundly moving in its simplicity and meaning. Only briefly did they miss their family and friends around them. They had wanted to start their new life together absolutely on their own. After the reception they went around the famous sights of Rome in a romantic horse-drawn landau.

A balmy, gentle night breeze stirred the fine, draped net curtains on the tall windows as they stood arm-in-arm on the balcony of their hotel room, sipping Torre Ercolana wine. They looked down on the Baroque fountains below, with their gushing arcs of sparkling water, and the gossiping, laughing crowds carrying out their 'passeggiata'. The lights of the open-air restaurants twinkled and flickered across the piazza and fussing waiters wove their way through the animated diners. A nearby quartet played Vivaldi. The sights, sounds and smells of Rome made a heady cocktail.

Later they lay on the bed, naked and curled close in the relative coolness of the night, and made love that was sweetly satisfying.

They woke to breakfast of delicious rolls and preserves and strong Italian coffee served by a young waitress who teased them about being newly marrieds.

She wrapped them up a picnic lunch and told them to buy a bottle of local wine somewhere and to enjoy nature in a field along the route.

Since their effects would be shipped out later, they had only a few bags to throw into the Fiat sports car they had hired. Now it was first stop new farmhouse, new home, Casa Maitland, to whom it concerned. They drove between hills of terraced vineyards, with the tops of the hills crowned by villages clinging to the slopes and topped off by the spire of a little church piercing the blue sky. Tuscan towers proclaimed the larger towns and the dark black-green up-strokes of the cypress trees gave the landscape perfection of perspective and scale. The noon-day air seemed full of anticipation and Pam stole an occasional glance at her much-loved Cas. He seemed to fill his being by coming to this place, the blood of its people running in his veins. They would have great fun tracing his family tree, and maybe they would find some interesting relations who might visit them.

They by-passed Siena and made straight for the district in which they would live, and when Pam saw the farmhouse they would occupy, she knew she was home. They drove up the avenue between blue-green and silver fields of olive trees, and stopped at the large, round sandy area in front of the house. The warm, reddish colour of the eighteenth century building thrilled her, and the great wooden shutters gave the house an air of strength and protection. The house blended into the undulating landscape, broken here and there by yellowish stone walls, and the rich, blue Tuscan sky brought into orderly perspective the genius of nature. Before they got out of the car, Cas and Pam hugged one another with delight.

'Oh darling Pam,' Cas said, 'I could never have made this change without you. You were made for me. Our new life now starts from this minute.' He laughed and looked at his watch. 'We'll have to celebrate this moment every year.'

'Silly old fool. I want to see the house', Pam laughed. Then she literally ran up the staircase which was positioned sideways against the front of the building. It had served as a granary and the entrance was on the upper storey. She had all the energy of someone starting a new life, and she stood for a moment on the small platform once used for threshing grain before entering the glass-paned door. It led straight into a large anteroom paved with brown and reddish flags, well worn by farming footwear down the years, and her heart sang at the sight of the huge, open fireplace stacked with logs.

Pam went ahead from room to room, throwing open shutters to let in the sunlight. She would run the business from here, which would give them enough to live on while Cas was sorting out the property in Arezzo which his mother had made over to him on his marriage. He would derive an income from that, and he would paint, and paint well, and sell his work in the smaller galleries in Siena and Florence frequented by visitors looking for a piece of Tuscany to bring home with them.

It was a good-sized house with a panelled reception area, and a large kitchen with a refectory table running the length of one wall. Tall windows at the other side gave a view over the valley, and the cook could nourish her mind as well her body any time she liked by admiring the panorama. A very old and well polished free-standing cupboard held crockery produced by a local pottery in Tuscan colours of sand, bluish-green and tiny flecks of red or mauve, echoing the wild flowers in the fields. Glass goblets for drinking the purple red and pale yellow local wines were lined up and boxes of cutlery completed the store.

Bedrooms opened off a corridor at the other end of the house and there seemed to be plenty of bathrooms, which would make it convenient when they had guests. And the house was centrally heated against the sudden cold snaps in winter. A large room on the north side of the building had a great window set into it, presumably by someone who had used it as a studio, and Cas would paint there now. For Cas, following along behind her, the house was both a revelation and a feeling of déjà vu, as old family photographs had featured country houses not unlike this one.

When Pam woke very early next morning beside a slumbering Cas, she looked at the clean white-washed ceiling and lay back to experience waves of pure gratitude at the hand which fate had dealt her. She vowed that she would start each day this way, so that she would never lose her sense of wonder and privilege in coming to live in such a beautiful place. She slipped out from under the cotton bedspread, with its hand-embroidered daisies, careful not to wake Cas, and she stopped briefly to admire the oval ceramic panels of wild flowers set in the wrought iron head and foot of the bed. In slippers and housecoat, she went to the kitchen and made her first pot of coffee to greet the day. Then she put on waterproof boots and, still in her night wear, went outside across the sanded yard to the surrounding fields.

The meadows had been cut over the previous days and now the scents of freshly mown thyme, lemon geranium, lavender and other plants rose in the early morning sunlight. Drops of moisture lingered on herb leaves and on the dewy grass, and she stopped here and there to pick some of the wild growth and press it against her face. A combination of factors touched her deeply: the scent of the dewy herbs, the feel of the rough grass, the early animal sounds in neighbouring farms, and the rich taste of thyme, as she nibbled it curiously, standing transfixed by the loveliness of everything about her. It was surprising to think that the city of Siena was a mere five miles away. She would need a few minutes every day to render thanks for all this.

And Cas wanted a family too, a child or maybe two. He wanted their children, Tuscan-Irish, Irish-Tuscan, what did it matter, for wasn't he a blend of the two himself. He wanted them to be known as the Maitland family, settled in Tuscany, but with Irish roots.

EPILOGUE

The Galleria Vecchia in Siena phoned Cas to say that some of his paintings had been sold, and if he had replacements they would be happy to display them. And his cheque was ready – would they post it, or would he collect it when he called in? When he told Pam about his sales, they did a little dance around the kitchen and decided to celebrate that evening in Siena. He spent the morning selecting a small number of finished canvases, and then stacked them in the station wagon, and they drove off together to Siena. Pam was amused to see him jauntily setting out wearing an old shirt, paint-stained jeans, in sandals and with his thick black hair tied back with an elastic band. How far removed from the tense collar-and-tie person he had been back in Dublin. All the same, she packed a change of clothes for their evening out.

Cas had worked tirelessly for the previous seven months and the Galleria Vecchia had decided to promote his work, as visitors were seeking the type of paintings he did – strong brushwork, a wide range of colour and remarkably evocative scenes of Tuscan scenery and everyday life.

'Your cheque is made out to Signor Felce, is that all right?' said the gallery owner.

'Thank you that's fine,' said Cas.

An elderly man, who was studying the pictures approached Cas.

'Excuse me, are you Marco Felce, the painter?' He gestured towards Cas's work.

'Yes,' said Cas. 'That's me. I saw you looking at the paintings. Do you like them?'

'Very much. Forgive me, your accent is not Italian, but your name is.'

'No, my name is Maitland, but we thought the paintings would sell better with an Italian name. It's my mother's maiden name. She's Italian.'

'I'm interested also because my name is Felce too! Giuseppe Felce. How do you do?'

Cas smiled and shook his hand. 'Are we related?' he joked. Then he introduced Pam, his wife, feeling proud to do so.

'It's an unusual name, only found in these parts. I think we could be related,' said Signor Felce. He mentioned the area where Cas's mother had been born and it appeared that they were distant cousins of some degree. Delighted with the encounter, Cas, Pam and Giuseppe Felce arranged to meet for dinner, a double celebration, as it turned out.

The following night Cas and Pam also dined al fresco, this time on the terrace of their home, with their cousin and guest Giuseppe, and as the red wine in large goblets reflected the fat yellow beeswax candles in their hand-wrought holders, the atmosphere was relaxed. A chorus of cicadas rehearsed endlessly in the warm night air, and the conversation at the table roved from one subject to another. Giuseppe had told them that he lived with his now depleted family in Verona and how he occasionally came to Siena on business. He always looked in at the galleries there, and liked the Galleria Vecchia particularly, as it supported talented new artists. And he was constantly on the look out for talent. While officially retired, he had taken on the post of artistic co-ordinator for the opera company which staged performances in the Verona Arena. Would they come and visit the family there?

Cas leaned forward in his chair and gave a low whistle. He had been in Verona briefly on a sight-seeing visit with Pam, and had done some sketches there. Would Giuseppe like to see them? That Roman Arena in the centre of Verona was magnificent. Nearly as big as the Colosseum in Rome, but in better repair. Pam and he had been planning to go back to see an opera performance before too long.

'You'll be our guests,' said Guiseppe smiling broadly, 'special concessions for family members!' Cas brought out the Verona sketches, one of which had been finished in his studio. It was based on the Monatgue and Capulet saga, and showed the famous Romeo and Juliet balcony in Verona.

'It's a fake, I know,' laughed Cas. 'The balcony – not the painting! It's just an invention for visitors who had to have a balcony to be happy with their visit to Verona.' It was an experimental stylised painting which he had greatly enjoyed doing, more like a stage set, and Giuseppe became quite excited about it. He offered to buy it as the basis for an opera set design if Cas agreed. Cas agreed all right, and it was the beginning of a set of commissions for the opera company in Verona. Luck falls into the lap of the prepared, and without his back-up of months of hard work, Giuseppe Felce and he would have passed one another without recognition.

The soaring voices of the singers swelled against the blackness of the Verona night sky and Pam and Cas sat closely together in the packed, open-air, stone-tiered arena. They could have had more expensive seats, but they preferred to be among the crowd, and to hire cushions and sit up high where the vastness of the amphitheatre and the bright lighting of the stage constituted drama, before the performance even began. Cas had spent almost more time in Verona than Siena over the past couple of months, making sketch after sketch until he had produced the required effect, a stunning backdrop to the lavish production they were about to see. He was in his element and so was Pam. At the end of the performance the audience rose to give a sustained ovation and the air filled with the muffled explosions and crackling of fireworks.

Cas scanned the crowd absently as it began to flow slowly out of the arena. At first he wasn't sure, and then, as people separated to go through different exits, he saw her clearly. Chloe! Chloe, of all people! Here in Verona! It was definitely she. He was about to pluck Pam's arm, and point out Chloe when a rocket burst above them, sending a shower of light cascading over their heads, and everyone looked up and gasped. When Cas checked back Chloe was not there any longer. On reflection he said nothing to Pam.

The excited and chatting crowd moved slowly to the exits and as they emerged on to the street Cas felt a tap on the shoulder. He turned and there was Barry, laughing delightedly, with Chloe beside him. All four spoke together as they met, and Chloe then stood slightly apart, looking amused at the unexpected meeting. Cas realised that Pam and Chloe had never met, and he was surprised to find himself feeling awkward as he introduced them. Pam slipped her arm into his affectionately and Chloe noticed the gesture immediately.

'We're staying in Padua tonight', Chloe said. 'We came over by coach for the opera, but tomorrow we're going on to Venice. Italy's swell, isn't it?' Pam and Cas were staying overnight in Verona, but would have invited Barry and Chloe back home to Siena if time had permitted.

'Have we time for a quick drink?' Barry asked.

'Love to,' said Cas. 'There's a birreria. Let's go over.'

'Chloe and I are doing the Grand Tour,' said Barry, putting his arm around Chloe. 'We call it the Grand Tour because it's costing us a grand each per week to tour.' Everyone laughed.

'Come on, quick,' said Pam, 'not a minute to lose, and we have to hear what's happening back in Dublin.'

'How's your business coming on, Pam?' asked Chloe as they crossed the street.

'Couldn't be better,' Pam smiled, giving no details. 'And the film business?'

'It's all go.' As they sat around the pavement table chatting, Pam caught Chloe stealing occasional thoughtful glances at Cas, through the smoke of her cigarette.

'Anyone see the Giraffe these days?' asked Cas. 'It was a hard blow about Rita. I know I was really shocked myself. I was very fond of Rita.'

'Barry pointed him out to me in the foyer of the Shelbourne only last week,' said Chloe.

'He had some man up against a pillar, convincing him of something,' laughed Barry. 'I still remember your agency stories, Cas.'

'How did he look?' asked Pam.

'He looked – sort–of – I don't know – smaller,' said Barry. 'Somebody said they saw him a few times in the Queens, and he seems to drop into The Club a bit too. The car is often parked outside, apparently. But I hear he sold the Vico palace and lives in solitary grandeur in a penthouse over the Gresham Hotel.'

'A la Howard Hughes,' Chloe couldn't resist the movie reference.

'Not quite,' said Barry. 'He's still out and about touting for business and the agency seems to be going from strength to strength.' He looked at Cas. 'Martin O'Neill has taken over as Managing Director though. Did you know that?'

'Yes,' said Cas. 'Celine Dunphy – one of the girls in the agency – wrote a rambling note to Pam a while ago. I've known from way back that MD was the job Martin always wanted.'

'Coveted,' said Pam.

'And what about the curls-a-bobbin' Liz?' asked Chloe. 'She about?'

'She left Ted,' said Pam, 'and went to a job somewhere else, but it didn't work out very well. They didn't accept her airs and graces and she didn't have Ted to boost her.'

'Then she invested in a cosmetic company that went belly up,' said Cas.

'Celine has no idea what she's up to now. Or where she is.'

'What about –' Barry sipped his beer. 'What's his name – Bennett. Paul Bennett?'

'You knew him?' asked Pam.

'Knew of him. There was something about a boating accident involving his wife.'

'Ah yes, lovely Tessa,' said Cas.

'She nearly drowned,' said Pam. 'And then she had a miscarriage immediately afterwards. Poor girl. There was an awful lot of trouble there. They separated, but they're back together again now. They live in Waterford and Paul works for Tessa's uncle. Not a lucky couple.'

Barry and Chloe filled them in on the various activities

in Dublin, and Cas said he might be back in a year or two to mount an exhibition.

Pam slipped into bed beside Cas that night in their hotel. 'A lira for your thoughts?' He was sitting up stripped to the waist, his hands behind his head. 'I was just thinking. All those places in Dalkey with Italian names. Sorrento Road, Sorrento Terrace, Sorrento Park, Vico Road ....'

'Nerano Road,' said Pam. 'Torca Road – is that Italian?'

'I'm not sure. And the houses – Monte Alverno, Villa Nova, Milano ....'

'Roncalli, Siena, Ravenna ... there must be more.'

'And Killiney Bay, always compared to the Bay of Naples. Someone once said it's like a reversed negative of it. Dalkey should be twinned with some Italian town.'

'Which one?'

'I don't know.' He turned to Pam. 'One thing I do know ....'

'What's that?'

'I'm very happy here.'

'So am I.'

Flynn & Malby seemed a galaxy away.